Visions of the Past

Catriona shielded her eyes, trying to see past the afternoon glare. "B-but it can't be you!" she said.

The man cocked his head in a way Catriona found very familiar. "Excuse me?" he said. His voice was pleasant and warm, like a summer's day—like the day he and Catriona had spent near the waterfall in his hidden kingdom.

"You're dead!" Catriona blurted. "I saw you die!"

All the others, including the handsome man, looked puzzled.

"Milady," the man began, "I don't know who you think I am, but—"

"*Alric!*" Catriona said. "You're Alric Arngrim!"

THE NEW ADVENTURES

GOODLUND TRILOGY
BY STEPHEN D. SULLIVAN

Volume One
WARRIOR'S HEART

Volume Two
WARRIOR'S BLOOD
(May 2007)

Volume Three
WARRIOR'S BONES
(November 2007)

ALSO BY STEPHEN D. SULLIVAN
THE DYING KINGDOM

THE NEW ADVENTURES

GOODLUND TRILOGY

•

VOLUME ONE

WARRIOR'S HEART

STEPHEN D. SULLIVAN

COVER & INTERIOR ART
Vinod Rams

MIRRORSTONE

WARRIOR'S HEART

©2006 Wizards of the Coast, Inc.

Cover art by Vinod Rams
Cartography by Dennis Kauth
First Printing: November 2006
Library of Congress Catalog Card Number: 2005935548

9 8 7 6 5 4 3 2 1

ISBN-10: 0-7869-4187-1
ISBN-13: 978-0-7869-4187-2
620-95784740-001-EN

U.S., CANADA,
ASIA, PACIFIC, & LATIN AMERICA
Wizards of the Coast, Inc.
P.O. Box 707
Renton, WA 98057-0707
+1-800-324-6496

EUROPEAN HEADQUARTERS
Hasbro UK Ltd
Caswell Way
Newport, Gwent NP9 0YH
GREAT BRITAIN
Save this address for your records.

Visit our web site at www.mirrorstonebooks.com

To the gang I first worked with at TSR more than twenty-five years ago. That's a lot of years and a lot of friendship. Thanks.

And to the memory of
Keith Parkinson and Dave Sutherland III,
friends gone too soon.

Acknowledgements

Special thanks to the Alliterates and, especially, the guys in The Shire. I couldn't have finished this one without your unflagging confidence and support.

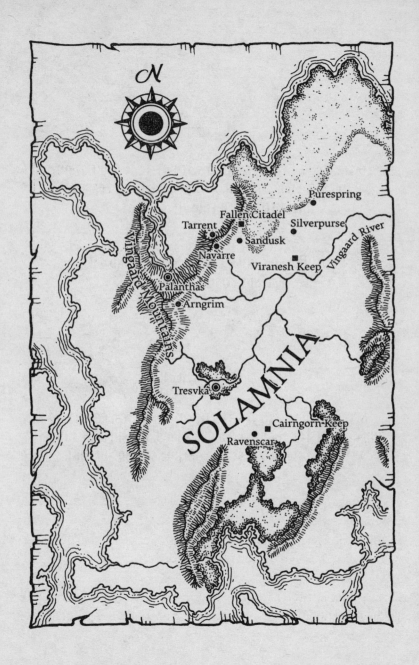

TABLE OF CONTENTS

CHAPTER

1   On the Road to Nowhere

A familiar, smiling face peered at Catriona over the wagon's tailgate as she woke with a start. She sat up, smacking her head on the low tarp covering the wagon she was riding in.

"Rohawn?" Catriona asked blearily. Warm afternoon sunlight filtered in through the canvas overhead. She felt hot and her body ached as the cart bounced over the rutted trail.

"Sorry," Rohawn said. "I thought you were awake."

"I'm awake *now*," Catriona replied. She took her hands away from her weapons—the wicked-looking curved blades were called dragon claws—and rubbed her fingers through her flame red hair.

"You shouldn't sneak up on me like that," she said. "I might have killed you."

"You wouldn't have killed me," Rohawn said confidently. "Besides, I have some people I want you to meet. That's why I woke you up. They're guarding this caravan."

Catriona rolled her eyes. "I've met caravan guards before. Lots of them. Frankly, I'd rather go back to sleep."

"But they want to meet you," he said. "I've been telling them all about you. And they're"—Rohawn's voice dropped, and he smiled sheepishly—"they're standing right behind me."

She frowned at him.

"I've been telling them all about you. About our adventures, I mean," he said. "There's an elf in the caravan too. A half-elf, actually, I think. She seems very nice."

Catriona stretched and adjusted the fit of the chain-mail shirt under her forest green tunic. Sleeping in armor was a good habit, but an uncomfortable one as well. She felt stiff and crabby, not at all in the mood to meet new people.

A head poked over Rohawn's shoulder. "Good afternoon—or should I say morning?" said a girl who looked to be about Cat's age. "It seems we've interrupted your sleep. Shame on you, Rohawn—we could have waited until your mistress woke up!" The brown-haired girl's tone was light and pleasant, but the arched eyebrows beneath her silver-winged helmet suggested she wondered why Catriona had been sleeping in the middle of the day. Cat squinted at the newcomer, who had to be mounted because she looked so much taller than Rohawn.

"This is Karise Tarn," Rohawn blurted. "Karise is guarding the caravan until we get to Silverpurse. Karise, Catriona Goodlund. Catriona is training me to be a knight."

Catriona crawled out of the wagon, fussing with her hair and clothes to make herself look a bit more presentable. "Sorry about my appearance," she said. "I wasn't expecting to meet anyone new today." She frowned in her squire's direction. Rohawn's shrugged his eyebrows and kicked a stone in the roadway.

Karise's blue eyes lit on the dragon claws hanging from Catriona's belt. "Planning on fighting during this trip?" Karise asked. "Or are you looking for work after you get to Silverpurse?"

"Neither," Catriona replied. "I'm carrying the weapons, but not using them. I'm kind of taking a rest."

"A rest?" the girl said. "In this godsforsaken place?" She nudged her fine white gelding into motion again to keep up with the caravan. As they moved, Catriona noticed a fiery copper medallion dangling at the girl's throat. A token of faith—which meant Karise was a cleric.

Catriona bristled at the girl's comment about the landscape, though the insult rang true as well. Flat, arid land surrounded the wagon trail in all directions. Patches of stunted, brownish grass clung to the parched earth. There were few flowers, even fewer trees, and almost no signs of water. To the north the plains melded into vast, trackless deserts. To the south lay the beginnings of the fertile Plains of Solamnia, the heart of Ansalon. To the west, the Vingaard Mountains poked their heads above the dusty horizon. Northeastward, and still out of sight, lay the caravan's goal—the trading town of Silverpurse.

Silverpurse wasn't Catriona's goal, though she wasn't about to mention that to Karise. It was merely a stopover on a journey Cat felt increasingly nervous about making. She'd grown up a lot in the last few years. She'd been forgiven for many of her mistakes and worked hard to redeem others. But still . . .

Rohawn cleared his throat. "Here's the next person I wanted you to meet," he said. He pointed to a young woman in a plain silk tunic, full-length skirt, and simple leather sandals, walking on the other side of Karise's gelding. "Shara is the half-elf I was telling you about."

Shara bowed slightly. Swirling patterns in brown, earthy red, and yellow ochre decorated her clothing. She walked with a casual, unhurried grace, as though she were strolling through a field of green grass rather than down a hot and dusty road. Catriona bowed in return. She wondered how old Shara might be. Elves, even half elves, aged much more slowly than humans did. Shara appeared to be Catriona's age, but she might, in fact, have been fifty or sixty.

Rohawn looked around. "There's one more person I wanted you to meet, Catriona," he said. "He's around here somewhere . . ."

As the caravan continued slowly northeastward, Rohawn spotted a man on horseback riding beside a cluster of merchants and waved him forward. As he came closer, Catriona's jaw dropped and she felt the blood drain from her face. "I—I—" she stammered. "You!"

The man's face remained shadowed by his wide-brimmed hat, but Catriona would have recognized that tall, muscular, rugged figure anywhere. Several days' beard growth adorned his square, regal chin. Silver decorations trimmed his dark tunic. An ornate long sword hung from his hip. Everything about him spoke of nobility.

Catriona shielded her eyes, trying to see past the afternoon glare. "B-but it can't be you!" she said.

The man cocked his head in a way Catriona found very familiar. "Excuse me?" he said. His voice was pleasant and warm, like a summer's day—like the day he and Catriona had spent near the waterfall in his hidden kingdom.

"You're dead!" Catriona blurted. "I *saw* you die!"

All the others, including the handsome man, looked puzzled. "Milady," the man began, "I don't know who you think I am, but—"

"*Alric!*" Catriona said. "You're Alric Arngrim!"

"Catriona," Rohawn said, "this is Gillean Rickard, the other caravan guard I told you about."

The young man took off his hat and bowed to her from the saddle. "Gillean Rickard the Third," he said, "at your service."

"B-but," Catriona sputtered. She blinked and wiped the sweat from her brow. As Gillean drew up alongside her, the shadows on his face changed and Catriona got a better look at him. No, it wasn't Alric, a fact which both relieved and disappointed Catriona.

Gillean did look similar to Alric in both face and stature. But his eyes were actually more blue than gray, and they lacked that wild, desperate quality that marked Prince Alric's gaze. Gillean's eyes were kind and sympathetic.

"I'm sorry," Catriona said, "but the resemblance is uncanny." She and the others kept pace behind Catriona's wagon as they talked.

Gillean nodded politely. "Did you say this man you knew was from Arngrim?" he asked. "My family is descended from people in Arngrim—legend has it from the royal line. But whether I'm descended from royalty or just from impoverished nobility, I'm very pleased to meet you, Catriona Goodlund. Please, call me Gil."

"Thank you, Gil," Catriona said, her cheeks burning. She noticed now that Gillean's garments were *not* black as Alric preferred, but rather a deep midnight blue. And the silver decorations on his clothes and sword were owls, not the lions of Arngrim. Not many young lords became caravan guards—this young man was nearly as much a mystery as he would have been if he'd been Alric.

"So you met someone from Arngrim, Catriona?" Gillean said.

"Yes," Catriona replied, still a bit flustered. "I knew their prince— Prince Alric."

Gillean rubbed his unshaven chin. "That's curious," he said. "As I understand it, the kingdom of Arngrim vanished from Ansalon centuries ago."

"It's a long story," Catriona said. Wanting to change the subject, she turned to Karise. "I couldn't help but notice your token of faith. Which god do you serve?"

"I'm devoted to the god Sirrion," Karise replied, "the fiery god of passion and creativity."

Rohawn looked puzzled. "I thought from the wings on your helmet that you might be devoted to Shinare," he said.

Karise nodded. "Sirrion is Shinare's companion," she said. "To tell you the truth, my goal is to serve them both. That's why my vestments incorporate symbols from both gods."

"I don't know much about Sirrion," Rohawn said.

"Careful, Roh," Gillean put in. "Kari will chew your ear off about the gods if you let her."

Karise glared at him, though the corners of her mouth tugged into a slight smile.

"Sirrion's religion is not well established in this area," Karise explained. "I hope to change that, even if Gil here doesn't seem to take my devotion very seriously."

Gillean bowed in his saddle. "I meant no offense," he said. "I take the returned gods quite seriously."

"As befits one named after a god," Shara commented.

Gillean smiled and told her, "It's spelled differently, though it sounds similar."

"Good thing," Karise said. "We wouldn't want you starting your own priesthood."

"Perhaps I should join yours instead," Gillean replied.

Karise nodded. "Perhaps you should."

As Gillean and Karise bantered, Catriona quietly observed the pair. She'd had trouble with mercenaries before, and a glib tongue sometimes hid sinister intentions.

As if reading Catriona's thoughts, Rohawn pointed to Karise's mace. "So, you're a warrior priestess?" he asked. "Is that usual with your sect?"

"Very little is 'usual' with Sirrion," Karise replied. "His religion is quite free-form. That's why I can devote some of my time to his consort too. Sirrion favors striving and passion, while Shinare is patron of merchants and travelers. So, here I am, indulging my passion for riding while serving a band of merchants."

"Shinare approves of caravan guards," Gillean said, "so long as they're well paid."

"Shinare is the goddess of *wealth*, not greed, Gillean," Shara said.

"See?" Karise said, looking at Gillean. "What did I tell you? Commerce is important to Shinare, but it is not the *only* tenet of her religion. However, as to my being *well* paid, well, why don't you ask his lordship here what kind of money we're making?" She hooked her thumb toward Gillean, and the two exchanged a knowing glance. He laughed.

"Would you like to ride with us, Cat?" Gillean asked. "Kari and I need to patrol the caravan line and stay alert for trouble, but we'd love to have you for company."

"Oh, yes," Karise said. "We could continue our sparkling conversation."

Not sure the cleric meant it, Catriona replied, "My squire seems to have misplaced my horse."

"No I haven't," Rohawn said. "It's right over there!" A moment later, he mimed slapping his head. "Oh. I see," he said. "It was kind of a joke."

Everyone laughed but Shara, who stared at the western sky, brows furrowed.

"Is something wrong?" Catriona asked.

Shara pointed toward a bank of low clouds swirling between the caravan and the distant mountains.

"Look there," she said.

The clouds parted and a group of hideous winged creatures dived out of the clouds. They circled once, as though searching for something, then streaked toward the caravan.

CHAPTER

2   Best Laid Plans

The caravan came to a sudden halt to stare at the approaching intruders. From a distance, Cat could see their craggy, blood red skin and the wicked talons that grew from their bony fingers and toes. Wide, batlike wings held the monsters' armored bodies aloft. The creatures shrieked and keened as they swarmed out of the distant clouds toward the startled travelers.

"Draconians!" Rohawn gasped.

"No," Gillean said. "These are something else."

Shara shielded her hazel eyes from the sun with one hand. "Gargoyles," she said.

"Gargoyles aren't red," Karise told her. "They're gray—made of stone."

"Nevertheless," Shara replied.

Gillean shouted to the merchants, "Take shelter! Move into defensive formation!" Aside to Catriona, Shara, and Rohawn, he continued, "It's time for Kari and me to earn our keep."

Rohawn drew his greatsword. Catriona's hands rested atop her dragon claws. Both followed Gillean as he rode toward the front of the caravan, shouting orders.

"We can help," Rohawn said.

"Stay put, the both of you," Karise told them, turning in the other direction. "Take shelter in your wagon, along with the rest of the paying customers. We'll call if we need you." She rode toward the rear of the line, positioning herself between the caravan and the oncoming gargoyles.

Rohawn looked hopefully at Gillean, who nodded. "If you're that eager to pitch in, I've got a job for you," he said. "Help me pull the caravan in. Then we'll see."

"Where do you want me stationed?" Catriona asked.

"Actually," Gillean replied, reining his horse to a stop, "you can sit this one out, if you want."

The fine hairs on Catriona's neck prickled.

Sensing her annoyance, he added, "I mean, if you really want to fight, that's fine with me. But your squire told me this trip was supposed to be a vacation for you. So, with your leave, fair Catriona, Kari and I will try to keep it that way." He bowed slightly from the saddle.

Catriona's heart fluttered. At that moment, Gillean Rickard the Third looked very much like Alric Arngrim. "But—" she began.

"Really, don't worry about it," Gillean insisted. "Like Kari said, we can always call if we need you."

Catriona watched the distant flock of gargoyles draw closer. She counted five, which seemed a lot for two mercenaries of unknown quality, but probably not too many with Rohawn helping.

"What kind of mercenary would I be if I couldn't handle a fistful of gargoyles?" Gillean asked, as though reading her mind. "They aren't that bright anyway."

"All right," she said. "I'll wait with my wagon—for now. Go ahead, Rohawn. A squire can always use the practice."

Rohawn beamed.

"All right, kid," Gillean said. "Tell the front of the line to fall back to the middle. We don't have time to circle the wagons, but we need everyone as close together as possible. Oh, and blinders on the horses—we don't want the animals getting spooked."

"Right," Rohawn said. He ran to the front of the caravan while Gillean resumed his ride through the center of the line. Karise was already pushing the rearward wagons toward the center.

The mercenaries' strategy impressed Catriona. Clearly, Karise and Gillean had done some defensive planning in advance.

"So you will sit and wait, Lady Knight?" Shara asked.

Catriona jumped. She'd forgotten the quiet half-elf was there.

"I'm not a knight," Catriona replied. "I never took the tests. Besides, if Gillean and Karise think they can handle the gargoyles, I'm willing to give them a chance. They seem to know what they're doing."

Shara nodded, but didn't seem quite convinced. "I will wait here as well," she said.

"Can you defend yourself?" Catriona asked.

"If fate wills it."

Catriona didn't know what to make of that. "Do you want to sit in the wagon with me?"

"Like your squire, I will stand on my own two feet," Shara replied.

Catriona frowned, unsure whether the reply was intended as a jab at her decision to sit out the battle. She hopped into the back of her cart and watched as the monsters flew closer.

Her wagon halted near the middle of the caravan. The merchants around Catriona dutifully hid in their wagons or took shelter beneath them. Shara stood a few yards away. She seemed unconcerned by the coming attack. Catriona's nerves jangled.

"Gillean and Karise said they could handle it," she told herself. "They said they'd call if they needed help." She remained unconvinced. The mercenaries *seemed* to know what they were doing, but until the fighting started, who could really tell? She dangled her legs over the back of the wagon nervously as she waited, ready to jump in if needed.

Karise, stationed in the rear of the caravan, hefted her spiked mace. Gillean reined his horse to a stop several carts in front of the cleric. Rohawn waited deeper inside the wagon formation, between Gillean and Catriona. The caravan's horses stamped the ground and whinnied in fear. Even with their eyes covered, they sensed the gargoyles' approach.

Gillean's strong voice boomed over the assembly. "Stay calm!" He drew his longbow and fitted a gray-fletched arrow to it.

The screeching gargoyles closed within a hundred yards.

Gillean aimed and let fly. His arrow pierced the stony throat of the lead gargoyle. The creature squawked and crashed to the ground, landing a dozen yards away from the frightened merchants.

The other gargoyles kept coming. Gillean stowed his bow and drew his long sword. He and Karise rode out to either side, away from the wagons, making themselves easy targets for the stony predators.

But the gargoyles didn't attack the mercenaries, nor did they fall upon the rear of the line, as Gillean had expected. Instead, the four remaining monsters dived for the center of the caravan.

Karise cursed. She and Gillean wheeled their horses around and charged to meet the threat.

A gargoyle landed two yards away from Rohawn. It looked past the boy and sniffed the air as though searching for something.

Rohawn leaped forward, swinging his greatsword at the gargoyle's neck. The monster ducked and the blow glanced off the stony horns atop its head. It slashed at Rohawn's midsection.

The young squire stepped back out of the way, but bumped into a wagon behind him. The monster leaped forward, claws extended. Rohawn rolled aside and the gargoyle's talons splintered the wagon's side board.

A second gargoyle swooped past. Its claws raked huge holes in the canvas cover of the wagon beside Rohawn. The merchants inside the wagon screamed, but the attacking gargoyle didn't seem interested in them. It, too, sniffed the dry summer air.

Gillean and Karise galloped to the center of the line as the two remaining gargoyles landed amid the wagons with frightened merchants huddled underneath. The two beasts seized a wagon not twenty feet from where Catriona was sitting. They ripped the wagon's tarp covering off and smashed its wooden sides. They began rocking the vehicle, trying to tip it over. The family that was hiding in the wagon dived out, barely avoiding the gargoyles' flailing claws. The cart flipped sideways, toppling perilously toward the family's youngest boy.

Catriona jumped out of her wagon and ran to help. What *had* she been thinking? How could she let Rohawn and the others do the fighting when there were innocents in jeopardy? She cursed herself for letting Gillean's good looks and charming manner cloud her judgment.

The parents seized the boy and dragged him out of the way just in time. Finished with the wagon, the gargoyles turned toward the family. Cat leaped cart harness. There too many obstacles between her and the victims! All five members of the family screamed as the gargoyles lurched toward them.

Gillean reached the monsters while Catriona was still dodging between the wagons. He rode up behind the first gargoyle and hacked with his long sword. The blade chopped through the monster's wing, severing it near the shoulder.

The one-winged gargoyle howled. Both it and its companion spun to face the young nobleman. The wounded monster stood its ground and slashed at Gillean's horse. The second gargoyle took to the air, flying straight for Gillean's face.

Gillean ducked and parried. His sword blade turned aside the talons of the grounded gargoyle, but the winged monster struck him as it flew by. The chain mail beneath Gillean's tunic stopped the flying gargoyle's claws from gutting him, but the force of the blow knocked him from his saddle.

Catriona vaulted a low wagon and landed between the nobleman and the gargoyle. Instantly, her dragon claws sprang into her hands. The wounded gargoyle glared at her, then slashed at her belly. Catriona parried and the blade of her left-hand weapon cut off two of the gargoyle's fingers. The monster shrieked. She stabbed with her second dragon claw, but the gargoyle backed away.

The gargoyle's companion swooped low and seized a fifty-pound bag of flour from the overturned wagon. It hurled the bag at Catriona just as the wounded monster lunged again.

Catriona blocked the attack from the one-winged gargoyle, but she couldn't stop the heavy missile. It hit her full in the chest, and she toppled backward over the low wagon she'd vaulted earlier. The wind rushed out of her lungs and her surroundings swam for a few seconds.

The wounded gargoyle turned back to Gillean. The young nobleman staggered to his feet, sword ready.

Catriona watched, dazed and unable to help. The one-winged gargoyle leaped at Gillean. But at the last moment, Karise rode between the monster and the mercenary. She smashed her spiked mace into the head of the wounded gargoyle. The beast crumpled to the ground, though the blow didn't kill it.

Karise shot Gillean a wry smile. "I'm supposed to be protecting the merchants, you know," she said, "not *you*."

Gillean shook his head to clear the cobwebs. "I'm sure I'll return the favor before the fight's over," he replied.

Catriona got to her feet. Gillean and Karise seemed to have these two creatures under control for now, so she looked to see how Rohawn was doing.

Two gargoyles trapped the squire between several overturned wagons. Clusters of panicked merchants raced around the carts, blocking Rohawn's retreat. The boy couldn't protect himself without endangering the very people he was trying to help.

As Catriona raced to help him, a shadow fell across the wagon beside her. She spotted it out of the corner of her eye and instinctively threw herself flat on the ground.

As she did, another blood red gargoyle swooped over her. The monster's claws passed within inches of her head.

"Where did *that* one come from?" Catriona wondered aloud. Two gargoyles were fighting Gillean and Karise, and the other two were battling Rohawn. The remaining one had been killed by Gillean's arrow, hadn't it?

The fifth gargoyle landed a short distance away, right next to Shara. It threw its arms wide and lunged for the half-elf.

Shara dropped to the ground, twirling her staff. She swept the weapon across the monster's legs, knocking its feet out from under it. As the gargoyle fell forward, Shara sprang to her feet and clouted it on the back of the skull. The monster crashed into a wagon, splintering the side of the vehicle, and lay still. The half-elf walked calmly away.

Catriona got up and ran to help Rohawn. Panic still seized the caravan merchants. The tradesmen ran screaming in all directions, many fleeing from dangers that didn't actually exist. A fat man in magenta robes nearly bowled Catriona over.

"Watch out, you fool!" she barked.

She dodged around the man and ducked between two wagons, hoping to reach Rohawn before the gargoyles killed him.

Rohawn chopped his greatsword deep into the shoulder of the gargoyle on his right, but his blade stuck as he tried to pull it out. The gargoyle grinned back at him, unfazed by the wound. It clawed at Rohawn's midsection while its companion circled around behind the squire.

Catriona leaped over some spilled barrels and landed behind the second gargoyle. The monster sensed her and turned, clawing at her face. She brought her left blade up defensively and caught the monster's talons on the weapon's inner curve. At the same time, she slashed with her right-hand blade.

Her dragon claw bit deep into the gargoyle's chest. The beast grunted, startled. Catriona yanked the weapon out and stabbed it into the monster's heart. The gargoyle fell onto the roadway with a thud.

As Rohawn cheered, the remaining gargoyle head-butted him. The squire staggered back, dropping his greatsword. The gargoyle spread its wings and took to the air with a low, laughing grumble.

Catriona gauged the distance as it rose. Its shoulder wound hampered its flying and Cat thought she could reach it by vaulting off a low cart between them. Before she could act, though, something seized her ankle.

CHAPTER

3 GARGOYLES

Catriona yelped as stony talons pierced her left boot and cut into her heel. She whirled and saw the gargoyle she'd stabbed lying in the dust behind her. It *wasn't* dead. The monster grabbed her other foot and rose to its feet, upending her.

"By Paladine!" Catriona cried, wondering how the beast could still be alive. She kicked loose from its grasp and rolled across the roadway, only to slam hard into a wagon wheel. The breath rushed out of her lungs and stars flared before her eyes. The gargoyle loped forward to kill her.

Rohawn retrieved his greatsword and ran at the gargoyle's unprotected back. It spotted the boy and turned to defend itself, but not in time. Rohawn's blade bit into the creature's chest, plunging to where the gargoyle's heart should have been—the same spot that Catriona had stabbed earlier.

Again, the monster didn't die.

"What does it take to kill you?" Rohawn asked. He grunted as he pulled the weapon out and swung again. Just then, the second gargoyle swooped down on him from above.

Nearby, Karise and Gillean dismounted as the gargoyles they were fighting retreated into the tangle of wagons. Both mercenaries had stabbed and smashed their stony foes dozens of times. Long gashes and deep holes marked the monsters' craggy red skin, but the wounds barely seemed to slow the gargoyles down.

Shara was facing similar problems. Many dents from her carved staff marked the stony skin of her foe, but the monster refused to die. Slowly, both mercenaries and the half-elf fell back to the center of the caravan, toward Rohawn and Catriona.

As the flying gargoyle bore in on Rohawn, Catriona leaped up and slashed at its left wing. Her weapon tore a long gash in the thin membrane, and the gargoyle couldn't stay airborne. It crashed into a nearby cart, but rose again immediately.

"Form a defensive circle!" Catriona called to her friends. "The gargoyles seem more interested in us than the rest of the caravan!"

"Kill us, and the rest will be easy pickings," Karise pointed out. But she, Gillean, and Shara quickly did as Catriona suggested.

The five warriors stood back to back, surrounded by the five blood red gargoyles. The one Gillean had originally shot hissed at them, the nobleman's arrow still protruding from its throat.

"Does anyone know how to kill gargoyles?" Rohawn asked. Sweat covered his muscular form and grim determination filled his dark blue eyes. He hacked at one gargoyle as it came in, but the monster backed away, cackling.

"They're enchanted beasts," Shara replied. "There is no single way. Every group is different." She turned smoothly from one foe to the next, staring the gargoyles down.

"I just hope they *can* be killed," Gillean added. One lunged at him and he put his long sword into its eye. The creature staggered back, half blinded, but it didn't die.

"Demons of the Abyss!" Karise cursed. She smashed a huge dent into the head of the gargoyle fighting her, but it still kept coming.

Catriona cut high and low. The gargoyle facing her blocked the first attack, but the second nearly severed its left arm. The monster didn't seem to mind. It came in again, trying to get through her guard.

Catriona blocked the blow and kicked the creature in the chest, sending it reeling back. Her eyes darted around the circle, looking for some sign of weakness that she and her friends might exploit.

The gargoyle with Gil's arrow in its neck swiped at Shara. The half-elf dodged smoothly out of the way and struck the creature in the neck with the end of her staff. The blow hit right next to the embedded arrow. The gargoyle staggered back, gasping and faltering for a moment.

While Cat focused on the gasping monster, Rohawn's sword deflected a blow meant for her. She nodded her thanks as her mind raced.

"Rohawn, hold mine!" she called. Before he could respond, she ducked forward under the monster's grasp and stepped in front of the one Shara had been fighting.

The gasping creature turned, but not in time. Catriona stabbed with her right dragon claw. The gargoyle reached out and batted it aside, just as Catriona wanted. Her other blade flashed in a quick arc, separating the monster's ugly head from its shoulders.

The gargoyle flopped backward to the ground and crumbled into reddish dust.

"That's it!" Gillean cried. "Lop off their heads!" He stopped fighting defensively and began attacking: high and low, left and right.

Catriona and Shara turned to help Rohawn. The two gargoyles bore in on the teenager, their flailing claws almost sneaking past his guard.

Shara swept the legs of one with her staff, and it went down. Catriona leaped over it, dragon claws flashing. The second gargoyle didn't see her coming. Her blades met in the middle of the monster's neck and its head fell to the earth. Rohawn decapitated the one Shara had knocked down. Both gargoyles crumbled.

Cat turned back to Gillean, who pressed forward, his attacks escalating in power and savagery. His monstrous foe fell back, though it still showed no fear. He stabbed through its flashing talons and into its neck. The monster's head toppled to the ground and its body turned to dust.

On the other side of Gillean, Karise muttered a prayer and her left hand filled with burning embers. The one-winged gargoyle swiped at her face. She ducked to the side and tossed the embers into its eyes, which burst into clinging, bright orange flames.

The monster roared and clawed at its eyes. Karise smashed her mace hard across the back of its neck. The gargoyle fell to its knees, but didn't die. "A little help here!" Karise called.

Before the creature could recover, Gillean stepped forward and severed its head. The gargoyle's body crashed into the roadway, its remains scattering into dust as it hit.

All five defenders breathed a deep sigh of relief.

"Well, that was harder than I would have liked," Karise said. She pulled off her winged helmet and wiped her brow.

Gillean turned to the rest of the caravan. "It's all over now," he said. "Nothing more to worry about. Pick up your belongings and we'll get started as soon as we can."

The caravan traders crept from their hiding places.

Rohawn kicked at the reddish dust, which was all that remained of their foes. "Dark magic!" he said.

"But why?" Gillean asked. "Why attack this caravan?"

"For loot, obviously," Karise replied. "That's why the caravan boss hired us in the first place—because he knew someone might be after his steel."

"Gargoyles have no interest in coin," Shara said.

Catriona shrugged. "Sometimes there is no why," she said. "Sometimes it's just warrior's luck. Occasionally battle finds you, even when you're not looking for it."

"Is that good luck or bad luck, then?" Gillean asked.

"It depends on whether you're looking for a fight," Rohawn replied.

"Well," Karise said, "I can think of easier ways to earn my pay." She gestured to a long gash down the left sleeve of her tunic. A fair amount of blood stained the golden yellow fabric.

"Are you all right?" Rohawn asked.

"I will be," Karise replied. She rolled up her sleeve and bared the wound. The cut's ragged edges extended almost from her elbow to her wrist.

Rohawn and Gillean gritted their teeth in sympathy, and Catriona winced. Only Shara showed little concern.

"Don't worry," Karise said. "I've had worse." She muttered a prayer, closed her eyes, and laid her right hand on the wound. As she did, pale blue sparks formed around her fingers. The tiny flames danced from her hand to the open wound. The fire lingered for several moments, seeming to burn across the gap in her flesh. When the sparks died away, Karise's arm was whole once more. Not even a trace of a scar remained.

"Wow," said Rohawn. "I mean, I've seen people healed before, but never a cleric healing herself."

"A nice trick," Gillean agreed.

"No trick," Karise said sternly. "The power of the gods."

"Sorry," Gillean said. "I didn't mean to offend."

"Is anyone else wounded?" Karise asked.

"Nothing worth mentioning," Catriona replied, rubbing her heel. Gillean and Rohawn had received only minor cuts and bruises, and Shara didn't appear hurt at all.

"Someone's coming," the half-elf said.

All of them turned as a bright-eyed man dressed in colorful silks puffed through the stalled wagons toward the group, looking sweaty, anxious, and none too pleased.

"The caravan boss," Gillean explained. "I expected him sooner. Come on, Karise, we should see what he wants."

"He better not want to cut our pay," the warrior-cleric said. "It's not our fault his caravan got attacked." She and Gillean hurried off to intercept the man.

"No," Shara said quietly. "I'm sure the gargoyles weren't after you." She glanced toward Catriona and Rohawn.

Catriona frowned. What had she meant by that? Surely the gargoyles didn't have anything to do with Rohawn and her. All their enemies were dead, or at least, very far behind them now.

Rohawn watched her go. "Strange girl," he said.

Catriona nodded.

CHAPTER

4   Rohawn's Journey

Rohawn couldn't believe that Catriona really would go back to sleep after their brutal fight with the gargoyles, yet that's exactly what she did. As soon as they'd repaired the wagons and gotten the caravan back under way, his mentor lay down in her shaded cart, closed her eyes, and immediately dozed off.

The young squire shook his head and went to water their horses. How could Catriona sleep with so many interesting things going on? Even the bleak landscape fascinated the teenager.

The shift from golden southern plains to seemingly endless desert in the north was remarkable to behold, like the slow encroach of a sandy tide. Rohawn stared at the tall, rocky formations dotting the landscape.

He wondered what had made the formations. Had the huge rocks been dropped there by the gods? Did the huge fiery boulder that had destroyed the Kingpriest become the towers of stone pieces in the rocky terrain? Had the rocky pillars been thrust up from below by massive magical battles beneath the earth? His mother had once told him a tale about a dwarf battle that lasted thirty years, after which all the dwarves turned to stone.

Rohawn had heard the caravan merchants whispering of dwarves in the area—evil dwarves who rose from below and carried young children off as slaves. He'd assumed those were merely tales to frighten children. But what if they weren't? What if the stones had been thrust up from below in titanic battles between warring tribes of evil dwarves?

Rohawn finished tending their horses—which had escaped the battle unscathed—then jogged over to talk to Shara, who was walking between the wagons a dozen yards back. Of all the people he'd met during this trip, Shara seemed the wisest.

She acknowledged his presence with a glance, but didn't say anything as he fell into step beside her.

"Are there dwarves around here?" Rohawn asked.

"Undoubtedly," she replied, neither looking at him nor breaking her pace.

Rohawn frowned. She'd answered him precisely, but the question wasn't exactly what he'd wanted to ask. "I mean, do you think there are dark dwarves around here?"

Shara turned toward him and arched her sand-colored eyebrows. Somehow her eyes seemed to be green and brown and blue all at the same time, depending on how the light hit them. "Where did you get that notion?" she asked.

"I heard some of the merchants talking," Rohawn said.

Shara nodded and turned her gaze once more toward the road ahead. "There are many types of dwarves in the world," she said, "and we are not too far from the Vingaard Mountains. Dwarves, both good and evil, dwell there."

"But do you think there are—or were—any dwarves *here?*" Rohawn pressed. "Here?"

"Yes," he said eagerly.

"No."

"Well, thanks," he replied, trying not to look too crestfallen.

She inclined her head slightly in a polite nod. "You have quite an imagination, Rohawn," she said. "Be sure to put it to good use." She smiled at him ever so slightly, and then returned her focus to the road.

Rohawn jogged toward the back of the caravan, scratching his head as he went. He'd hoped the half-elf might be a source of fascinating lore, as his bard friend Kelenthe had been. Shara's answers remained maddeningly obscure. What he needed now was some less-mysterious company.

Gillean and Karise rode together toward the rear of the line of wagons. Their clothing was soiled and slashed in places, and both were bruised and bloodied. Neither looked as gallant as they had when Rohawn first met them. But then, Rohawn figured he probably looked just as bad after all that fighting in the dust.

"Hey, Roh!" Gillean called as the squire approached. "Everything in order at your wagon? Your horses are all right?"

Rohawn smiled, trying not to appear nervous or awkward. "Yes," he said. "Everything's fine. Catriona's napping."

Karise laughed. "I could use a nap myself," she said. "But then, I'm being *paid* to guard this caravan."

"Paid or no," Gillean said, "I'm glad she decided to help out when she did. She was useful in the fight."

"That's what she does," Rohawn said. "She helps people. That's why I decided to become her squire."

"Did you say earlier that she had Solamnic training?" Karise asked.

"Yes," Rohawn replied. "She was a squire once but"—and here he realized he should be tactful—"she left the order. She's agreed to train me in the Solamnic ways, though, so that I can take the tests at Palanthas. That's where we're going."

"Um, Roh," Karise said. "I don't know how to tell you this, but we're not heading toward Palanthas. We're going in almost the opposite direction."

Rohawn's cheeks warmed. "I-I know that," he said. "I meant that we're going there *after* we go where we're going now. Catriona has some things she needs to take care of before seeing the White-stone Council again."

Gillean's blue-gray eyes lit up. "Ah, so the fair Catriona is on a mission. She's a mercenary, then." He rubbed his stubbly chin. "It's strange for a mercenary to be training a knight-to-be, though many things have been strange since the war."

Rohawn felt unsure how to reply. Gillean assumed a lot of things that just weren't true. "Catriona's not a mercenary," the squire began, "and she's not—"

"Not a mercenary?" Karise broke in. "A do-gooder, then? Is there any steel in that?" She looked perplexed. "Only fools risk their lives without a strong cause."

"Catriona is *not* a fool!" Rohawn protested.

Again, Karise laughed. "Sorry. I didn't mean to offend you," she said. "And I certainly didn't mean to besmirch your mis-tress's honor or intelligence." The cleric's eyes twinkled playfully. Rohawn couldn't discern whether she was joking.

Gillean broke in. "I think what Karise meant is that it's very rare to find people willing to fight, and possibly die, with no chance for profit."

"Our profit is making Krynn a better place," Rohawn said. He felt both angry and confused, though he remained determined not to show it. Were the mercenaries making fun of him and Cat?

Gillean nodded. "Of course, we *all* hope to make the world a better place," he said. "It's just that most of us can't afford to do so for free. Even the Knights of Solamnia have resources to support them."

"We get by," Rohawn said, still feeling defensive. "Sometimes the people we help give us a place to stay or something to eat.

Other times, they insist we take a small reward for something we've done."

Karise laughed again, a high, clear sound that grated on Rohawn's nerves. "I hope you're not waiting for a reward from the caravan master!" she said. "If so, you should know that his 'generosity' nearly extended to firing Gil and me."

"For not preventing the gargoyle attack," Gillean added. "How we were supposed to do that, he didn't say. Maybe he thought the beasts were on our payroll." He looked sternly at the warrior-cleric. "Karise, did you hire those gargoyles to attack the caravan and make us look good?"

"Not I."

The young nobleman shook his head ruefully. "We'll be lucky if the old skinflint doesn't short our pay."

"*He'll* be lucky if he doesn't, you mean," Karise said. "If he withholds so much as a copper, he and I will have . . . words." She patted her mace in a way that said the weapon would do her talking.

The thought of the young woman fighting her employer didn't seem right to Rohawn. "I thought clerics were supposed to be forgiving," he said.

"Forgiving, yes," Karise replied. "But we're also supposed to get paid."

Gillean smiled at her and laughed. "Clerics trying to win the favor of Shinare take their wages very seriously," he told Rohawn.

"As do young noblemen trying to prop up their family fortunes," she shot back.

"Point won," Gil said, bowing slightly. He laid his hand on the side of his mouth and spoke to Rohawn as if Karise couldn't hear him, though clearly she could. "She's displaying her passion for sarcasm right now," he said in a stage whisper. "I'm sure that pleases Sirrion greatly. He likes passionate clerics."

Karise smiled at him. "I *might* develop a passion for clouting you on the head," she said, "if I thought you were making fun of my beliefs."

"You won't be surprised to learn," Gillean said to Rohawn, "that Sirrion's clerics are also sometimes known for their fiery tempers."

Rohawn felt completely out of his depth. Unlike his companions, he had little talent for banter. It would probably take him the rest of the afternoon to work out the meaning of all their jabs and counterthrusts. He smiled to make it look as though he hadn't missed the jokes completely.

Gillean stood up in his saddle and peered ahead of them. "Our travails may soon be over," he said. "I believe that's Silverpurse."

Karise stood in her saddle too and shielded her eyes. She nodded. "We should reach the town well before nightfall," she said. "That's good. I could use a bath and a warm bed."

"What will the two of you do once we get to Silverpurse?" Rohawn asked.

"I'll be looking for work again," Gillean said. "I imagine that Karise will be doing the same."

She nodded again.

"Alone, or together?" Rohawn asked. It had suddenly occurred to him that the two mercenaries might be a couple, though neither one had actually said anything to that effect.

Karise shrugged. "Either way," she said. "Whatever the gods have in mind is fine by me."

"We were both lucky to have found a job with this caravan," Gillean added. "Kari, perhaps you could put a word in 'upstairs' and find us something better in Silverpurse." He glanced toward the sky as he said it.

"Sirrion and Shinare help those who help themselves," Karise said.

Gillean put his hand to the side of his mouth and spoke to Rohawn in a stage whisper again. "See?" he said. "That's why I've never been religious. It seems to me that the gods should be helping those who *can't* help themselves. Everyone else is already doing fine on their own."

"Spoken like a true heretic," Karise said fondly. "It's a good thing that neither of my deities believes in conversion by the sword."

"Or the mace," Rohawn put in, pleased that he'd come up with something to add to the banter. Ideas about weapons came to him much more quickly than ideas about other things. Gillean and Karise laughed, which made him even more pleased, as he'd done the banter correctly.

He still wasn't sure if the two were a couple, though. So he just asked straight out. "Are you two a couple?"

Gillean and Karise looked at each other for a moment and then laughed again.

Rohawn frowned. "Is that a 'yes' or a 'no'?"

"Gods, no," Karise said between chuckles.

"We only met on this trip," Gillean added.

Rohawn scratched his head. "But it seems as if you've known each other for ages," he said.

"Life is like that sometimes," Gillean said.

"After all," Karise said, "your mistress thought she'd met Gil before."

"That's different," Rohawn protested.

"Maybe not," Karise replied. "There are only a few types of people in the world. When you travel a lot, you meet plenty of folks who remind you of other folks you've known."

"Some people you take to right away," Gillean added. "Others can take a whole lifetime to appreciate."

Rohawn scratched his head. "I guess I just haven't traveled enough," he said. "I've hardly gotten started, really."

"Give it time, kid," Gillean said. "No one grows up overnight."

"And why would you want to anyway?" Karise concluded.

As Karise had predicted, the caravan reached the town of Silverpurse well before sunset.

Clearly, Silverpurse had once been a thriving community with numerous businesses and homes. Some of the buildings lining the main street were quite grand. As Rohawn looked more carefully, though, he noticed that many of the buildings were old and ill repaired. Boards covered the doors and windows of some of the homes and businesses.

"With a name like Silverpurse, I thought this would be quite a town," Rohawn said. "But it looks kind of shabby."

"Sorry to disappoint you, kid," Karise said.

"What do you think happened here?" Rohawn asked.

"It's just another town struggling on the edge of civilization, I'm sure," Gillean replied. "Settlements spring up where there's a resource to exploit. Then, when the resource is gone . . ." He gestured to the buildings around them and shrugged. "I just hope they have enough going on that I can find a decent job."

"And one for me too, please, thank you very much," Karise added.

"But where have the people gone?" Rohawn asked. "Why did they leave their homes and businesses?"

"Trade routes change," Karise said. "The ebb and flow of commerce is like the currents in the river of life. People must follow where those currents lead them. The gods teach us that."

Rohawn nodded.

"Perhaps the war changed the pattern of trade," suggested a voice beside them.

Karise, Gillean, and Rohawn all jumped. None of them had seen or heard Shara approach. Her sandaled feet made no noise on the dusty road.

"Wars change many things," the half-elf concluded.

"Or maybe people just got tired of the place," Karise offered. "It doesn't look very interesting."

Rohawn didn't agree. He'd never seen anything quite like the buildings here. They were almost entirely timber-built, constructed from long slats of wood, arranged either horizontally or vertically. Many of the buildings were two stories tall and had balconies above their covered porches. The largest of the buildings had shingled roofs and were brightly painted, though most of the paint had faded.

Many of the wooden structures seemed in need of repair too. Rohawn thought he knew why. He'd seen very few stands of trees on the way into town. The residents of Silverpurse would have to go a long way to find timber for their repairs.

Rohawn wondered if trees were the resource that had dried up. Maybe the townsfolk had cut them all down to make the buildings and now they didn't have any more and the town was dying because of it.

He was about to suggest this theory when the caravan stopped at one of the large stables on the edge of town. The merchants staying in Silverpurse began unpacking their wares. Those traveling onward secured their wagons and went to make arrangements for the next step of their journeys.

"Here at last," Gillean said.

Rohawn nodded. "I'd better wake Catriona."

CHAPTER

5   CATRIONA'S MISSION

Remembering how Catriona nearly drew her dragon claws on him before, Rohawn tromped over to the wagon that he and Cat shared, trying to make enough noise not to startle her. Shara followed along with him, making no more noise than an afternoon breeze.

Catriona lay rolled up in her blanket, sound asleep. Apparently, his stomping around hadn't roused her a bit.

"Catriona," Rohawn said quietly.

Instantly Catriona sat bolt upright, reaching for the hilts of her dragon claws. Then she noticed her squire and the half-elf standing quietly beside the wagon.

"Not more gargoyles, I hope," she said.

Rohawn shook his head. "Nope. We've reached Silverpurse."

She climbed from the back of the wagon and stretched. "About time," she said.

"Did you sleep well?" Shara asked.

"Pretty well," Catriona replied. "As well as one ever does when wearing armor."

"The battle with the gargoyles took a lot out of you," the half-elf observed.

"Not really," Catriona said. "I'm just on holiday, remember? I came here to get some rest."

"And to put other things *to* rest, I think," Shara said.

Both Catriona and Rohawn frowned at her. Rohawn wondered if the half-elf knew more than she was letting on.

"The sleeper wakes at last!" Gillean called as he and Karise walked toward the others.

"Where are your horses?" Rohawn asked.

"They were just on loan," Karise explained.

"I thought the merchant might give them to us for meritorious service," Gillean said. "But . . ." He shrugged and smiled in a way that said he really hadn't expected any such reward.

"You got paid, though?" Rohawn asked.

"In full," Karise said, patting a slightly bulging money pouch attached to her belt.

"Karise can be very persuasive when it comes to cuts in wages," Gillean noted with a grin.

Rohawn glanced at the spiked mace hanging from Karise Tarn's belt. There didn't seem to be any new bloodstains on it. He felt a bit relieved.

"So, Catriona," Gillean said. "I really admired the way you handled those gargoyles. Without your help, someone could have been hurt—or worse."

"You two were doing fine on your own," Catriona said. "I'm sure you could have handled it without me."

"Hey, thanks," Karise said. Rohawn wasn't sure whether she was being sarcastic.

"Be that as it may," Gillean continued, "I thought that maybe all of us could have dinner together and discuss future prospects."

"I have to keep traveling," Shara said, her voice dreamy and distant. "My road lies ahead."

"Oh," said Gillean. "That's too bad. Perhaps another time, then,

Shara." Rohawn guessed that Gillean hadn't meant to invite her to begin with. Nevertheless, the young nobleman handled Shara's decline very politely.

"Perhaps," Shara replied. She bowed to each of the companions in turn, and then walked down the main avenue toward the eastern side of town.

As she disappeared among the merchants populating the dusty streets, Karise said, "A few birds shy of a flock, that one."

Catriona shook her head. "I don't think so," she said. "She clearly has different concerns than the rest of us. I wonder what nation her elf family is from."

"She was a good fighter," Rohawn commented.

"Yes," Gillean said. "I noticed that too. Still, each of us must go our own way—unless, perhaps, some of us could go together." He smiled at the rest of them. "Speaking of which, I meant to bring this up over dinner, but perhaps I should mention it now. Rohawn says that you're on some kind of a mission, Catriona."

"I—" Rohawn began. He had intended to say he had never said that, but Gillean kept talking and didn't give him a chance to break in.

"I was hoping that perhaps I—or Karise and I—might tag along," Gillean concluded. "We're good in a fight, as you've seen, and if there's enough coin to share . . ."

Catriona shook her head. "I think you've misunderstood my squire," she said. She reached into the back of the wagon, grabbed Rohawn's traveling pack, tossed it to him, and then retrieved her own. She gathered her horse and Rohawn's and handed the animals' reins to a stable boy standing nearby, slipping him a few coins. The boy nodded and took the animals away.

Catriona turned and walked to a three-story wooden-sided building nearby. A sign hanging on the front of the building promised food and lodging.

Gillean and the rest hurried to keep up with her.

"I never said there was a mission!" Rohawn blurted.

Gillean frowned at him. Rohawn cursed himself silently. He'd become fairly adept at dealing with people during his adventures with Catriona, but somehow, being with Gillean and Karise made him feel very young and foolish. Maybe it was because both mercenaries were so clever in their bantering and so cheerful at the same time. They were very different from the cold-blooded mercenaries of the Northern Star, who partnered with his friends only to betray them.

"But surely some kind of work brought the two of you here to this godsforsaken place," Gillean said to Catriona.

Catriona didn't reply. Instead, she pushed through the swinging doors at the front of the inn. She found a table near the door, dropped her pack on the floor, and sat down.

Rohawn sat down next to her, miserable, embarrassed, and sure that she was mad at him. Karise took the chair next to him. Gillean paused long enough to order drinks for all of them, then sat down as well.

Karise leaned over the table and touched her fingers to the wick of the unlit candle. She muttered a prayer, and immediately the taper lit itself. Rohawn gaped, but Karise ignored him and stared over the flame, looking intently at Catriona.

"Your squire told us that you were taking him to Palanthas," the warrior-cleric said. "But that's opposite the direction the two of you were traveling. Why come out here to the middle of nowhere if there wasn't some coin involved?"

Cat laughed quietly and shook her head. "I agree that this is a godsforsaken area," she said. "And I'll agree that there's little chance of making a decent living this far north—especially for mercenaries. I know this area well. So I don't blame the two of you for wanting to tag along and see if I have a job for you."

"Catriona, I never said—" Rohawn began.

"Hush," Cat said. "I understand. They've just jumped to the wrong conclusions."

The innkeeper brought their drinks, a foggy-colored root ale. Gillean took a long quaff to wash away the dust, then asked, "What other conclusions could we reach? A fine warrior like you, venturing in to the middle of nowhere while claiming to be on the way to a city that's leagues away—in the opposite direction."

"A good, high-paying mercenary job is the only thing that makes sense," Karise agreed.

"Is that why the two of you came to Silverpurse?" Catriona asked.

Both Karise and Gillean squirmed in their seats. "Well, no," Gillean said. "We just took a job that came to hand."

"It was a *job* that brought us here, though," Karise said. "And if not a job, I ask again, what brings you to this godsforsaken place?"

Catriona's green eyes scintillated with reflected candlelight. "Because," she said, "this godsforsaken place is on my way *home*."

Both Gillean and Karise leaned back in their chairs. The warrior-cleric shook her head in disappointment.

"I tried to tell them, Catriona," Rohawn said. "But they just wouldn't listen."

Gillean sighed and put his boots up on the table. "Home," he said. "I guess that makes sense. I'm sorry. I assumed far too much. It's just that—as you know—jobs are hard to come by in these parts, and—"

"I'm sorry about that godsforsaken crack," Karise put in. "I'm sure this place is much nicer than it looks." She flashed a smile at the innkeeper who was working nearby. He glowered at her.

"Silverpurse isn't my home," Catriona clarified. "My home is in the desert nearby."

"Does the town you come from have a name?" Gillean asked.

"Purespring," Catriona replied.

"I've never heard of it," Karise remarked.

"I'm not surprised," Catriona said.

"Have you been away long?" Gillean asked.

A dreamy, far-off look washed over Catriona's face. "Too long," she finally said. She took a long drink from her mug.

Gillean nodded and said, "So, do you want some company on this trip?"

Catriona shook her head. "I'm going alone."

"Except for me," Rohawn put in.

She looked at him and Rohawn felt suddenly nervous.

"No, Rohawn," she said gently. "This is something I have to do by myself."

"But—" Rohawn began. His stomach felt as though it had suddenly been tied in a knot.

"I'm sorry," she said. "This isn't something you can help me with. What I have to do at home is going to be tough enough without other people watching. Thank you, everyone, but no. This is one trip I'm making alone."

"But how can we go on to Palanthas if I don't go with you?" Rohawn asked.

"You can wait here and I'll come back for you," Catriona said. "I promise. My trip to Purespring won't take long, a couple of days at most."

"But I wanted to see where you grew up," Rohawn said.

"It's nothing special," she replied. "Just another small village in the middle of nowhere."

"But it's where you grew up," Rohawn insisted.

"Another time," Catriona said firmly.

"So I should just wait for you here, then."

"Yes."

Catriona pushed her chair back from the table and stood.

"And do what?" the squire asked peevishly.

"Practice your swordsmanship," she replied. "Maybe Gillean or Karise would be willing to help you."

"If we're not busy," Karise said. Again, Rohawn couldn't tell whether or not she was being sarcastic.

"I'm going to get Rohawn and myself rooms," Catriona said. "Then I'm going to prepare for tomorrow before I go to sleep."

"Don't you want supper?" Gillean asked.

"He said he'd pay," Karise reminded her. "It's a sin to pass up a free meal when it's offered."

Catriona chuckled. "Maybe some other time," she said. "Maybe when I get back."

"Assuming we're still here," Karise said. "We *will* be looking for new employment, remember?"

Catriona nodded. "If you're still here."

Rohawn crossed his arms and tried not to look as angry as he felt. "I'll be up later," he said.

Catriona found the innkeeper and paid for their rooms, then went upstairs.

After Cat left, Karise said, "She's a difficult one to figure out."

Gillean nodded. "Perhaps."

"No matter what she says, I'm going with her," Rohawn insisted. He felt angry and hurt and confused all at once.

One thing he knew for sure, though: he wasn't going to let Catriona leave without him.

Rohawn woke as the first ray of dawn crept through the gauze-curtained window in his tiny room at the inn. Pale light illuminated his cotlike bed, the inn's worn wooden floor, and the cracked plaster on the walls.

He got up, went to the window, and peered out. The entire town lay asleep. Everything looked gray and still in the predawn light. Only the distant sound of animals from the stables broke the silence.

Rohawn yawned and stretched. Then he donned his clothes and strapped his greatsword to his back. He scratched his head sleepily as he stumbled into the hall.

He paused outside of Catriona's room, next door to his, and took a deep breath. Then he knocked quietly.

"Catriona," he whispered. "It's Rohawn. I'm ready to leave. Should I fetch the horses from the stable?"

She didn't respond.

"I know what you said," Rohawn continued, "but I'm going with you."

Silence.

"I mean it. I know you need some time by yourself, but it can be dangerous out here in the wilderness. The gargoyles proved it."

Again, only silence.

"C'mon, Cat. Don't be like this. I won't get in the way, I promise."

Rohawn held his breath and waited.

"Please?"

"If you're looking for Catriona," said a voice behind him, "you won't find her."

Rohawn whirled, reaching reflexively for his sword. A strong hand fell on his wrist, preventing him from drawing the weapon.

"Gillean!" Rohawn gasped. "What are you doing up at this hour?"

"I'm a light sleeper," Gillean replied. "That's why I know Catriona left a couple of hours ago."

"A couple of hours!" Rohawn said, crestfallen. How could she leave without him?

"She gave me a message for you," Gillean continued. "She said that once she'd finished her errand, she'd come back and take you to

Palanthas for training—just like she promised. She left the horses too. Said there was no need to take them into the arid wastes. She said both you and the animals should rest up and be ready for when she gets back."

Rohawn's disappointment turned to anger. He crossed his arms and fumed. So now he was no better than a horse, was he?

"She also said that you shouldn't worry about her," Gillean continued. "She said that this is something she has to do on her own, and that you can't help her, even though you want to. She said she'll be back in a few days—a week at the outside."

"Why didn't she tell me all this herself?" Rohawn grumbled.

Gillean smiled wearily at the youngster. "I thought she did—last night," he said. "Besides, she seemed pretty convinced that you'd follow her if she gave you half the chance."

"And I *would*, if I had any idea where she went," Rohawn said. "She's my knight and I'm her squire. We're supposed to travel together. We're supposed to work together."

Gillean Rickard shook his head and shrugged. "All that's true," he said. "But face it, kid, when she said she wanted to go alone, she meant it."

CHAPTER

6   THE ROAD HOME

By the time the sun peeked through the curtains in Rohawn's room at the inn, Catriona
Goodlund had left Silverpurse far behind.

The countryside to the northeast became more hilly, dipping and
rolling as she traveled. The gentle, dusty hills quickly obscured the
village from her view—and obscured her from the view of anyone
in Silverpurse as well.

Catriona knew that leaving Rohawn behind the way she had was
a rotten trick, but Rohawn would never have let her go by herself. For
some reason, she felt she needed to face her family alone. She thought
she had forgiven herself long ago, but the old feelings gnawed at her
when she thought of what her family might say. There was still a long
road ahead—more than enough to make amends. And, gods willing,
she'd left most of her mistakes behind.

Taking Rohawn as her squire had definitely *not* been a mistake.
The youngster was strong and reliable, a better knight than she'd
been at a similar stage of training. Even though she was leaving
him behind, she *couldn't* let him down.

"I'll return and take him to Palanthas as soon as I can," she
said quietly.

40

She felt glad that she'd bumped into Gillean before leaving. She hoped the mercenary would faithfully relay her message to the boy. She hadn't known Gil for very long, but she thought he'd watch out for Rohawn. Maybe it was his resemblance to Alric that made her want to trust him. She pushed that thought aside and focused on the road ahead.

The growing light of day revealed a familiar landscape around her. Northward, in the direction she was headed, the rolling terrain turned more arid. As she walked, the vegetation became sparser and less healthy looking, every shoot and leaf struggling just to stay alive. The jutting rock formations common to the area became even more numerous. Shaped by centuries of wind and sand, the stones stood like petrified titans surveying the bleak countryside.

Catriona knew that these contrasts would increase the farther north she went. Sand and rock would replace grass and brush, dry ravine and gully would replace rolling valley, scorpion and snake would replace hare and wild goat. And then she would reach the last oasis on the edge of the trackless desert—Purespring, her home.

The idea of coming home sent a tumult of emotions swirling through Catriona's mind. Feelings of dread threatened to overwhelm her. Should she turn back and abandon her personal quest?

She considered the possibility for many long minutes, though she continued to walk homeward. How much simpler it would be to guide her squire to the Knights of Solamnia than to go home!

What would that gain her, though? After taking Rohawn to Palanthas, she would still have to face her family someday.

She had abandoned her knight—who was also her aunt—just when she needed Catriona the most. She pictured that day again, how easily the bandits had captured Catriona as she fled from them, how nobly Aunt Leyana had disarmed herself to save Cat. Even though the Whitestone Council had given her clemency, Cat couldn't expect her family to be as lenient.

How would her father react? Would he be glad to see her, or would he shun her? What would her younger sister, Syndall, say? Catriona had abandoned her in a way too, by being too cowardly to return home and face the consequences of her actions. Would Syndall ever forgive her?

An image of her sister's bright eyes and hopeful, upturned face flashed unbidden into Catriona's mind. The memory should have been pleasant, but instead, it felt like a dagger in her breast. How could she face her sister again?

Seeing her mother would be worst of all. Aunt Leyana was her mother's sister. They shared the name of Goodlund, an old and honorable name, a name so well regarded that Catriona's father had chosen it for his own.

Catriona had taken that name, taken generations of the family's good work and reputation, and thrown it all into the dust.

"How can they ever forgive me when I can't forgive myself?" she wondered aloud.

Catriona stopped, her heart too heavy to proceed. She sat down on a long, flat rock at the top of a ravine and wept until her tears ran dry.

The day crept from morning toward noon. The sun's gentle rays warmed her body and dried her tears. She wiped her eyes, stood, and began walking once more.

As she walked, she talked to herself, trying to build up her courage. "Good," she said. "It was good to get this out now. I have to be strong when I return home. I have to be willing to take whatever punishment my family thinks appropriate. I can't run away, and I can't be cowardly. I must face my fate bravely—as Leyana did."

Cat picked her way down a steep-sided defile. It was hot, but not unusually so for the time of year. She marched forward resolutely, pausing only briefly to eat and drink. By the time the sun set and the stars peeked into view, she'd covered more than half of the distance to Purespring.

The sandy, arid landscape surrounding her as she made her campfire looked very familiar indeed. She should reach the village by late afternoon.

Catriona sighed and tossed another stunted branch on the fire. As she did, the campfire flared and sparks shot up into the starry sky.

The brief blaze of light reflected off something in the darkness.

Eyes. Two green eyes lurking just beyond the edge of the firelight.

Catriona leaped to her feet, drew her dragon claws, and sprang into the darkness. The eyes disappeared.

Cat stabbed at where she thought the eyes might have been, but found nothing. She cursed. Sitting by the fire, her eyes hadn't grown used to the darkness.

The eyes reappeared, several feet away. Catriona lunged for them. This time, something she couldn't see was thrust between her feet. She tripped, sprawling onto the dusty earth. She quickly rolled onto her back, bringing her dragon claws around in a defensive arc.

But nothing attacked her.

She scrambled to her feet. Fighting in the darkness was doing her no good. The enemy had the advantage here. She retreated into the firelight and called, "Come out! Whoever or whatever you are, come out!"

"Do you intend to attack me again?" a quiet voice asked.

Catriona frowned. "It depends," she said. "Do you intend to attack *me* again?"

"I did not intend to attack you in the first place."

"All right, then. I won't attack," Catriona said. "Not if you don't."

In answer, a slender figure emerged from the darkness. Her ochre and brown clothing blended almost perfectly into the landscape. Her eyes twinkled green, then brown, then—as she drew closer to the fire—blue.

"Shara!" Catriona said, relieved. "You shouldn't sneak up on a person like that!"

"I was unaware that I had been sneaking," the half-elf replied.

Catriona's feeling of relief gave way to anger. "How did you get here?" she snapped. "How long have you been following me? Why did you attack me?"

The half-elf remained impassive. "I was no more following you than I was sneaking," she said. "And, as I said, I did not attack you. I merely defended myself. Are you all right?"

Catriona nodded. Her ankles smarted where she'd been tripped, but otherwise, she felt fine.

"Good," Shara said. Without asking permission, she sat down on the sand next to Catriona's fire.

Annoyed, Catriona sat down as well. "If you're not following me," she said, "then what are you doing here?"

The half-elf shrugged. "Here, there . . ." she said. "There is little difference."

Shara's word games fanned the fire within Catriona's gut. She clenched the handgrips of her weapons and did not sheath them. "It makes a difference to *me*," she said. "This is a trip I intended to make *alone*."

Unexpectedly, Shara smiled at her. It was a genuine smile, forgiving, disarming.

"Life seldom gives way to our intentions," Shara said.

"But you *were* following me."

"No."

"Then why—" Catriona began. Suddenly, she felt foolish and paranoid. She loosened her grip on her dragon claws.

"It seems that, at present, our fates are running along the same course," Shara said. She picked up a dry twig and cast it into the fire.

Catriona put her weapons away. "Well, you can stay the night," she said, "but tomorrow—"

"Tomorrow will bring what it brings."

"Would you like something to eat?" Catriona asked. "I haven't much, but—"

"Then perhaps I can share some of mine," Shara said. She produced a water skin from her pack and several leaf-wrapped bundles. The bundles contained a round, flattish bread, which Shara toasted over the fire. She took one for herself and offered the other to Catriona, who accepted and nodded her thanks.

Shara took a bite of her bread, and Catriona did the same. Cat smiled. A warm mixture of cheese and vegetables filled the bread. It was tasty, much more savory than the bread and dried meat Catriona had brought.

"Thanks," she said around a mouthful. "It's very good."

Shara nodded and offered Catriona the water skin. Cat drank freely. She felt a bit less cautious since trying the half-elf's food. The water tasted vaguely sweet. It was cooler than Catriona expected too.

"Thank you," she said, passing the skin back to its owner.

Again, Shara nodded. The two of them finished their meal in silence and then prepared to sleep. Catriona unrolled her blanket and laid it out carefully. Shara merely arranged her silken garments, curling up inside them.

Catriona sat down with her back against a nearby boulder. "I'll take first watch," she said.

Shara nodded and fell asleep quickly. Catriona watched her companion in the firelight, both annoyed at the half-elf's presence and at the same time glad for the company.

Rohawn paced the balcony outside Gillean's room at the inn. The balcony ran along the front of the structure, and several rooms had doors leading out onto it. Rohawn's small room was not one of them.

The squire gazed to the north, across the wooden rooftops of Silverpurse. He didn't know exactly what he was looking for, but he was pretty sure that Catriona had gone north—northeast probably. He wished he knew where Purespring lay so that he could follow her.

Inside the room, Gillean and Karise were sitting at a small table, eating breakfast. Both wore dressing gowns—quite nice ones—and neither seemed in much hurry to begin their day. They talked quietly, dallying over their eggs, bacon, and flat bread. Rohawn scowled, annoyed that neither of them felt the urgency that he did.

"Come inside and have something to eat, Roh," Karise called.

"I'm not hungry," Rohawn growled back.

"You can't conquer the whole world on an empty stomach," Gillean said. "Come back inside. Relax."

Rohawn came inside through the balcony door, but he didn't stop scowling. He stood near the table with his arms folded across his muscular chest. The breakfast table had been set as well as the small inn could set it, though the larder was clearly no better than the dingy white tablecloth.

Still, the fare suited the two mercenaries, in Rohawn's opinion. Both the inn and his new friends were trying to seem wealthier than they actually were.

"Try some of the tea," Karise suggested. "It's not half bad. They claim to import it from Abanasinia."

Rohawn shook his head. "I'm not interested. Thanks."

Gillean sipped his tea and leaned back in his rickety wooden chair. "Catriona said she wouldn't be back for a few days or maybe even a week," he reminded the teen. "What are you going to do between now and then?"

"Wait," Rohawn replied.

Karise arched her dark eyebrows at him. "That seems a waste for a warrior of your talent," she said. "Why don't you come job hunting with us?"

"You've got a strong arm and you're good in a fight," Gillean observed. "We could use someone like you. Throw in with us for a while. You might profit from it."

Karise nodded and slurped down a runny fried egg. "With caravans moving through this place, there has to be some work for three hardworking mercenaries," she said.

Rohawn winced at the word *mercenaries,* though he tried not to let his friends see his distaste. He'd dealt with mercenaries before, and though Karise and Gillean seemed more trustworthy than the Northern Star, he would never want to be like them.

"Shinare willing," Karise continued, "we can turn up enough business to keep all of us occupied—at least until Catriona returns." She smiled genuinely at Rohawn, but it didn't make him feel any better.

"I can't," he said stubbornly.

Gillean offered him a piece of flat bread dabbed with honey. Rohawn was about to refuse, but Gillean shot him a look that said it would be an insult to turn the bread down.

Gillean smiled. "Well, if you're not going to look for work," he said, "what are you planning to do? Tell me that you're at least going to have some fun."

Rohawn licked the honey from his lips. The food was good. He felt foolish for almost refusing it. "Fun?" he asked.

"You can't spend all your time staring northward, waiting for her to come back," Karise said. "You should see the sights, enjoy yourself, meet some new people—a young lady or two, maybe. Even a dingy town like this must have *something* for a handsome young man to do."

"I hadn't really planned—" Rohawn began.

"Just because you're a knight doesn't mean you have to lock yourself away from the world," Gillean observed. "Go out. Enjoy life!"

Rohawn felt his face redden. "I think I'll just wait," he said. "Catriona will be back soon." He turned and walked outside onto the balcony once more.

Gillean and Karise shrugged and returned to their breakfast.

Rohawn stared off into the distance. Cat was a good fighter. He knew she could take care of herself. Yet, despite all that, he couldn't help but worry about her.

CHAPTER

7   THE LURE OF PURESPRING

The warm morning sun shining on her face roused Catriona Goodlund from a deep slumber. At first she felt peaceful and serene, as though she were tucked safely in bed, surrounded by impregnable castle walls—the walls of Arngrim. Then she realized that she wasn't and woke with a start.

She sat up and looked around, worried. Shara was supposed to wake her for the early morning watch. Why hadn't she? Was everything all right?

The half-elf sat placidly by the fire, warming two pieces of her stuffed bread. As Catriona sat up, Shara nodded at her.

"You seemed to need the rest more than I did," Shara said, anticipating Cat's question. "I don't sleep as much as most people." She handed one of the pieces of bread to Catriona.

She took it, though she still felt slightly suspicious of the half-elf. Why did Shara have to act so oddly? She wasn't anything like Elidor or the other elves Catriona had met previously.

"Shara," Catriona said, "what kind of elves were you raised by?"

Shara arched her dusky eyebrows. "I don't recall saying I was raised by elves," she replied.

"So you were raised among humans, then?" Catriona said.

Shara took a bite of her stuffed bread and nodded.

"Are your people from around here?"

Shara shook her head.

Catriona frowned. "Then why are you here?"

"To see," Shara replied.

"See what?"

"To see what there is to see."

Catriona stood and looked to the north. "Well, there's not much to see where I'm going," she said.

Shara finished eating and stood beside her. "It is along my path," she said.

Catriona tied her hair up off her neck, taking a moment to think of how to say what she was thinking. "I'm not sure what to make of you," she said bluntly.

The half-elf smiled. "Why try to make anything at all? Why not just accept me as I am offered?"

"And what are you offering?"

"Companionship on a difficult journey."

Catriona took a deep breath and nodded. "All right," she said. "You can come with me. But there really isn't much to see."

"I think I shall judge that for myself," Shara replied.

Catriona headed northeast and Shara followed. The half-elf said little, seldom speaking except when Catriona spoke to her first. Shara's hazel eyes took in everything, though: rocks, scrub, sand, sky. Catriona got the impression that the elf would be able to follow this path again, should she ever desire to.

Cat wasn't sure how she felt about that. The location of Pure-spring was no secret, but Catriona felt as though it were a secret part of herself.

"Tell me about your home," Shara said after a long silence.

"It's not much," Catriona replied, unsure whether she resented or welcomed the conversation. "Just an oasis near the edge of the desert—a small town. Everybody knows everybody else's business."

"Is that why you left?"

Something squirmed inside Catriona, but she tried not to let her discomfort show. "No," she said.

"What, then?"

Catriona took a deep breath. "In a town like Purespring, everyone has a place. I just . . . didn't fit in."

"You didn't know your place?"

The former squire paused. "I knew my place wasn't there," she said.

Shara nodded.

They walked for another mile or so before the half-elf spoke again.

"You said earlier that there was nothing to see in this place," she said, her multicolored eyes scanning the landscape all around them. "Yet on the road we have taken, I have seen many, many things."

"I didn't mean there was *literally* nothing," Catriona replied. "Just that everything here is so . . . barren. Hardly anyone goes to Purespring nowadays."

"But people used to go there in the past?" Shara asked.

"Yes."

"But they don't any longer."

Catriona nodded. "Purespring used to be quite an attraction—before the war. Before the gods returned."

Again, Shara arched her eyebrows. "How did the war and the return of the gods affect your village?"

Images flooded through Catriona's mind—images of when she was a child playing with other children in the town's dusty streets, watching her parents work their looms, participating in the sacred rituals of the Wellspring. Happier times.

"Purespring is an oasis," Catriona began. "The spring is the heart of the village. We divert the water from the spring into a pool within the Wellspring Temple. They say the water has healing properties. Pilgrims used to come from all over the area to visit the town, bathe in the pool, and pray for healing."

"And the war ruined the spring's curative properties?" Shara asked.

"No," Catriona said. "I don't think so. No one ever said it had. But we'd never had a lot of pilgrims, even in the best times. The war made it dangerous to travel, especially out near the desert wastes. Purespring was never on a major trade route. The town had just kind of . . . sprung up where the water was. The healing waters were an amazing boon to everyone who lived there."

"Including your family."

Catriona nodded. "But then the gods . . ." She took a deep breath. "Well, when the gods returned and granted miraculous powers to their clerics . . ." She shook her head, not sure how to continue without seeming impious.

"I understand," Shara said. "People grew impatient with the old ways. Why bathe in a spring for a week and pray for healing when a gifted cleric like Karise can heal you immediately?"

"Yeah," Catriona said. She spat the dust from her mouth.

"Does your family tend the spring?"

"Not exactly," Cat replied. "But most of the people in town depend on the spring in one way or another. My mother is a weaver. She makes the robes required for the Wellspring ceremonies and for pilgrims to enter the sacred pool. She works very closely with the Wellkeeper."

"And your father?"

"My father also weaves, but he specializes in rougher merchandise, like the burlaps and ropes that merchants use. He wanted me and my sister to go into the family business, but . . ." She patted the twin dragon claws hanging at her hips.

"Both your parents remain living, then?" Shara asked.

"Yes," Catriona replied, then added, "last I knew. But it's been a long time, and I haven't heard from anyone." She suppressed a cold shudder at the idea that anything might have happened to her family during her absence. But everything would be fine at home—it had to be. She'd walk down the village's main street to see children playing just as she once had, and as she turned a corner, she'd hear the shuttle of her mother's loom clacking in tandem with her father's. Catriona had never written home since Leyana's death; most likely, they'd never written to her for the same reason.

A wistful look crossed Shara's face, and Catriona suddenly realized that the long life of an elf or half-elf could be a burden. It meant that you would probably outlive many of your friends and loved ones. Likely, a half-elf would lose one parent—the human parent—relatively early in life, while the other parent would remain young and vital for decades, or perhaps centuries.

"Are your parents still alive?" Cat asked, hoping not to stir up any painful memories.

"My father," Shara replied. "At least, he was well when last we met."

"Is he your human parent or—?"

"Yes," the half-elf replied. "My human parent. My mother died in the war."

"I'm sorry," Catriona said. "My family . . . I lost someone around then too."

"Many did," Shara said, her voice quiet and distant. "Far too many. Did you leave home to fight in the war?"

The question stung a bit, but Cat decided to answer it. She would have to face painful questions from her family soon enough. Better that she should get used to such things now.

"Sort of," she replied. "I ran off to squire for my mother's sister—my Aunt Leyana. She was the one I mentioned . . . the one who got killed just after the war ended."

Shara nodded.

"It was my fault," Catriona blurted. "I was captured by bandits. She sacrificed her life to save me."

Again, Shara nodded.

"I hated myself for a long time because of that," Catriona finished.

"And now?" the half-elf asked.

Cat frowned. "Now . . . it's mostly in the past for me. I know hope exists, even if I don't always feel it. I know that life goes on. But sometimes I still hate myself. If I could change just *one* thing in my life . . . !"

"A river flows in only one direction," Shara noted.

Catriona nodded. "Unfortunately."

"The death of your aunt . . . is that why you've been away from home for so long?"

Catriona nodded again, but couldn't muster the voice to reply for a moment or two. Finally she said, "I couldn't face them. I couldn't face my parents or my sister. I can barely talk about it, even now. I can hardly stand to think of it."

"If such painful memories lie ahead of you, why are you returning home?"

"Because I have to," Catriona said firmly. "Because I need to face my family before I take Rohawn to the Council. My aunt was a full-fledged knight, you see. And even though the order has officially forgiven me for my . . . cowardice . . . I . . ." Her voice failed her again.

Shara put a gentle hand on Catriona's shoulder. "If your order has forgiven you, surely your family will as well."

Catriona shook her head. "But the order only lost a knight," she said. "They still have plenty of knights left. My mother . . . she lost her only sister."

"It seems," Shara said, "that she lost a daughter as well."

Catriona took a deep breath. "That's why I'm returning home," she said. "Whether my family disowns me or not, I *will* face them. I'll tell them the truth and beg their forgiveness."

Shara nodded, empathy in her face. "A noble goal."

They walked in silence for a while after that, stopping only briefly to eat during the middle of the day. The terrain became rougher as they traveled. Scorched badlands scarred by deep gullies replaced the rolling, dusty planes.

As the sun arced toward late afternoon, Catriona recognized more of the terrain. Catriona's heart began to pound in her chest, and the weight of her aunt's broken sword, stowed safely in her pack, became almost unbearable.

"Purespring is just over those dunes," she said, pointing to several sandy hills a mile or so distant. "The stream leading from the spring lies in the ravine ahead of us. We can follow the watercourse all the way to the village."

"Where does the stream flow after it leaves Purespring?" Shara asked. "I've seen no ponds or lakes here."

"It goes back underground," Catriona said. "If it didn't it would just evaporate in the heat."

"Your village is lucky to have a reliable water source," Shara said. "In the desert, water is more precious than steel."

Catriona nodded and began picking her way down the rocky slope of the defile. Shara, surefooted and agile, followed right behind.

As they reached the floor of the ravine, Catriona stopped. She looked around, puzzled.

"What's wrong?" Shara asked.

Catriona knelt down and scooped up a handful of dry, reddish dirt. "The stream should be here," she said. "This is where it flows after it leaves the sacred pool."

Shara shielded her eyes and looked up the defile, toward the hills Catriona had indicated. "It has been very hot lately," she said. "Perhaps the stream is evaporating before it can return underground."

Catriona didn't reply. Instead, she began running toward the hills. After a moment, Shara followed.

Catriona began sweating, not just from exertion, but also from fear. Why was there no water in the stream? Why didn't she hear the sounds of village life ahead? Why didn't she see the smoke of cooking fires above the nearby hills?

She dashed through the defile, weaving between the intervening dunes. Only one hill remained between her and the village of Purespring. Leaving the dry stream bed, Catriona hurried up the steep rise. The sand kicked out from under her feet, slowing her progress. Several times she nearly fell. The afternoon sun beat down mercilessly on her head. Sweat poured down her pale skin. She hadn't felt the heat while walking, but now . . .

With one last, determined surge, she crested the hill and skidded to a stop, gaping at the crumbling ruins of the village that had once been Purespring.

CHAPTER

8   ERIKOFF

Rohawn strode down Silverpurse's Main Street for about the twentieth time. He'd been pacing the long avenue most of the day, pausing only occasionally to eat or drink, or to talk to Gillean or Karise.

The two mercenaries were friendly and Rohawn liked them a lot, but they didn't seem to understand his determination to stay in Silverpurse and wait for Catriona.

The squire paused at the western end of the street and stared off to the northeast.

"Looking for something?" an unfamiliar voice asked.

Rohawn turned and saw a young man leaning against the rail of a livery fence. At least, Rohawn assumed the person was a young man from the voice. It was hard to tell for sure. A golden mask covered the youth's face—all except his dark eyes. Orange robes, similar to those worn by a mage or cleric, draped the stranger's slender frame.

"There's not much out there except desert," the youth said. He brushed the dust off his robes. "I know—I just got in."

"From the north?" Rohawn asked.

"No," the youth said. "From the west. I'm Erikoff." He extended his hand.

Rohawn shook it. "I'm Rohawn."

"So," Erikoff said, "what are you looking for out there?"

"Someone," Rohawn replied, not sure what to make of the masked youth. Erikoff seemed friendly enough, but the smooth golden mask—with only slits for Erik's nose and mouth, and slightly larger openings for his eyes—was off-putting.

"A friend who's lagging behind?" Erikoff asked.

"Not exactly," Rohawn said. He kept staring toward the northeast.

"Someone you're waiting for, then."

"Yes."

"But you don't know when he's coming back," Erikoff ventured.

"She."

The masked youth nodded. "Don't know when *she's* coming back."

"Yes."

"Is she late?"

"No. Not yet."

"But you're worried."

"No. Not really."

Erikoff shrugged. "So there's nothing better to do in this town than just stare into the distance?"

"Are you asking for me, or yourself?" Rohawn asked, a bit peeved at Erikoff's ceaseless questioning.

Erikoff chuckled. "Myself, mostly. I'm supposed to find something to occupy me—it's part of my training with the order."

Rohawn stopped staring into the distance and looked more carefully at the young man. "What order?" he asked.

"The Fellowship of the Phoenix," Erikoff replied.

"Are you a wizard or a cleric?" Rohawn asked. Then he added, "It's hard to tell with the mask and all."

"I'm a mage in training," Erikoff said. "The mask is part of my order's vestments."

"Which moon do you serve?"

"Lunitari, the red moon."

"Oh," said Rohawn, somewhat suspicious. Devotees of the red robe walked the balance between light and darkness. He'd heard of good red wizards, but the only one he'd ever known hadn't been so good. "So, what are you supposed to do?" he asked.

"You mean magically?"

Rohawn frowned. "No. I mean, what kind of training mission did your superiors send you on?"

"I'm supposed to help people."

"Help people," Rohawn mused. "Is that all?"

"You're dressed like a Solamnic Knight, aside from the lack of armor," Erikoff said. "Are you one?"

The change of subject confused Rohawn a bit. "What?" he said. "No. I'm not one yet. I'm training to be one."

"And as a squire, then, what are you supposed to do?" Erikoff asked.

"Um . . . whatever my knight tells me to."

"Yes, but beyond that, what are you supposed to do?"

"Um . . . I'm supposed to fight evil."

"Why?"

Now Rohawn felt really puzzled. "Because that's what's right. It's what we're supposed to do."

"I understand that's what you're supposed to do," Erikoff said patiently. "But why? Why are you supposed to do it?"

"To help people, of course," Rohawn said.

"Aha!" Erik said. He threw his arms wide and his orange robe fluttered around him. "See? You and I are on the same mission."

Rohawn scratched his head. "I guess we are at that."

"Good!" exclaimed Erikoff. "So, who is there to help around here?"

"I don't know, really," Rohawn said, ashamed. He'd been so busy waiting for Catriona, it hadn't occurred to him that anyone in Silver-purse might be in need of assistance—the kind a knight in training could provide.

Erikoff put his arm around Rohawn's shoulder, though it was a stretch for the shorter, orange-robed mage. "Let's find out, then."

Rohawn nodded his agreement and the two of them walked back toward the center of town. "We could start at the inn, I guess," Rohawn suggested.

"A fine idea," Erikoff replied. "I could use something to drink. My mouth is positively caked with dust."

They reached the inn and found Karise and Gillean sitting at a table, enjoying an early supper. Rohawn introduced Erikoff, and the two of them sat down. Erikoff ordered a drink for himself and one for Rohawn as well.

"Does your mask come with a golden straw?" Karise asked Erikoff. "Or do you have some magic that allows you to drink through that mouth slit?"

"Perhaps I've merely practiced doing so," Erikoff suggested.

"Have you?" Rohawn asked. In his mind he imagined how a mage might do that.

"No, not really," Erik replied. "I usually tilt the mask up when I eat or drink."

"And you always wear it otherwise?" Gillean asked. "It must get very hot."

"It can," Erik said. "But wearing the mask in most situations is part of my order's discipline. They tell me it builds character. Mostly, I think it builds sweat."

All of them laughed.

Karise danced her fingertips over the flame of the table's sole candle without being burned. "So the mask isn't welded to your face in some kind of secret magical ceremony or anything."

Erikoff laughed. "No. Of course not." He tilted the faceplate back, onto the top of his head. The face behind the mask was lean and angular with deep brown eyes. Locks of his short-cropped blond hair stuck out of the mask's eyes and mouth holes.

"I've heard of mages wearing white robes, red robes, and black robes," Gillean said, looking a bit wary of the newcomer, "but never orange robes."

Rohawn silently cursed himself for overlooking the obvious. He knew better than that. He'd asked Erikoff which moon he served, but it never occurred to him that the wizard's clothes were out of the ordinary. Could Erikoff have been lying about serving the red moon?

Erikoff took Gillean's remark in stride. "Mine is a new order, an offshoot of the red robes, as it were." He smiled. "Would you like to see some magic?"

"I don't think that will be necessary," Gillean said.

"Yes!" Rohawn blurted at the same time.

Erikoff chuckled. He pulled his mask back down over his face and muttered some words that Rohawn couldn't understand. The mage opened his left hand over the table, and a small flame danced in his palm.

Karise smiled, impressed. "That could be useful," she said, "if it were larger."

She opened her right hand, where a taller flame sparked to life.

Erikoff nodded and his flame grew to equal hers. "Are you a devotee of Sirrion, by chance?" he asked.

Gillean laughed. "Well deduced, Erik!" he said.

Both Erikoff and Karise closed their hands, and the flames died away. Rohawn stared, amazed by their casual use of magic.

"I'm a bit puzzled by your winged helmet, though," Erikoff said to Karise.

"You're not the first," Gillean joked.

"That's in honor of Sirrion's wife, Shinare, also known as 'Winged Victory,'" Karise put in.

"Karise is trying to appease both sides of the holy family," Gillean added.

"That explains it," Erikoff said. "Things are not so simple as most people assume, are they? Your multiple devotions, my offshoot band of wizards . . . There are just all sorts of oddities in the world." Behind his golden mask, the mage's dark eyes glittered.

Karise's bright blue eyes sparkled playfully in response. "Very few things in life are simple," she said, leaning toward Erikoff.

As the others spoke, Rohawn pondered the conversation. He knew that there was more going on than there seemed on the surface. He knew that the mercenaries were using their casual, friendly conversation to discover what kind of person Erikoff might be, though he wasn't sure exactly how.

He wished that Catriona were there to help him sort it out. She understood non-warriors and subtle language much better than he did. He'd decided to keep his mouth shut and see what he could learn from watching. Just then, the innkeeper arrived.

"Drinks at last!" Erikoff said. "I was beginning to fear that I might perish of thirst!" Erik's tone was light and jovial, but the innkeeper scowled at him.

"If you're gonna die, do it outside," the man said.

"I'll remember that if it comes up," Erikoff replied.

"See that you do," the innkeeper grumbled.

Erikoff laughed, a short, barklike burst, though the feeling seemed genuine enough. Karise and Gillean laughed as well.

The wizard cupped his hand aside the mouth slit of his mask and said to Rohawn, "It's a dangerous business matching wits with people you've just met. Even the most unseemly bartender may turn out to have a rapier tongue." Erik spoke in a mock-confidential tone, clearly intending the others at the table to hear.

"You'd better remember that yourself," Gillean said.

"Indeed I shall," Erikoff replied. He lifted his mask and took a long draught of his drink.

Gillean finished the last of his shepherd's pie and stood. "I hate to eat and run," he said, "but I'm finished eating . . . and I have to run."

"Did you find a job?" Rohawn asked.

"Yes," he replied. "Kari and I were hired as guards for a southward journey."

Karise finished her food and stood as well. "We'll be gone about four days. There's an opening for another caravan guard, if you're interested, Roh."

Rohawn shook his head.

"What are you guarding the caravan from?" Erikoff asked. "I didn't see anything bigger than a lizard on my trek here."

"You were luckier than we were," Rohawn said. "We got attacked by gargoyles on our way in."

"Really?" Erikoff said. "I thought gargoyles liked mountainous regions or ruins. This place may be run down, but it doesn't qualify as a ruin yet. Is your new boss worried about more gargoyles?"

Gillean shrugged. "I overheard one of the drivers worrying about an army of raiders."

"Oh, that's a fine thing to tell me now, *after* I've hired on!" Karise said. Rohawn couldn't determine whether she was actually worried or just bantering.

"You know how merchants are," Gillean said. "They see a vulture circling high in the clouds, and by the time the caravan reaches town, the bird has become a dragon. I'm sure that, in local lore, the five gargoyles we fought have become a legion of draconians by now."

"We should be so lucky," Karise said. "Having people believe we fought off a legion of draconians would raise our fees considerably." The look on her pretty face told Rohawn that the warrior-cleric wouldn't mind benefiting from such an exaggeration.

"I'm sure all the credit will go to Catriona, though," Gillean joked. "And our Rohawn, of course."

"Who's Catriona?" Erikoff asked.

"My knight," Rohawn explained.

"Oh. The one you were waiting for," said Erikoff.

Rohawn nodded.

"Speaking of which, are you sure you won't change your mind and go with us, Roh?" Gillean said.

"You should go, Rohawn," Erikoff urged. "It's better than sitting around and waiting."

"I told Catriona I'd wait," Rohawn replied.

Karise smiled at him. "A man of your word," she said. "I admire that."

"But not enough to give up some steel and wait with him," Gillean added with a grin.

She shook her head. "Nope," she said. "Sorry, Roh."

"Do what you have to do," Rohawn told her.

"What about you, mage?" Karise said. "We could probably use a few spells on this trip—especially if that 'army' shows up. The pay wouldn't be much, but—"

Erikoff shook his head. "I just got here," he said. "There's no way I'm running off again without at least a *little* time to relax. If you like, though, I could send something with you. Giving out charms is one of my order's budding traditions."

He reached into a concealed pocket within his robe and pulled out two small trinkets. Both were made of gold and about the size of a man's thumbnail. One was a tiny golden feather; the other resembled a bird's eye. "The feather and eye of the phoenix," he explained. "If you rub the feather, it will create sparks—for lighting a campfire or something. If you rub the eye, it will glow for about ten minutes."

He gave the feather to Gillean and the eye to Karise. "Courtesy of the Fellowship of the Phoenix," Erik said.

"How much light does this give off?" Karise asked, examining the bauble.

"About as much as a tiny candle," Erik replied. "You can use the token's powers about once an hour."

"And does the magic last forever?" Gillean asked.

Erikoff laughed his short, barking laugh again. "I wish!" he said. "Only the good luck the tokens bring lasts indefinitely. The other effects last about a month. If we meet again, I can recharge the charms for you."

"Or give us new ones," Karise said, flashing a winning smile.

"Perhaps," Erikoff replied. "Since I'm in the giving mood, here's one for you as well, Rohawn." He handed Rohawn another golden feather. Rohawn, Karise, and Gillean pocketed the tokens.

"That's it, then," Gillean said. "We're off. See you in a couple of days, if you're here when we get back."

"Yeah. See you," Rohawn replied.

Karise patted him on the back. Then she and Gillean grabbed their bags from beside the table and left through the inn's swinging doors.

Erikoff leaned back in his chair. "They seem nice enough—for mercenaries," he said. "Have you known them long?"

"Not very," Rohawn said. "They guarded the caravan Catriona and I were traveling with."

"Well," said the mage, "let's hope that the next few days are uneventful for them and interesting for us. After a long, dull journey, I could use a bit of excitement."

CHAPTER

9   DARK HOMECOMING

Catriona stood frozen in her tracks, staring at the ruins below. She recognized the outline of the village, but nothing else matched her memory of the vibrant oasis community. Could this blasted wreckage actually be Purespring?

The town's adobe houses lay crushed and toppled. Roof timbers stuck out of the rubble like bones protruding from a disturbed grave. All the plant life—the trees, the gardens, the flowerbeds—had been scorched and trampled. Nothing moved. The only sound was the wind and a loud throbbing drumbeat—a sound Catriona suddenly recognized as the pounding of her own heart.

She ran down the hillside, shouting, "Mother! Father! Syndall! Where are you?" Her cries echoed off the ruined buildings, but no other answer came. "Is anyone here?"

Catriona dashed through the rubble-strewn streets, looking from house to ruined house. She found no one—no sign of life. Not a single edifice remained unscathed.

She turned a corner and skidded to a stop outside a horribly familiar building. The wooden door lay trampled on the ground. It had been torn from its hinges, and the walls on either side of it were demolished. The home's roof was gone. Piles of burned timbers and ash filled the interior rooms. Only a big, stone chimney remained standing—a chimney Catriona remembered her father building with his own hands.

She leaned heavily against the door frame, unwilling to venture inside, yet unable to tear herself away.

"Was this your home?" Shara's quiet voice asked behind her.

Cat couldn't find her voice to answer, so she merely nodded.

"I'm sorry," Shara said. "What happened to your family? Is there any sign of them?"

Catriona could hardly bear to find out. Steeling herself, she pushed through the rubble into the ruined home and sifted through the debris. Cold fear gripped her. After a moment, Shara came inside to help her. They searched the ashes, moved aside broken beams, and probed under the fallen walls.

As the sun dipped low in the west, Catriona wiped her brow and shook her head. "Nothing," she said. "There's nothing here. No bodies. All the valuables are gone too."

Oddly, she felt both relieved and more worried than ever. What could have happened to her family? What had happened to Purespring?

"We should look in some of the other houses," Shara suggested.

A terrible notion arose within Catriona's brain.

"The Wellspring Temple!" she gasped, dashing from the house and into the ruined streets. She ran toward the sacred precinct of the healing waters. Shara sprinted along with her, just a few paces behind.

"Would the people have taken refuge there?" Shara called.

"Maybe," Catriona called back. "Even if they haven't, I need to see . . ."

She didn't elaborate and Shara didn't ask.

Cat leaped over wreckage in the alleys, dodged around fallen walls, and scampered up piles of rubble that had once been houses. As she ran, she noticed bodies lying in the street. Most had been picked clean by vultures or other scavengers. A few, though, showed the remnants of charred flesh.

Catriona didn't stop to examine the corpses. There would be time for that later.

As she ran, the Wellspring Temple—the center of life in Purespring—came into view above the rest of the ruins. The temple's marble walls lay smashed, its columns toppled. The blue-painted dome covering the main building looked like a broken eggshell balancing atop the few remaining walls. More than half of the dome was missing.

Catriona fell to her knees. "Is there nothing left?" she gasped.

Shara stopped beside her, standing silently as the evening slipped into night.

After a few minutes, Catriona stood and wiped the tears from her face. She steeled herself, then walked to the front door of the temple.

The great lintel over the entrance had broken in two and fallen, blocking the doorway. The wall above the door had crumbled away, leaving only a V-shaped gash where a grand and glorious entryway had once stood.

Catriona climbed over the rubble and into the room beyond the entryway, which had been an antechamber for greeting temple guests. Once, a blue tile roof had covered the chamber, but the room now lay open to the twilight sky. To the right, an angled passage led away to changing rooms and the sacred bathing pool. An identical passage on the left led to the quarters of the Wellkeeper and her staff. Both hallways were strewn with rubble, but passable.

Nevertheless, Catriona ignored them and walked across the fallen roofing. She stopped before the huge double doors on the far side of the chamber. The tall, red-painted doors still stood, but their hinges had been bent and smashed. The doors hung askew, leaving only a small, triangular void in the middle. Though a very little bit of light remained in the sky, the space beyond the gap remained dark.

Cat took hold of the brass handle belonging to the straighter of the two doors and heaved, but the door didn't move. She huffed, concentrated, and pulled again. The door grated open toward her, but only slightly. She frowned.

"Help me clear some of this rubble away so we can open the door," she said to Shara.

"What do you hope to find?" Shara asked.

"I don't *hope* anything," Catriona said. "I intend to find out what happened to the Wellspring."

Shara nodded and the two of them cleared away most of the smaller rubble from in front of the right-hand door. They pushed aside several stones that were too large to carry.

Catriona took a deep breath and grabbed the brass door handle again. Shara took hold next to her, and the two pulled with all their might.

The door groaned and rumbled like a giant waking from a deep sleep. Gradually, inch by inch, it swung open. They pulled it ajar a couple of feet, wide enough for one person to pass through. Catriona let go of the handle and slipped through the crack into the sanctum of the Wellspring.

Again, Catriona's memory of the place fought against reality. In her mind, the room was a magnificent domed chamber: Votive niches, each holding a delicately carved statue of a sea elf, lined the room's curved walls. In the middle of the room stood a blue stone fountain, carved in the shape of falling waters. And atop it, at the center of the temple, sat a gold and crystal artifact, summoning Purespring's healing waters from deep inside the earth. The waters flowed into a wading pool that was twenty feet wide and several feet deep. Tiles arranged in designs of waves and fish lined the wading pool's bottom and sides. A three-foot-wide channel exited the Wellspring chamber, bringing healing water to the sacred bathing pools beyond. At least, that was Cat's memory.

Now the dome stood cracked and broken, open to the moonlit sky. The statues lay toppled and crumbling. The chamber's curved walls remained, though they were badly cracked and scarred. The sacred pool was empty, bone dry. Worst of all, the blue stone fountain had ceased to flow and a foot-wide gap stood at the fountain's apex.

A weight pressed on Catriona's chest, as if she'd been struck. "It's gone!" she gasped.

"What's gone?" Shara asked.

"The Heart of Purespring," Catriona replied. "This is the well—the center of the temple—and the Heart is what made the water flow."

The half-elf cocked her head in curiosity. "Was the Heart some kind of machine? A pump?"

"Not really," Catriona said. "No one really knows what it was or where it came from. Legends say that the founder of the village brought it with her from far away and used it to locate the pure waters beneath the sandy soil. It rested atop the Wellspring fountain and summoned the healing waters to the temple."

"What did this artifact look like?" Shara asked. "Did you ever see it?"

Catriona nodded. "I saw it many times during the well ceremonies and examined it up close when my mother delivered the sacred robes to the temple." She relaxed and let the picture form in her mind's eye. "It was like a large piece of jewelry, a golden latticework of bars—about as big around as your finger—encircling a glittering gemstone set into the center. The gem was huge, about the same size and shape as a person's head."

"A gem? So someone might have stolen it because it was valuable."

Catriona sat down on the edge of the empty pool. "It was priceless."

"Worth destroying a whole town to steal?"

Catriona put her head in her hands and closed her eyes. "Maybe," she said. "I don't know. Who could have done such a thing?"

Shara sat down beside her. "I don't know," the half-elf said. "Nor do I think we'll discover the answer tonight. We've come a long way. We should rest."

Catriona lay back on the stone and tile floor and gazed at the moonlit sky through the shattered dome. "I don't know if I can sleep," she said. "I should *do* something."

"What can you do tonight?" Shara asked. Her voice was calm, soothing. "Perhaps tomorrow, in the bright light of day, we'll be able to discover the truth."

"Yes," Catriona said. "Tomorrow."

"I will take first watch," Shara offered.

Catriona agreed and laid her bedroll out on one side of the chamber, away from the main door. Shara took up a position opposite, near where the water once flowed into the bathing room. The half-elf sat with her back against one of the fallen statues.

As Catriona drifted off, a sleepy thought occurred to her: in the dim light, Shara almost looked like one of the temple's carved sea elves come to life.

CHAPTER

10   Last Gasps

Cat awoke gasping for air, a heavy pressure bearing down on her chest. A wild-eyed skeletal face leered down at her, drooling hot spittle.

The thing was smaller than Catriona and far less muscular. But it was sitting on her chest, and already had its hands around her neck, its bony fingers tightening around Catriona's throat.

"Give it back to me!" the creature snarled. "Give it back!"

The thing's eyes burned with anger. Its long, tangled hair scratched across Catriona's face. Catriona tried to heave upward, but the thing leaned forward, pressing her back down.

"Give it to me!" the creature hissed, its haggard head silhouetted against the brightening sky.

Amid her struggle, Catriona felt puzzled. The sun was already rising, but where was Shara? Why hadn't she woken her? Why hadn't she slain this creature or, at least, cried out for help?

"Give it back!" the thing cried.

Catriona tried to respond, but she had no air to speak. Already, spots were dancing in front of her eyes. The creature kept her arms pinned under its knees. She couldn't reach up to break its grasp.

Cat groped desperately around on the floor. Amid the rubble she found a fist-sized rock. She seized it and flicked her wrist as hard as she could, flinging the stone at the creature.

The rock bounced off its left temple. The impact wasn't hard, but it broke the creature's concentration. It blinked in confusion.

Catriona heaved and the creature tumbled off her. She rolled to the right, down the slope, and into the empty Wellspring pool. She scrambled to her feet and drew the dragon claws from her hips, holding them before her in a defensive stance. She glanced around, fearing she might be fighting an army of loathsome beasts.

But there was no one, just Catriona and her enemy alone in the Wellspring chamber—and Shara. The half-elf lay crumpled by the far wall, lying on her stomach facing the empty pool. Even in the dim morning light, Catriona could see the nasty bruise on her left temple.

"Thief! Defiler!" the creature screamed. It charged down the slope of the empty bowl toward Catriona, its eyes feral. Tattered rags covered its bony form. Suddenly, Catriona recognized it.

"Stop!" she said, stepping aside. The thing barreled past her, nearly crashing into the carved fountain at the Wellspring's center.

The creature whirled, slashing at the young warrior with its decrepit fingernails. "You took it!" it rasped. "You took it! Give it back to me! It belongs to the village!"

"Stop!" Catriona cried. "Mother of Waters, stop! It's me, Catriona Goodlund!"

The creature paused and some of its wildness ebbed.

In the lull, Catriona saw that she had been right. This was no monster, but a human being like herself—a human being she had once known.

"Mother of Waters," she said again, "I am not your enemy. I am Catriona, daughter of Ariana and Connal, older sister of Syndall."

The feral old woman crouched low, as though she might spring at any moment. "You lie!" she said, her voice a rasping cough. "Catriona left long ago. Her shame made her dead to all of Purespring."

"But I am *not* dead," Catriona replied calmly, "and I have returned to face my shame." To emphasize her point, she lowered her weapons and dropped to one knee. "I have returned," she repeated, "to make amends." She bowed her head slightly, though she kept her eyes on the haggard old woman.

The Wellkeeper's wild eyes softened and her aged jaw trembled. "C-can it be?" she asked. "Or am I finally mad?"

"You are not mad," Catriona said. She slowly stood and opened her arms to greet the old woman.

Tears budded in the Wellkeeper's eyes. She staggered to Catriona and embraced her. Catriona hugged her back, ignoring the stench of her unwashed body.

"I dreamed that a deliverer would come," the Wellkeeper said. "But I did not dream that it would be you."

"I'm no savior," Catriona replied, "but I will do what I can." She stroked the old woman's head tenderly. As she did, her eyes returned to the corner where Shara lay unmoving.

"Mother of Waters," Catriona said gently, "I need to check on my friend." She released the Wellkeeper, though she maintained eye contact.

"What friend?" the haggard old woman asked.

Catriona pointed to where Shara lay. "Do you know what happened to her?" she asked, pretty sure that she already knew.

"I hit her," the Wellkeeper answered. She grinned sheepishly and then coughed. "I thought she was a bandit. I didn't recognize either of you."

Catriona nodded and knelt beside Shara. Her pulse was strong and she was breathing regularly, despite the bruise on her head.

Catriona got her water skin, then cradled Shara's head in her lap and gently washed the girl's face. Shara's eyelids flickered. "Water . . ." she gasped.

The red-haired warrior dribbled some onto the half-elf's lips. She looked up at Catriona.

"What happened?" she asked.

"I was hoping you could tell me," Catriona said. "Why didn't you wake me for my watch?"

"I thought you needed the sleep more than I did," Shara replied. "Besides, I don't need as much sleep as most people."

"Yes," Catriona said. "You told me before."

Shara sat up, wincing and holding her head. "Did I?" she asked. She spotted the Wellkeeper, who was now sitting cross-legged near the center of the dry fountain. "Is that who hit me?"

Catriona nodded and handed Shara the water skin.

The half-elf drank. "I'm sorry," she said. "I got up to stretch just before dawn. The old woman leaped from the shadows and clouted me on the head before I could react."

"She's quicker and stronger than she looks," Catriona said, rubbing her neck.

Shara nodded. "Who is she?"

"She's the Wellkeeper," Catriona told her. "Most people in town referred to her as the Mother of Waters. She's the high priestess of the Wellspring Temple."

"She certainly seems zealous in her duties," Shara said. She touched the dark red bruise on her forehead gingerly.

"Yes," Catriona replied. "But apparently, she couldn't save the temple—or the Heart of Purespring."

"Did she tell you what happened?"

"No. We didn't have time to discuss it yet. We can find out now if you're feeling better."

"I'll live. My family is known for being hardheaded," Shara said without a trace of a smile. "We also heal quickly."

"Glad to hear it," Catriona said. She stood and helped Shara up.

They walked to the center of the empty pool where the Wellkeeper was sitting. "Mother of Waters," Catriona said formally, "this is my friend Shara."

The half-elf bowed slightly. The old woman rose shakily and did the same.

"Shara," the Wellkeeper mused. "That's an unusual name. Are you from around here?" She gazed questioningly into Shara's hazel eyes.

"Not really," the half-elf replied.

The Wellkeeper's eyes narrowed. "Can she be trusted?" the old woman asked Catriona.

"I think so," Catriona replied. She still wasn't quite sure what to make of Shara, but now wasn't the time to mention that.

The Wellkeeper looked back at the half-elf. "Did you take the Heart?" she asked.

"No," Shara replied.

The Wellkeeper thought for a moment. "I don't think she's lying," the old woman finally told Catriona, "but you never can tell with elves."

Catriona shot Shara a sympathetic glance, but said nothing. The half-elf remained silent and impassive as well. The Wellkeeper smiled beatifically, completely unaware that she might have insulted Shara.

"Mother of Waters," Catriona began after a long, uncomfortable silence. "What happened to the town? Where are the people? How was Purespring destroyed, and who took the Heart?"

The old Wellkeeper slowly sat down, as though every move she made now caused her pain. She lowered her haggard head and said in a very low voice, "It was a *dragon*."

Gillean Rickard took turns riding at the front and rear of the caravan with Karise Tarn. The half dozen merchants in the wagon train seemed nervous to the young nobleman. The tradesmen milled around between their fourteen wagons, muttering among themselves, but seldom spoke to Gillean. When they did say something to him or Karise, it was usually about some perceived fault in the mercenaries' routine.

Both he and Karise bore the insults stoically, not wanting to jeopardize their pay. When the two of them changed places in the line, they often lingered near the middle of the caravan and chatted a bit. They spoke quietly to keep their conversations private.

"Any trouble?" Karise asked as she moved from the back toward the front.

"Other than our employers, you mean?" Gillean replied. "No. I'm getting a bit tired of explaining to them what we're doing. If they didn't think we'd make good guards, why did they hire us?"

"Maybe we were all they could afford," Karise said, flashing him a sly grin.

Gillean nodded back. "With the wages they're paying us, that certainly could be the case."

"We should have held out for more," Karise said. "They were anxious to get going and might have upped their offer."

"Spoken like a cleric of Shinare," he joked.

"I'm not there yet," she replied. "Maybe some day. Until then, I'm happy to dedicate my money-earning creativity to Sirrion."

Gillean cast his eyes up and down the small wagon train. "You'd think they'd be happier getting guards of our quality at bargain prices," he said.

"They do seem jumpy," Karise agreed, "even for merchants."

"Any idea what it's about?" he asked.

She shook her head. "None. Unless they're worried about that mythical army of raiders." She laughed her light, musical laugh.

"I doubt it," Gillean replied. "One thing's for sure: anyone attacking this caravan won't be doing it to steal the food. I may have to start a mutiny if we don't get a better cook."

"Mutinies are at sea," Karise said. "I think it's rebellion on land. But let me know if you intend to start one so I can throw in with you." Her bright blue eyes sparkled.

"I just might do that, Kari," he said, smiling back at her. He felt surprised at how fond he'd grown of her in the short time they'd traveled together. "You know, I'm glad we met up. These trips would have been boring without you."

She raised her eyebrows. "Even with the gargoyles?" she asked.

He shrugged. "Gargoyles notwithstanding."

"And what about that girl Catriona?" Karise said. "It seemed to me that you had your eye on *her* as well." Again, her eyes flashed.

He shrugged. She'd hit the mark, though. He *had* grown fond of Catriona as well. "She seems nice enough," he replied.

Karise made her voice deep and morose. "Assuming you like your women grim and focused," she said. She pulled her face into a dour expression.

Gillean laughed. "I take women as I find them," he said. "There's no sense trying to do otherwise."

"That's a good rule to apply to men as well," Karise said. "I'll have to remember it the next time I'm in the market."

"And are you?"

"Am I what?"

"In the market?"

"Are *you?*"

He paused, unsure for a moment what to say. Then something in the southeastern sky caught his attention.

"What is it?" she asked.

He squinted and shielded his eyes. "I can't be sure from this distance," he said. "But I think it might be a *dragon.*"

CHAPTER

11   RUMOR OF DRAGONS

Y ou're joking," Karise said.

Gillean continued to shield his eyes and peer southeast. "I never joke about these kinds of things—not when I'm working."

Karise swore and shielded her eyes as well. In the distance, high up near the clouds, she saw a small, dark speck. A cold shiver ran down her spine.

"It could be a bird," she suggested.

"Not at this distance," he said. "I've never heard of any bird that large. Worse, I think it's coming this way."

She swore again. "So much for Erikoff's good-luck charms! We'd better tell our employers."

He nodded and rode toward the back of the caravan while she rode toward the front, both passing the grim news through the line as they rode.

Rather than panicking, as Karise had expected, the caravan leaders nodded grimly and requested a brief conference with her and Gillean. They met near the center of the wagon train.

"We were afraid of this," the merchant leader, a woman named Rabe, said.

"Really?" said Karise. "You expect *dragon fighters* at the wages you're paying?"

Rabe grew red in the face. "Our wages are what they are," she said. "Didn't you wonder why we were in such a hurry to leave, or why no one else had taken the job? Did you think we were just waiting around for you and your handsome friend to show up? Everybody knows there's a dragon on the prowl around here."

Karise frowned. "Well *we* didn't," she said. "Next time, I guess we'll know to ask. So, now that we've seen a dragon, what do you want to do?"

"You're the experts," Rabe said. "That's why we hired you."

Gillean kept his eyes on the distant shape in the sky. It was still a long way off, though definitely growing closer by the minute.

"We don't have a lot of time," he said. "I suggest we scatter and hide. With luck, it may pass us by."

"Unless, of course, it's looking for this caravan and that's why you hired us in the first place," Karise put in.

"No," Rabe said, scowling at her. "They wouldn't be coming for us personally. We don't have anything of great value."

"Which we could have guessed from the wages," Karise said. She and the merchant boss glared at each other, and for a moment Karise thought Rabe might strike her.

"Kari, that's enough," Gillean said. "We have to get all these people and wagons under cover." He pointed to a wide swath of scrubby brush nearby. "Madame, have your people move off the trail and camouflage themselves and their wagons."

"Put blinders on the animals," Karise ordered. "Muzzle them and muffle their ears and noses, too, if you can."

"People who aren't used to dragons should hide as deep in the brush as they can," Gillean added. "Dragonfear is a terrible thing. The last thing we need is some fool running out from under cover and alerting the beast to our presence."

"Perhaps you should restrain yourselves, as well," Karise added. "When the dragon comes, we need everyone to stay absolutely silent and still."

Rabe looked indignant. "Gag and tie ourselves up?"

"She's right," Gillean said. "The urge to cry out or run when a dragon passes by is very great. A gag and tied legs would be a good idea."

"Then how would we flee if it actually comes after us?" Rabe asked.

"Don't worry about that," Karise said. "If the dragon comes after you, you're dead whether your legs are tied or not. And if you know any good prayers," Karise said, "now would be the time to start saying them."

Rabe nodded. She directed her companions to prepare as Gillean and Karise had suggested. The merchants rushed around, moving the wagons off the road, cutting brush, and looking fearfully toward the sky.

Gillean and Kari helped out wherever they could. Some of the merchants had brought green tarps with leaf designs painted on them, which they quickly threw over their wagons.

"If we'd seen those earlier," Karise said to Gillean, "we'd have realized they were serious about fearing an attack."

The young lord nodded and continued chopping brush with his sword, glancing toward the oncoming dragon from time to time. In the clear skies of the desert, he could see a long way, and the dragon was still pretty far away.

The group worked quickly and efficiently. Inside of a quarter of an hour, they'd cleared nearly all traces of the caravan from the road. The merchants, their wagons, and their animals huddled underneath camouflage tarps and chopped brush. Many bound and gagged themselves, as the mercenaries had suggested.

Rabe and the other merchants glanced nervously at the sky. While they prepared for the attack, the dragon had flown much closer.

"You'll tell us when it's gone?" Rabe said, pulling a blindfold over her own eyes.

"Of course," Karise told her.

"You'll probably feel when it's gone, anyway," Gillean added. "Once the dragonfear passes, you'll know it."

He and Karise made their horses lie down. They blindfolded the animals' eyes, tethered the steeds tightly, and covered both the horses and themselves with cut brush.

Then they waited.

"A fine thing to do to my good clothes," Karise mused, extracting a twig from the sleeve of her tunic.

"Better a few twigs and snags than scorch marks from dragon breath," Gillean pointed out. They'd arranged their shelter to observe the enemy's flight path.

The dragon moved toward them with great power and swiftness. The morning sun glinted off its scaly armor, though it was still too far away to see what color those scales were.

"What do you think it wants?" Karise whispered to Gillean. The beast was still about two miles away, but somehow she didn't dare to speak in normal tones.

Gillean shook his head. "Loot? Food? Who knows?" he whispered back, then paused. "Is that someone riding it?"

Peering toward the distant threat, Karise spotted what he had seen—another, smaller shape perched atop the back of the huge flying monster. "A dragon rider!" she gasped.

Gillean nodded. His face looked grim. His blue-gray eyes glanced to the makeshift thickets where the merchants, their animals, and their wagons lay hidden.

Gillean had done an excellent job concealing their employers. If Karise hadn't known where to look, she probably wouldn't have seen them. She hoped the dragon wouldn't be able spot the group either.

STEPHEN D. SULLIVAN

The brush concealing the merchants barely moved, and Karise wondered if they were paralyzed with fear. She was starting to feel nervous herself. She'd seen a dragon once before, but it had been a copper—one of the "good" dragons—and even that had made her feel a bit uneasy.

It was coming close enough that she could see that the beast was a blue, a servant of the Dark Queen. Though a human might be riding the dragon, it certainly had no love for humankind—or for clerics that didn't serve Takhisis. Karise swallowed hard and tried to force her stomach to calm down.

With each passing moment, the dragon drew closer. Its huge wings buffeted aside low-lying clouds as it came. The rumble of its breath sounded like distant thunder. It scanned the surrounding landscape looking for . . . for what? Karise hoped it wasn't looking for them.

Had the merchants lied to her? Were they actually carrying something valuable, something the dragon wanted? Karise hated to think that she might throw her life away defending this conniving lot.

Yet she had been hired to do a job, and her code demanded that she finish it. Sirrion might put up with clerics changing their mind on a whim, but Shinare expected her worshipers to follow through on a transaction. If Karise ever hoped to join the ranks of Shinare's clerics, she had to see this to the end.

But what good would keeping her word do if she were dead?

She discovered that she was clutching Gillean's hand tightly, though she didn't remember doing it. Her palms sweated profusely, as did the rest of her. She felt faint, lightheaded.

Gillean looked at her, concerned. "Are you all right?" he whispered.

"I—it's the dragon," she replied, her voice a hoarse whisper.

He nodded. "I feel it too. It's dragonfear. Try not to let it take hold."

He glanced toward the hiding merchants once more. "I hope those bonds and gags hold. If any of them bolt out into the open . . ."

He didn't need to finish the sentence. Karise could already see the result in her mind: Several frightened merchants would run from the cover and the dragon would spot them. It would turn and blast them with its lightning breath. Then it would search the area until it discovered where they'd come from.

The dragon would find all of them then—and then the killing would start. By the time the beast finished, no one, not merchant nor mercenary, would remain alive.

The dragon followed the roadway they'd been using until it passed directly over Karise's head. She felt as though a cold hand had clenched around her heart. She wanted to tear her eyes away, but she couldn't. She wanted to scream, but her voice remained stuck in her throat.

She could see the monstrous scales on the dragon's belly—impenetrable armor protecting its near-immortal heart. The sound of its breath crashed against her ears like the rushing surf. Her head throbbed with the pounding of her own heart. She squeezed Gillean's hand until she thought she would break it.

He said nothing. She couldn't tell if he was watching the dragon or not. In that moment, only two things existed: the dragon and a world filled to overflowing with fear. She felt a shriek building up within her. Her legs wanted to run, either to escape or—if that proved impossible—to go to the dragon and quicken her own demise.

Nothing could be worse than this fear. Nothing. Not even death. Her lips parted. She would scream, scream with all her might, just as soon as she found her breath.

A strong, gloved hand clamped firmly over her mouth.

"Karise! Snap out of it!" Gillean hissed.

And the spell was broken. She saw the dragon arcing away, leaving behind the caravan, its cowering merchants, and its hidden guards.

Karise closed her eyes. Her head fell to her chest, and she let out a long, low breath. She let go of Gillean's hand.

"Thanks," she whispered, opening her eyes once more.

He nodded. "You shouldn't have looked."

"Did *you* look?" she asked.

"Yes," he said.

"Well, then why should I have kept my eyes closed?"

"Because I've been around dragons before."

"When?"

"My family has . . . rather, *had* money, remember?" he said. "With money comes influence, and sometimes, danger. I met a good dragon or two during the war, and saw more than my share of the evil ones as well."

"And all that helped you get over the fear?"

"Some of it." He smiled at her. "I still wanted to scream like a baby, though."

She chuckled. "I almost did. I've seen a lot of things in my travels, but never anything like that. Do you think it's safe to come out?"

Gillean watched the dragon as it flew into the distance. "Not yet," he said. "Let's give it another half hour at least. We need to make sure it's not coming back."

"Should we tell the merchants to stay put?"

He shook his head. "I don't think we'll need to."

It was a tense half hour, but the dragon did not return. Karise smiled at Gillean, happy that he'd been beside her during the crisis. "Maybe Erikoff's good-luck charms work after all," she said.

"They certainly didn't hurt," Gillean replied. The two of them emerged from their shelter and rousted the rest of the caravan.

"It's safe now," Gillean declared. "You can all come out."

"We should get back on the road," Karise added. "Keep moving, just in case."

Rabe and the other merchants removed their gags and grumbled their agreement. They untied themselves and their animals and emerged from the conglomeration of brush and tarps. Rabe shook hands with both mercenaries. "I wasn't sure about you two," she said, "but you handled the situation perfectly. Thank you."

"Our pay will be thanks enough," Gillean replied.

"Yes, of course," Rabe said, yanking a tarp off a cart. "Once the journey is over. With a little luck, we won't have any more trouble."

"Speaking of which," Karise said, "you seemed to be expecting a dragon—perhaps even this dragon in particular. Why?" She grunted as she and Gillean helped Rabe pull the cart back onto the road.

"Rumors have been flying around Silverpurse for months," Rabe said. "Rumors about a new lord named Viktor and his dragon, Thane. They live in a fortress in the western mountains and are terrorizing the surrounding countryside. Many local villages are subject to them already."

"What about the Solamnic Knights or the wizards in Palanthas?" Gillean asked. "Why don't *they* do something about this Viktor and Thane?" He harnessed a horse to its wagon.

Rabe shook her head. "The Solamnics and their allies are stretched thin, even though the war is over. They're concentrating their efforts in the more populated areas to the south, from what I hear. Viktor and Thane don't dare to raid Solamnic territory. Perhaps someday they will, if their army grows powerful enough. Many dark creatures have joined the dragonlord's cause already."

"Creatures like gargoyles, maybe?" Karise asked.

"Maybe," Rabe said. "As their power expands, Viktor and Thane roam ever farther afield, seeking new people to pay them tribute, new villages too weak to fight a dragon."

"Which would be about everyone," Karise said.

Rabe nodded. "Those who do not pay are destroyed. That's why we're leaving this cursed area. I doubt any one of us will ever return.

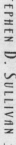

The land near the desert is becoming too dangerous to be profitable. And besides, since the war, few people travel this way anymore."

"No wonder we've had trouble finding jobs," Karise remarked.

Gillean looked over the line of wagons. "The caravan seems ready," he said. "Let's get going."

He and Karise saddled up, and the merchant train moved down the rutted road once more. They traveled as quickly as they could. Gillean and Karise kept their eyes peeled for thickets—which appeared from time to time as they moved southward—and other places they could use for cover. No one wanted to be caught unprepared if the dragon should return.

As they traded places in the line once more, Gillean caught Karise's eye. "You were right," he said. "They're not paying us enough."

"Does anyone ever?" she replied. A sudden knot twisted in her gut and she reined in, stopping for a moment.

"What is it?" Gillean asked, seeing the worry on her face.

"Gil," Karise said, "I just had a terrible thought. The direction the dragon was flying . . ."

"Yes?"

"It was headed north."

"Yes, what of it?" Gillean asked.

Karise swallowed hard. "Silverpurse is in that direction."

CHAPTER

12   THE FATE OF PURESPRING

A cold chill ran down Catriona's spine. "A dragon?" she asked.

The ancient Wellkeeper nodded. "Yes."

"When?"

The old woman coughed and shook her head. "Time?" she rasped. "What is time? Once I would have known, but now?"

A mixture of anger, guilt, and terrible longing welled up within Catriona. She fought hard to keep her voice from quavering. "I need to know," she said. "Was it days? Weeks? Months?"

The old woman's quiet, hoarse voice brimmed with painful memory. "Many months ago," she said. "The dragon arrived without warning. It swooped down upon our town like a jackal upon a hare. They said they wanted money, but . . ." She shrugged, and her bones seemed to shake.

Before Catriona could ask who "they" were, Shara asked, "Did you have defenses?"

"We are a peaceful people," the Wellkeeper said. She coughed again. With every moment, more life seemed to be seeping out of her.

"Purespring has never needed warriors," Catriona explained.

"Local traditions say the spring will dry up if blood is spilled in the town."

"And it has," Shara noted.

"But not because of the blood!" the Wellkeeper rasped, suddenly springing to her feet. "The water is gone because *he* stole it! He stole the Heart!" She looked around frantically, as though she might dash from the room and search out the villain.

Catriona put a calming hand on the woman's ancient shoulder. "Who?" Catriona said. "Who took the Heart of Purespring? The dragon?"

"No," the old woman said. "The dragon rider!"

"There was a rider with the dragon?" Catriona asked, trying to wrap her mind around the Wellkeeper's elliptical speech.

"A terrible man," the Wellkeeper said. "He demanded steel." She collapsed to the floor again as tears welled in her ancient eyes. "But since the war . . ." She shrugged. "We have so little. So few come to the spring anymore. I offered him what we had, but it was not enough." She put her head down and wept.

Catriona and Shara waited quietly her to continue. After a time, the tears stopped and the Wellkeeper found her voice once more. "They destroyed everything," she whispered.

"Just one dragon and rider?" Shara said.

The Wellkeeper nodded. "The town was defenseless. They destroyed everything and tore the Heart from Purespring."

"And the people?" Shara asked.

"All killed—blasted by the beast's terrible lightning or slain by its wicked talons and fangs."

Every muscle in Catriona's body felt tense, almost to the point of breaking. She could hardly speak through her clenched teeth. "What about . . . my family?"

The old woman shook her head. "All dead."

"You saw them?" Catriona said. "You saw their bodies?"

The Wellkeeper let out a long, slow breath and lay down on the cold tiles of the empty pool. "I saw many bodies," she said. "Too many to count. Too many to name."

"Then perhaps they survived," Catriona said, desperate for some small measure of hope.

The old woman's voice was barely a whisper now. "I lay trapped in the rubble of the temple for three days," she said. "I cried for help that entire time."

"No one came," Shara concluded.

"No one came," the Wellkeeper affirmed. "If any had survived, wouldn't someone have come to help?"

"Yes," Catriona said. She felt hollow inside. Everyone she grew up with was gone—her friends, her parents, her sister . . . everyone.

"I finally wormed my way free," the Wellkeeper said. "I crawled from the rubble of the temple and out into the corpse of the village. Vultures and jackals had come for what was left of the bodies by then. And after that . . . human jackals took the rest."

"What did you do?" Shara asked.

"I hid," the Wellkeeper said. Sadness made her ancient voice crack. "The Heart was gone. *My* heart was gone. What else could I do? I hid and I waited." She turned her aged, watery eyes toward Catriona. "But now, you have come."

"I—" Cat began.

"Now you have come," the Wellkeeper continued. "Now you know what happened. Now"—and here she sighed a long, deep sigh—"I can go too."

Catriona knelt beside her and took her wizened hand. "Mother of Waters," she said. "No. You can't."

"What else can I do?" the Wellkeeper asked.

"But our town," Catriona said. "Our history, our traditions . . . ." Tears streamed unbidden from her eyes.

"Our town, our history, our traditions, are . . . gone," the

Wellkeeper said. She squeezed Catriona's hand and leaned close. "But with you here . . . they are not . . . lost!"

The final words fluttered on the Wellkeeper's aged lips for a moment, and then her last breath carried them away. Her eyes closed and her body went limp.

Shara stood reverently beside the old woman. Catriona wept.

Finally, Catriona stood. "I waited too long to return."

"No one can know the future," Shara said. "The path before us is often unclear, but we must walk it as best we can. I do not think you have walked your path badly, Catriona."

Catriona spun on her, tear-filled eyes blazing. "I was *too late!*"

The half-elf remained calm. "Not for the old woman," she said.

"But for the town . . . for my family!" A sob stopped her.

Silence filled the well chamber for long minutes.

"What will you do now?" Shara finally asked.

"Bury her."

They chose a place outside the temple, where the earth had not been baked hard by the sun, and dug a shallow grave with boards salvaged from the ruins of a nearby house.

Catriona recovered some robes from one of the temple's less-destroyed antechambers. She wrapped the old Wellkeeper's body in the cloth, trying hard not to think about how the bodies of her family might have been treated after they died. Horrible images kept creeping in anyway. She saw her mother making this very cloth for the temple. She imagined her mother dying horribly, without even a burlap shroud to be buried in.

As they laid the Wellkeeper in the grave, sadness welled up inside Catriona again, but she fought back the emotion. "There will be time for tears later," she told herself. They piled stones on top of her body to keep scavengers away.

"Do you want to say something over the grave?" Shara asked,

WARRIOR'S HEART

standing solemnly at the graveside. "Are there special words that your people have?"

Catriona shook her head. It was all she could do to keep from crying.

Shara lowered her hazel eyes to the dusty ground. "The sands of life are ever shifting," she said quietly. "Some days they are soft and cool, others harsh and hot. All our days we walk the sand. Now this old woman walks no more. Now she returns to the sands that birthed her. When the wind blows, the dunes will whisper her name for eternity."

For a moment, everything fell silent, save for the wind.

"That was beautiful," Catriona said quietly.

"It's what my people say when one of our own dies," Shara replied. She gazed off into the distance for a moment.

Catriona wondered if Shara were looking toward her own home.

"What will you do now?" Shara finally asked.

Catriona took a deep breath. "My past is dead," she replied. "But not my future." She smeared the tears from the corner of her eyes with the back of her left hand. "I still have things to do. I made Rohawn a promise, that I would take him to Palanthas so that he can take his tests. I will keep that promise."

"So you will return to Silverpurse."

"Yes," she said.

"What about the lost artifact, the Heart of Purespring?"

Catriona shook her head. "What use is it to return a lost artifact to a dead village?" she said. "No. Searching for the dragon rider who did this is pointless. Now I must help the living, not avenge the dead."

"And that means guiding your squire?"

"Yes," Catriona said. "Rohawn. From now on, he is my family."

Shara nodded. "My path lies along a different road," she said.

"I understand," Catriona replied. She maintained a brave face, though secretly she was sad to lose the strange girl's company.

"Farewell, Catriona," Shara said. She adjusted her rucksack, turned to the northwest, and walked out of the destroyed town without looking back.

Catriona retrieved her pack from the temple and then turned to the southwest, back toward Silverpurse. As she left, she couldn't resist stealing a backward glance at the ravaged walls and burned buildings of Purespring.

She regretted it immediately. Tears flowed unbidden to her eyes and, try as she might, she could not stop them. By the time she reached the road to Silverpurse, she had no more tears to shed.

"To arms! To arms!"

Alarm bells sounded throughout Silverpurse. Townsfolk cried out in fear.

The sounds startled Rohawn out of his nap. He grabbed his greatsword from beside his chair and ran downstairs.

"What's wrong?" he asked the innkeeper as he dashed through the common room. "What's happening?"

The man ran into the back room, not stopping to answer him.

Outside the swinging doors of the tavern, a torrent of pale, sweating, frightened villagers raced past, running westward. Many glanced back over their shoulders, as though they were being pursued.

Rohawn exited the inn and ran in the opposite direction. He got to the eastern edge of Main Street just as the town militia was forming up.

They were a ragtag bunch of frightened-looking volunteers. Most had only a bit more armor than Rohawn. They wore mismatched helmets, chest plates, and—occasionally—an odd bit of chain mail. A few were obviously veterans of some previous campaign, perhaps even the War of the Lance. Those men and women had armor that actually fit, though none of it looked very well cared for.

Rohawn fell into line with them. "What's happening?" he asked. "What's going on?"

"Look, fool!" a gruff old veteran replied. "You have eyes, don't you?" He jerked his head to the southeast.

Rohawn gazed across the arid plain in that direction. At first he saw nothing—no approaching army, no marauding monsters, no bandits, nothing. Then he realized that he was looking too low— everyone else had their eyes fixed on the sky.

He looked up, and time froze as every detail of the scene burned itself into his memory. Below the clouds, a monstrous shape raced forward. It had bright blue scales and talons like swords. A long row of serrated spines ran along its arching back. A single horn and huge frilled ears framed its reptilian head. Its yellow eyes blazed bright with hatred.

Rohawn gaped. "A dragon!"

But that wasn't all. Perched on the dragon's back was a man dressed in crimson armor. A cloak flapped behind him as he and his mount surged through the air. He carried a long lance, and a broadsword hung strapped to his hip, while a rack of spears rested just ahead of his saddle. As he and the dragon bore in, he pointed his lance toward the small line of guards.

"Viktor!" gasped a man beside Rohawn. "It's Viktor and Thane!"

CHAPTER

13   THE BATTLE FOR SILVERPURSE

"Viktor and Thane!" gasped a youth in the rank behind Rohawn.

"I thought they were just a myth," said a woman on Rohawn's other side. "A fairy tale to frighten children."

"No such luck," replied the grizzled veteran. "Spread out. Don't give them a single target. If we stay calm, perhaps we can scare them off."

But the other members of the militia were already sweating. Several actually turned and ran back into the village.

Rohawn knew how they felt. His heart was pounding and his stomach felt as if fish were swimming around inside it. It was all he could do to keep his knees from shaking. He gripped his greatsword tightly and looked at the grizzled veteran.

"Can I help?" he asked.

The older man glanced back at him and said, "Son, I doubt that *anything* can help. But at least we can try."

Rohawn nodded and said softly, "If Paladine blesses our fury, we will win."

The dragon swooped toward them and backed his wings. Fierce winds buffeted the small group of guards, nearly knocking them **95** from their feet. Rohawn staggered, and dust stung his eyes.

The huge beast and the rider hung in the air, nearly motionless. The rider wore a horned helmet with a T-shaped slit in the middle that showed his cruel eyes and part of his bearded face. His bare arms bulged with muscles. Short suede gloves covered his hands, and matching maroon boots adorned his feet. His crimson armor glistened in the sunlight.

"We are Viktor and Thane," the man said. "New lords of all this countryside. As your rulers, we demand tribute—a small token of appreciation from those under our protection." His voice was high and reedy, belying his muscular physique. The high voice didn't make him seem any less threatening, though.

"We are poor folk," the old veteran replied. "We have little."

"Thane and I demand little," Viktor said, "merely forty percent of your earnings. Is that so much to ask for the protection of a dragonlord?"

"And if we do not pay?" the veteran asked.

Apparently, Thane had been waiting for just such a question, for without any signal from Viktor, the dragon opened his mouth wide and spewed a huge bolt of lightning toward the dusty street below.

Rohawn and the militia guards scattered as the street exploded. Dust and stones sprayed into the air, showering the guards as they dived aside. The blast caught one unlucky warrior and hurled her across the street. She crashed through a livery stable fence and lay unmoving in the horse pen.

Rohawn thought the dragon might pause to give them time to reconsider, but apparently Viktor and Thane were more interested in making an impression than in collecting any "tribute" this day. The dragon swooped low, over the scattering militia. As he did, Viktor took a spear from the rack in front of his saddle. The dragonlord hefted the weapon, took aim, and threw it directly into the back of a fleeing militiaman. The man cried out and slumped to the dusty street.

The old veteran screamed angrily, wheeled, and threw his spear at the dragon. The weapon struck Thane in the center of his chest, but bounced harmlessly off the dragon's scaly armor. The dragon seemed to smile, and bright white light seeped out from around his mouth.

"Look out!" Rohawn cried. He sprinted across the street and threw himself against the older man. The two of them hit the dirt just as Thane's lightning blasted over their heads.

The bolt of lightning struck the wooden roof of a nearby house and set it ablaze. Viktor laughed and hurled a spear at Rohawn and the veteran. Rohawn got to one knee and whipped his sword around. His blade connected with the shaft, knocking the spear aside before it could pierce Rohawn's chest. Viktor's spent weapon fell harmlessly to the dirt.

"Coward!" Rohawn called. "Come down here and fight like a man!"

Thane swooped down on them. Rohawn and the old veteran barely ducked out of the way in time. A smell like an approaching thunderstorm washed over them as they fell to the ground, and a faint crackle of electricity filled the air.

With a flick, the dragon's tail smashed the wall of a nearby stable, and a huge cascade of wood and mud bricks toppled toward Rohawn. He managed to scramble out of the way, but the militia veteran wasn't so lucky. Much of the rubble fell on his legs, pinning him.

"Don't worry," Rohawn told the older man. "I'll lead them away from you!"

"Forget about me!" the veteran said through gritted teeth. "Get out of here before you're killed!"

Viktor and Thane arced through a graceful turn and began another attack run.

WARRIOR'S HEART

97

Remembering something he'd seen in a nearby horse pen gave Rohawn an idea. He shouted an insult at the dragon, then sheathed his sword and ran around the corner of the stable, hoping to lead dragon away from the trapped veteran. Thane snarled a curse and turned to follow the squire. Behind the barn Rohawn found the haystack and the pitchfork that he'd remembered.

He pulled out the phoenix token that Erikoff had given him and rubbed the small golden feather vigorously. Just as the mage had promised, sparks shot out. The sparks hit the dry hay, setting the stack ablaze. He could hear the rush of the dragon's huge wings beating the air.

Thane's head appeared above the barn. Rohawn stuck the pitchfork into the burning hay and heaved with all his might.

Flaming straw flew up into the air, striking the dragon in the face. Thane reared back and roared with surprise. Viktor, who had been about to throw another spear, almost fell out of his saddle.

The dragon and rider tumbled through the air. Thane righted himself, but he couldn't stop the momentum. He crashed heavily into a mud-brick house beyond the stables. The house crumbled and debris flew up around both dragon and rider. The warlord threw up his arms, trying to protect his face from flying stones and dust.

Rohawn smiled, but only for a moment. Thane's head whipped around toward the squire. Hatred burned in the dragon's yellow eyes. He opened his mouth and breathed lightning.

The bolt of electricity seared across the intervening distance. Rohawn barely dived out of the way in time. He lost his grip on both the pitchfork and the golden phoenix token as he went. Electricity singed his hair and the back of his tunic as he rolled aside. His charm melted into a tiny blob of gold.

The lightning blasted into the barn behind Rohawn, blowing it to pieces. Blazing boards and flaming splinters flew in every direction. Rohawn covered his head as the burning debris pelted him. Blazing pieces of the barn fell onto other buildings, setting them alight.

Stupid! Stupid! Rohawn reproved himself. Never smile until the dragon's dead!

Thane righted himself, shaking debris from his scaly back like a monstrous dog shedding water. Viktor angrily dusted himself off and looked around for Rohawn.

For a moment, Rohawn considered charging and trying to force Viktor to fight him man-to-man. But he quickly realized that he'd never get the warlord to dismount from the dragon's back. Together, Viktor and Thane were more than a match for him.

Retreat is not defeat, Rohawn thought, remembering a favorite saying of Corrigan, his first knight. He ducked between two buildings and drew his sword once more. He kept going, hoping to outflank the dragon within the town's small maze of buildings.

He turned a corner, though, and found himself in a box alley that dead-ended at the back of the inn where he had been staying. The rear door of the establishment opened into the alley, as did several windows on the second floor. The windows were too high for him to reach. He tried the door, but he found the portal barred from the inside. No one came to let him in when he banged on the door and shouted.

Knowing the dragon would find him at any moment, he rammed the door with his shoulder. The air resounded with a deep thud, but the stout wooden planks refused to give way.

Rohawn cursed. "Just my luck to come up against the one sturdy door in the whole town!" He was about to give it another try when a high, reedy laugh behind him made him turn.

Viktor and Thane hovered at the far end of the alley, just above the rooftops. The dragon's huge body cast the dead end into deep shadow. His immense, spiked tail swished across the alleyway, blocking Rohawn's only possible exit.

The dragonlord laughed again. "Going somewhere?" Viktor asked. He retrieved a spear from the rack in Thane's saddle and reeled back his arm for a deadly throw.

As he did, a voice behind Rohawn said, "*Api sentak!*"

Suddenly, bright orange fire flared up around Viktor's helmet. The dragonlord gasped and dropped his spear. He reached for the helmet, but paused as the heat of the flames made his gloves smoke.

"Rohawn! This way!" a familiar voice called.

Rohawn looked up and saw Erikoff leaning out of one of the upstairs windows. The mage dropped the end of a bed sheet. Rohawn grabbed the makeshift rope and quickly scrambled up through the window.

"Thanks," he said. "I thought I was done for."

"We're not out of the fire yet," Erikoff replied. "The walls of this inn are scant protection against dragon breath."

The two of them dashed out the door of the room, with Rohawn in the lead. They ran down the hall and fairly flew down the stairs to the first floor. "I lost your good-luck charm," Rohawn said.

"Better to lose the token than lose your life," Erik replied.

The inn's big common room was devoid of patrons. "Where is everyone?" Rohawn asked.

"Hiding," Erik replied, "which is what we should be doing as well."

"In here?"

"No, outside," the mage said, pushing Rohawn toward the swinging doors that emptied onto Silverpurse's main street.

Just as Rohawn crossed the threshold, though, the entire building exploded. Rohawn toppled forward from the force of the blow. Debris flew everywhere, pelting his body. A large board crashed into his head and spots burst before his eyes.

He rolled onto his back just as Thane passed overhead. Pieces of the destroyed building fell from the dragon's huge talons. Thane snapped his barbed tail at the stunned teenager.

Rohawn rolled aside and the spikes gouged out a huge piece of the street next to him. Perched safely on the dragon's back, Viktor laughed. The dragonlord wore no helmet now, having apparently cast it aside to rid himself of Erikoff's clinging fire.

"Not so smart now, are you!" Viktor said as he and Thane swooped past.

"Smarter than you!" Rohawn muttered as he scrambled to his feet once more. The inn behind him lay in ruins. He didn't know whether Erikoff had survived or not, but Rohawn didn't have time to dig him out right now.

The dragonlord and his mount climbed high into the air, preparing to turn for another deadly attack run.

Rohawn tried to think. What did he know about dragon lightning? Did it rebound from stone? He seemed to remember something like that. At the moment, though, he couldn't recall if it was something he'd learned in his training or merely a rumor he'd once heard.

He remembered seeing a stone building somewhere in town. Where was it?

Yes! The big house at the western edge of Silverpurse—the mayor's home.

Hoping the building might provide him some protection, Rohawn ran as fast as he could through the deserted street toward the house.

Flames burned all around him. The whole town seemed to be ablaze. He ran through clouds of smoke and dodged burning embers as he went. He hoped that he hadn't added to the fires with his burning-hay trick, but even if he had, there was nothing to do about it now.

The mayor's building loomed up out of the smoke before him. To his dismay he saw that only the first floor of the building was made of stone. Would that make a difference? He didn't know. He wasn't even sure his trick would work. He had to chance it, though.

As he skidded up outside the house, he discovered the remnants of the town militia already assembled there. They were soot smudged and frightened looking, but seemed determined to make a final stand. Rohawn fell into line beside them.

He looked at the man on his left and the woman on his right. Both held their weapons in quivering hands.

Rohawn wished that he still had Erikoff's good-luck charm. But then, the charms hadn't saved the mage from being buried under the collapse of the inn. He wondered if Erik survived the tavern's destruction and vowed to dig his friend out, assuming he survived the coming battle.

Near the other end of Main Street, Thane turned and dived toward the town once more. Viktor stood up in his saddle and raised a spear high, sensing victory.

Rohawn looked at his trembling companions once more, trying to will himself to remember their faces, in case they should meet again past the Gate of Souls.

"At least," he whispered to himself, "I will have died bravely, as a knight should."

CHAPTER

14   A Wound That Does Not Heal

Catriona trudged down the dusty road leading back to Silverpurse. She felt weary to the bone, her mind still reeling from the events at Purespring. At that moment all she wanted in the world was a good night's sleep on a proper bed and to find Rohawn.

After that? She had no idea. She might just lie down and let the world wash away. What else could she do? Did her life even have a purpose anymore? She didn't know.

A more sensible part of her brain told her that was lack of sleep talking. She still had plenty left to do in the world. There were still plenty of people she could help—her friends among them. She wondered how Sindri, Nearra, and the rest were doing. Surely, even now, they would be glad for her assistance.

She told herself that, but part of her didn't believe it. As she topped a small rise in the road, though, a new sight snapped Catriona out of her grim reverie. Ahead, a smaller road merged into the main avenue. Riding on that road, very near the crossroads, were two figures she recognized.

"Gillean! Karise!" she called, waving.

The riders waved back and galloped down the road toward **103** her. "Do you want a ride, Cat?" Gillean asked, patting the saddle behind him.

She shook her head. "No, thanks," she said. "I could use the walk."

"I hope you did better than we did," Karise said.

"Trouble?" Catriona asked. It felt good to be thinking about other people's problems again, rather than her own.

"Nothing serious," Gillean replied as they continued west. "Just bad pay and a close call."

"With a dragon," Karise added. "Something our cheapskate merchant friends failed to mention when they hired us."

"And then, of course, they came up short on our pay after we reached our destination," Gillean said. "And this after we nearly saved their lives."

"Nearly?" Catriona asked.

"The dragon kept going," Karise explained. "Just flew over and gave everyone a good scare."

"Us included," Gillean added. He steered his horse around a chuckhole in the road, and Karise swerved to avoid him.

Catriona stepped out of the way without breaking stride. "So even after that, they shorted your pay," she said.

"They claimed that they didn't mean to," Gillean said. "They said they'd come up a bit short on expected funds and that they'd pay us in full if we waited until they'd made their sales."

"Which is going to take until the end of the week," Karise chimed in. "With no recompense for room or board while we wait, of course."

"Of course," Catriona agreed.

"So we took the horses," Karise said. She smiled and patted her brown-coated beast on its neck.

"Horse thieves can be executed in places like this," Catriona warned.

"We had them sign some papers," Gillean said. "Technically, they bought the horses from the stables and promised to pay the stable master in the future."

"Which he couldn't complain about, because he was one of the people the merchants were planning to sell their wares to later," Karise finished. "But, of course, he claimed not to have their money right at the moment, so . . ."

Catriona shook her head and sighed. "It's just an endless circle of people cheating each other," she said.

"Shinare wouldn't approve, of course," Karise said. "She demands honesty in business deals. Sirrion, on the other hand, admires the creativity of the accounting." She and Gillean laughed.

Catriona admired the easy camaraderie between the two. She was coming to trust them, though not as much as she trusted Rohawn or Sindri. Not yet. "Do you intend to keep the horses?" she asked.

"We're not sure," Gillean replied. "We may cash them out if we can get a fair price in Silverpurse."

"But if the job market—or the horse market—is slim there, we may just keep them and move on," Karise said. "They're not bad animals, though I doubt there are any champions in their bloodlines."

Catriona nodded and laughed. They'd come quite a way as they talked. Catriona gazed over the gently rolling hills before them. She noticed a gray haze hovering in the distance, but before she could figure out what it was, Karise asked, "How'd it go for you?"

Cat felt as though her feet had been kicked out from under her. Listening to the mercenaries' friendly banter, she'd almost forgotten the dire outcome of her own journey.

"It went badly," she replied.

"Oh?" Gillian asked, concerned.

She nodded. "My village had been destroyed by a dragon."

"That's terrible!" Karise cried. "Was anyone hurt?"

"Everyone," Catriona replied. "Everyone was gone. There was nothing left. No people, no buildings, nothing. Only a half mad temple priestess—and she died shortly after I got there."

"So, this dragon attack was recent," Gillean said somberly.

"No. It happened months ago. Only the gods know how the old woman managed to hold on so long. Not only did they kill everyone, they took everything of value in the town, even the Heart of Purespring. That's the sacred artifact that made the town's water run pure and clear."

"Catriona, I'm so sorry," Gillean said.

"There's nothing you could have done," she replied. "Nothing anyone could have done."

"What about your family?" Karise asked.

"Gone," Catriona said. "Just like all the others. Only a few burned bones left." She hung her head and shuddered as the memories threatened to overwhelm her again. The thoughts of all the fire and death triggered another notion in her mind.

She looked up and gazed at the haze forming over the distant hills. It wasn't haze, it was *smoke*—a lot of smoke, coming from the direction of Silverpurse.

"The town!" she gasped.

"Your hometown?" Gillean asked, misunderstanding.

"No," she said. "Silverpurse! It's burning!"

Now Gillean and Karise saw the smoke as well. "Climb up," the cleric said, reaching for Catriona's hand. The three of them rode as fast as they could toward Silverpurse.

It was almost dusk by the time they arrived. The small frontier town barely resembled the one they'd left just a few days earlier. Nearly half the buildings had been demolished, and most of those remaining showed scorch marks from some terrible battle. A few buildings were still burning, the blazes raging beyond the control of the feeble bucket brigades trying to contain them.

The three dismounted and helped out where they could, pulling people from wreckage and tending the wounded. Karise used her healing powers to aid the worst, though some were beyond her ability to mend.

"What happened here?" Gillean asked Karise. "Do you think it was . . . ?"

The warrior-cleric shrugged and shook her head.

"It's the same thing that happened to my town," Catriona said. "It was a dragon."

"The dragon we saw was heading this way," Karise said. "But we'd hoped—"

Gillean grimaced in anguish. "We didn't have any way to warn them! If only we could have!"

"There's nothing you can do about it now," Catriona said. "Let's keep moving." As they picked their way through the wreckage, her eyes searched for one particular face among the frightened and injured.

Overwhelming guilt welled up inside her. "I should have taken him with me," she whispered.

She lifted a fallen timber off a boy no older than seven. The child scrambled out from beneath it and ran off, bawling for his mother. How many children in Silverpurse would never run again? If only she hadn't been so anxious to move on!

"Have you seen him yet?" Karise asked.

"Who?" Catriona replied, coming back to the present.

"The kid," Gillean said. "Rohawn."

Catriona shook her head.

"Maybe he got out of town, like we suggested," Karise said.

"No," Catriona replied. "He wouldn't do that. He would have waited for me."

"Well then, maybe he had the good sense to stay out of the fight," Gillean said.

Again, Catriona shook her head. "No. He would never do that either." Her voice became low, almost inaudible above the chaos around them. "He would never have turned away from his duty as a Solamnic Knight in training."

"Wasn't that the inn over there?" Karise asked.

She pointed to a ruined hulk of a building standing near the western edge of town. Though all of them had stayed there only days ago, they barely recognized it. The upper floors lay in ruins around the lower floor. The tavern doorway with its distinctive swinging doors still stood, but the interior was filled with rubble. All the windows had been blown out.

On the ground outside the tavern sat a blond young man wearing torn, soiled orange robes—and more than a bit bloody. Below a golden mask sitting atop his head, a large cut traced down the youth's temple and onto his cheek. The big, bald-headed innkeeper knelt beside him, trying to tend the dazed, pale young man's wound.

Catriona didn't recognize the robed figure, but Karise apparently did, for she shouted, "Erikoff!" Both she and Gillean dismounted and ran to the young man's side. Catriona followed.

The innkeeper looked up as they arrived. "Returned, have you?" he asked the group rhetorically. "You picked a good time to be away, no doubt about it." He didn't seem bitter, just weary.

"Erikoff," Karise said. "What happened?"

"I ended up on the wrong end of a dragon," the young mage replied weakly.

"You look like you *came out* of the wrong end of a dragon," Gillean remarked.

Erik smiled slightly. "Yeah," he said. "The whole town does."

"Let me tend that wound," Karise said. The mage nodded his assent.

Karise removed her gloves and laid her hands on either side

of the long gash. She whispered a soft prayer, and it seemed to Catriona that the whole world grew still and silent.

Blue sparks ran out of the cleric's hands and into the wound. The cut blazed with blue fire for a moment, but Erikoff didn't cry out. The wound closed and as the fire died away, the scar faded away with it. In moments, Erikoff's angular face looked as though he'd never been injured at all. He still seemed exhausted, though.

"Nice trick," he told Karise. "You must teach it to me some time."

"You've decided to be a cleric now, as well as a wizard?" Gillean asked.

Erikoff smiled. "Maybe after I've slept," he replied. "Who's the pretty redhead? I don't remember meeting her before." He looked as though he might drift off to sleep at any moment.

"Erik, this is Catriona," Karise said.

"Ah," the mage said. "Rohawn's friend."

A chill ran up Catriona's spine. "You know Rohawn?" she said.

"They met before we left with the caravan," Gillean explained.

"Do you know where he is?" Catriona asked.

Erikoff shook his head. "We were together until the building collapsed on me," he said. "After that . . . ?" He shrugged.

The innkeeper looked grave. "The young man with the big sword? I know where he is," the man said.

"Where?" Catriona, Gillean, and Karise all asked.

"He's dead."

CHAPTER

15 ROHAWN'S FATE

W hat?" Catriona gasped. She felt as if she'd
been stabbed through the heart and had
her stomach kicked simultaneously. For a moment, the wreckage
of the whole world swirled around her.

"What do you mean, 'dead'?" Gillean asked.

"That's plain, isn't it?" the innkeeper replied.

"But how?" Karise asked, looking as stunned as Catriona felt.

The innkeeper waved his hand at the wreckage of the town,
indicating that they should look around. "Killed by the dragon and
his lord, like most other folk," he said. "There ain't hardly nothing
left of Silverpurse now."

"Tell me," Catriona said, forcing her voice to remain calm. "Tell
me what happened."

"The dragonlord was chasing Rohawn," Erikoff said quietly. "I
tried to help him. We ran through the inn, but the dragon smashed
it before I could get out. Thankfully, a large beam fell on me first—it
kept me from being crushed under the rest of the wreckage. This
man found me and dug me out."

"I saw the boy run out of my inn just before the dragon destroyed
it," the innkeeper continued. Anger and despair mingled on his

proud face. "He ran to the mayor's house, where the town militia had assembled to make a last stand."

"What happened then?" Gillean asked, his voice dry and unsteady.

"Whatta you think?" the innkeeper said. He raised one big, dirty mitt to his eyes, leaving dark smears as he brushed at his tears. "He died along with the rest of them."

"But how do you know?" Catriona asked. "How can you be sure?"

"I seen the bodies," the man replied. "I seen 'em burned and buried under the rubble of the mayor's house. Ain't hardly a stone left standing."

Catriona's knee's buckled and she sat down on a nearby pile of rubble. She couldn't weep. She could barely breathe. She'd failed Rohawn—failed to keep him safe, failed in her promise to take him to Palanthas. Failed utterly.

She wondered about her friends—Nearra, Sindri, Elidor, Davyn. Were they safe? Perhaps they were all better off without her.

"What about the dragon and his rider?" Karise asked. "Were they killed too?"

The innkeeper shook his head. "Not a bit," he said. "They're indestructible, I don't doubt. The dragonlord—Viktor, he said his name was—he said he'd return in half a year to collect his tribute. He said if we didn't have it, he wouldn't leave anything next time."

"Viktor!" Gillean said. "That's the dragonlord the merchants were worrying about—the one we narrowly avoided on the road. They said he's been extorting steel from every village from here to the mountains."

"Seems like he's added Silverpurse to his list of clients as well," Erikoff noted. He looked better now, more determined, almost angry.

"When Viktor returns, will the town pay?" Karise asked.

The man shrugged. "We'd have paid him now, if he'd given us half a chance. Look at our Silverpurse. Most of us spent our lives building this town. Of course we'll pay! What choice do we have?"

"You could fight!" Catriona said. Fire welled up inside her, and she rose to her feet once more. She shook her fist angrily at the innkeeper. "You could fight him and his dragon and drive them from Krynn forever."

"We *did* fight him!" the man shot back. "And look at what it got us! The town in ruins, our people dead, our livelihoods burned! Be a hero if you want, girl! The rest of us just want to live!"

For a moment, Catriona wanted to punch the man and knock some sense into him. Giving in to villains never solved anything—it only made matters worse. As she clenched her fist, though, Gillean laid a firm hand on her shoulder.

"Catriona," he said, "we all know what you're feeling. We feel the same way. But we can't march to Viktor's lair and fight him right this moment. The best we can do now is to help here."

Slowly, Catriona nodded. The fire of her anger subsided, replaced by compassion for the unfortunate villagers. Deep inside her, though, the spark of hatred burned brightly. "You're right," she said. "Let's do what we can here."

All of them worked the rest of that evening and throughout the night, pulling people from the wreckage, helping to put out fires, bandaging wounds, and whatever else they could do. Karise healed people until her energy was spent and she collapsed into a deep, troubled sleep.

Erikoff's fire-based magic proved exceptionally useful. His spells easily put out smaller flames and helped control the larger blazes until the bucket brigades could extinguish them.

The work that Catriona and Gillean did was mainly physical: clearing rubble, hauling water, bearing the injured way from the wreckage. Catriona relished it. The strain on her muscles and the ache in her back took her mind off her terrible loss.

As night crept on to morning, she and the others bedded down on a nearby hill, away from the smell of smoke and carnage.

"I found out more about the dragonlord from talking to the townspeople while we worked," Erikoff said wearily. "Viktor and Thane live in a fortress in the foothills of the northern Vingaard Mountains. They settled there after the war, and have been raiding farther into the countryside ever since."

"What color is this monster?" Catriona asked. She was lying down, like the others, but her mind raced with possibilities.

"Blue," Erikoff said. "The dragon is blue."

"Those are the lightning throwers, aren't they?" Catriona asked, wondering if she'd remembered her dragon lore correctly.

"Oh yes," Erikoff said. "I personally saw it shoot lightning from its mouth. Not something I'd care to see on a regular basis, but worth glimpsing once . . . if not for the devastation."

Catriona spoke quietly, as though the whole world hung on her words. "My home—Purespring—was destroyed by a dragon rider and his mount," she said. "I was told that lightning shot from the beast's mouth."

"You're thinking that the dragonlord who killed your people and this Viktor are one and the same," Gillean said.

"Yes."

"Did you ever meet this beast or its master?" Karise asked sleepily. "Did you do something to offend them?"

"No," Catriona said. "I've never met a blue dragon or a dragonlord."

Erikoff yawned. "Was your home near here?"

"Not close," Catriona said. "But not far either. Close enough to be a target for a predatory dragonlord, it seems."

"They're not only bandits and extortionists, this dragon and his warlord," Erikoff said. "They're slavers as well. Merchants I've spoken to say they take people from the towns they oppress and sell the abductees to dark powers."

"As if just killing and stealing weren't enough," Gillean said. He'd closed his eyes, and his voice was blurred and dreamy.

Despite her anger, Catriona found herself drifting off as well. "We need to stop them," she said. "We need to track them down and make them return what they've taken."

"Track down a dragon and dragonlord?" Karise mumbled. "That shouldn't be hard, but forcing them to give up their ways or make reparations—that's something else entirely."

"How do you intend to accomplish it?" Erik asked, his voice little more than a tired whisper.

Catriona yawned. "We'll figure that out after we sleep."

"That," Gillean said, "is the best idea I've heard all night."

Morning had crept into early afternoon by the time Catriona and the others rose. They made a spare breakfast of what little they could forage, plus the leftover provisions from previous trips.

"I'd complain about the fare," Erikoff said, "but it would seem churlish given the circumstances." He gazed down from the knoll where they'd slept to the ruined town below.

"What's our next move?" Gillean asked as he chewed on a piece of beef jerky and hardtack.

"I intend to find Viktor and Thane and kill them," Cat said.

"Well, I know that," he said. "And I'm willing to consider the proposition—Rohawn was a friend of mine too, though I hadn't known him nearly as long as you had. But how do you intend to go about it?"

"I suggest we scout out the villain's fortress," Karise said. "We can hire some more horses, beyond the two we have and the two

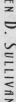

Catriona has—assuming her animals survived the attack."

Catriona winced.

"Sorry, Cat," Karise said. "I know that one of them belonged to Rohawn, but even though we want to avenge him, we still have to be practical."

Catriona nodded.

"So we have enough horses to ride, but we'll need to hire a horse or two to carry some provisions," Karise continued. "What little Gil and I have earned should be enough for that at least."

Gillean patted his nearly empty coin purse and winced at the suggestion, but said nothing.

"I think you'll have enough, especially with the newly depressed economy in town," Erik put in.

"After that, we scout out the stronghold and find out what we're up against," Karise finished. "If this Viktor has been raiding the countryside for months, there should be some kind of price on his head, or at least substantial loot to be recovered."

"I don't want anyone doing this for coin," Catriona said as she packed her possessions. "The chances that we'll be killed are probably greater than the chances that we'll recover any steel. The reason for going after Viktor and Thane is because it needs to be done. They killed Rohawn and a lot of other people, and they need to be brought to justice."

In her mind, she saw not only the dead of her village and Silverpurse, but also the stolen Heart of Purespring as well. If she could recover that—even though her hometown was gone—then perhaps she could do some good for the world after all. If the dragonlord had taken the Heart, maybe he still had it. If not, he could certainly be forced to tell what he'd done with it.

Gillean bowed slightly. "I hope you'll pardon the rest of us if our motives are not quite so noble, Catriona," he said. She couldn't tell whether he was being sarcastic or not.

"I once heard a proverb that said when you set out on the path of vengeance, you should first dig one grave for your enemy and another for yourself," Erikoff said. "However, I, too, have lost kinsmen to evil dragons. So I'm willing to go along with you—at least to see what opposition we might face."

"It's settled then," Catriona said, clipping the last item to the outside of her pack—the broken sword that once belonged to her aunt. The sundered weapon seemed even heavier than ever.

The four of them returned to Silverpurse to discover more about Viktor and Thane, and to help the townsfolk for one more day.

By sundown all of the fires in town had been extinguished. Those who could be rescued had been, and the mourning had begun for the settlement's many dead. Karise and Gillean purchased supplies and one more horse.

The four travelers met at the ruins of the inn.

Gillean examined his nearly empty purse and shook his head. "You were wrong about the horses, Erik," he said. "Neither the horse nor the provisions came cheaply."

Karise patted him on the shoulder. "With all this devastation, the remaining animals and supplies are all the more precious to their owners," she explained.

"Well, at least we had enough to get us going, right?" Cat asked. "We need to start the journey as soon as possible."

They rode out of town to the west, despite the approaching night.

"Viktor's lair is definitely in this direction," Erikoff said. "That's not only what the rumors say, but it's also the direction he flew off after assaulting the town."

Karise nodded. "The people I talked to agreed with that," she said. "They said he lives on the edge of the mountains, in a great fortress. 'Impregnable' is the word they used."

"No fortress is impregnable," Catriona said. "You just have to figure out how to breach it."

"With a dragon holed up there," Gillean said, "my guess is that very few people are thinking along those lines."

"I am," Catriona replied.

"On the bright side," Gillean noted, "with all the looting this Viktor has done, he's sure to have a substantial hoard."

"I told you before," Catriona said, "coin isn't our goal. Killing Viktor and Thane is."

"But once they're dead, it would be a shame to let their treasure just sit there," Gillean said.

They rode out into the desolate plains west of the ruined town, following a trail that veered southward to avoid the worst of the plains. When they stopped at about midnight, all they could see of Silverpurse was a dark halo of diffused smoke in the moonlight.

Erikoff gathered kindling. Karise lit the campfire and prayed to her gods, after which Catriona and Gillean cooked. Catriona took first watch, and was up again in time for Erik's watch just before dawn.

"Don't trust me?" the golden-masked mage asked when he saw her awake.

"The only people I trust are thousands of miles away," she replied. "Or dead."

"Those are pretty tough prerequisites," he said. "I hope you don't mind if I stick around and try to earn your trust the old-fashioned way."

A slight smile tugged at the edges of Catriona's lips. Then a memory of Rohawn—smiling and joking with her, just as Erik was doing—wiped it away.

"Well, if you insist on staying up, then I guess I'll get some more sleep," Erikoff said. "Try not to plant a dagger in my back while I'm dozing, would you?"

He took off his golden mask and lay down once more. In just a few moments, he'd fallen fast asleep.

Catriona wished her mind were that untroubled.

Though they had ridden late, she woke the others before mid-morning. They breakfasted quickly and then got on the road once more. They veered northward just before noon, leaving the trail and entering the trackless arid plains. The northern Vingaard Mountains loomed in the distance. The afternoon heat made their foothills undulate like waves upon a distant shore.

A few hours later, Catriona spotted a lone figure walking across the plains ahead of them. Something seemed familiar about the person, but from so great a distance, she couldn't be sure. The others noticed the figure as well.

"Should we avoid him?" Gillean asked. "He seems to be walking in the same direction that we're riding."

"Are you sure it's a him?" Karise asked.

"From this distance, it's hard to tell." Erikoff shielded his dark eyes with one pale hand and peered ahead into the glare.

"I can't see how one person could be a threat to us," Catriona said. "Besides, perhaps he or she knows something about Viktor and Thane that we don't."

"It's worth checking out, I guess," Gillean said.

They kept to their course, and the horses quickly overtook the walking figure. As they drew closer, they saw that it was a woman carrying a staff and dressed in an ochre shirt and brown skirt.

"Shara!" Catriona called as she recognized the girl.

The half-elf turned and Catriona rode up beside her. "What are you doing here?" the warrior asked.

"Walking," Shara replied.

"But where are you going?" Gillean asked as he and the others caught up.

In answer, Shara pointed to the mountains ahead.

"Silly girl," Karise teased. "Don't you know there's a dragon that way?"

"So I've heard," Shara said. "I mean to see it."

"Why?" Erikoff asked.

The half-elf cocked her head at him.

"Shara, this is Erikoff," Catriona said. "He's with us."

"So I gathered," Shara said.

"Erik, this is Shara," Catriona said. "She traveled with me . . . with *us* for a time."

"She came to Silverpurse with us," Gillean explained.

Erikoff nodded in acknowledgement.

Shara looked around the group. "Where is Rohawn?"

Catriona started to answer, but the words caught in her throat.

"The dragon killed him," Erikoff said flatly.

The half-elf bowed her head. "I'm very sorry to hear that," she said. "I will remember him and say a prayer under the stars tonight." She lifted her head again. "Is that why you're going to find this dragon?"

"Yes," said Catriona. "We're going to kill Thane and his rider."

Shara nodded. Catriona felt as though the half-elf's multicolored eyes were peering into her soul.

"You think this is the same man and the same dragon who destroyed your village," Shara said.

Again, words failed Catriona. Shara held her gaze.

"The road to vengeance is paved with the bones of those you love," the half-elf said.

"Yes," Catriona said quietly. "Yes, it has been."

The half-elf shook her head. "You misunderstand," she said.

"I understand perfectly," Catriona replied, her face grim with determination. "Now why are *you* going to see the dragon?"

"It is my job to see things," Shara replied.

"What things?" Gillean inquired.

"Everything," Shara said in response.

"Including the dragon?" Karise asked.

"Yes."

"I hope you don't mind if I kill it," Catriona said.

Again, Shara shook her head. "A path, once taken, is hard to turn aside from," she said. "Can you make the whole world safe, Catriona?"

Catriona rode away, heading for the mountains. Why did the half-elf have to be so cryptic? When the two of them traveled together before, Catriona had felt a bond with the girl, but now . . . now she felt only anger—anger at Shara, and Viktor and Thane, and the whole world.

"Since we're going in the same direction," Erikoff said to Shara, "would you like a ride? I'm lighter than my armored compatriots or the provisions on our pack horse, so I don't think you'd be much burden to my horse."

"There are other burdens besides physical ones," Shara said. "Those I have no wish to add to." She looked questioningly at Gillean and Karise.

"We'd be glad for your company," Gillean said.

"Don't mind Catriona," Karise added. "She's had a very difficult time of late."

"I know, and more difficult times to come," Shara replied. "But I will ride with you . . . for now."

Erik gave her a hand, and she swung up behind him on his saddle. The four of them followed after Catriona.

They traveled west for three more days as the landscape became more and more arid. They rode carefully through the desert, conserving their water and continuing to follow the hints the merchants had given them.

On the fourth day, the arid hills grew rockier and the defiles between them deeper. Gigantic pillars of weathered stone, like towering petrified trees, sprouted up out of the earth with increasing frequency. The horses stumbled often in the sand and scree, though fortunately, the sturdy mounts righted themselves immediately.

On the morning of the fifth day, they topped a tall hill and saw just how far they'd come. A long stretch of badlands—with towering pillars of natural stone and deep, craggy ravines—separated them from their objective. The Vingaard Mountains loomed above them like titanic walls of stone. And at the base of the nearest peak lay the fortress of Viktor and Thane.

Catriona's jaw dropped open.

Gillean gasped. "I don't believe it!"

CHAPTER

16 THE PRICE OF VALOR

L ying at the base of the mountain before them rested a huge rock, a rock nearly a quarter the size of the mountain itself. Atop the rock stood a fortress the likes of which none of them have ever seen. Its walls were made of blocks so large that only a god or a dragon could have moved them.

The citadel's walls wound through the rock with a sinuous grace, as though they had grown from the titanic boulder itself. Towers, barbicans, buttresses, battlements, all had been expertly positioned to give the defenders of the rock maximum advantage.

But something must have gone terribly wrong, because every wall, every stone, every building, every tower lay skewed at a crazy angle—tilted nearly twenty degrees to the north. The reason was obvious to Catriona: the mountain-sized rock that the fortress stood on had fallen from the sky.

"A sky fortress," Shara said.

Erikoff nodded. "With fortresses like this one, the dragonlords attempted to overrun all of Krynn—and very nearly succeeded."

"If not for the Heroes of the Lance and their allies," Cat added.

"I'd heard of such fortresses during the war, but I never believed they existed," Karise said. "I always thought they must be a myth, started by the dragonlords to frighten their enemies."

"The magic required to move such a thing must have been magnificent," Erikoff said.

Cat took a deep breath and steeled herself. "Well, it's not moving now," she said, "which will make attacking it all the easier."

Gillean shook his head. "Even grounded, I don't think there will be anything easy about it," he said.

"I wonder why it fell," Shara mused.

"The dragonlords exhausted its magic," Karise said. "It's like Erikoff said, it must have taken a lot of power to make a rock that big fly. It's still an impressive fortification, though."

Erik nodded and said, "Very impressive."

"Impregnable," Gillean offered.

"Maybe once," Catriona said. "But not now. Look." She pointed to a place where the great citadel wall met the mountainside. There the impact of the giant rock's fall had splintered the mountainside and the fortress wall as well. "And there . . . and there too." She pointed out two more places where the citadel had crumbled under the shock of falling from the sky.

"Why hasn't Viktor repaired those walls?" Gillean wondered.

"Perhaps he has neither the time nor the talent," Karise suggested.

"Perhaps he doesn't fear such small breaches in his defenses," offered Shara.

"Reaching those holes will take some hiking and then some climbing," Erik noted. He looked out across the landscape before them. It was fractured with a veritable maze of towering stone pillars and craggy ravines.

"Those breaches may seem small to a dragon and his rider," Catriona said. "But they're miles wide to us. Come on. We've found our way in." She urged her mount forward, but Gillean took hold of her reins.

"Hold on a moment," he said. "We hardly know anything about the place besides its outward appearance. Is there a battalion of draconians or other monsters waiting just behind those walls? We'd be crazy to rush in without knowing more."

Catriona's eyes narrowed. "Are you calling me crazy?"

"No, of course, not," he replied. "I'm just saying we need to think this through."

"I don't need to think anything through," she said. "The man who killed Rohawn is behind those walls. That same man destroyed my home. I intend to kill him."

"Aren't you forgetting something?" Karise asked.

"What?" Catriona replied.

"The dragon," the warrior-cleric said.

"I haven't forgotten him," Catriona said. "I'll kill him too if I can."

"Get yourself killed, more likely," Karise said.

Catriona cast a cold glance at the other four. "You don't have to come," she said. "None of you have to do this. But I do."

She looked at Gillean and added, "Take my horse." She swung down from the saddle and handed him the reins. "If I don't come back, you can sell him to cover your expenses for the trip."

She turned and began walking through the scarred and rocky landscape toward the fallen fortress.

"Wait," Gillean called after her. "It's not that I'm against assaulting the fortress, I just think we need to talk it over first—scout out the defenses."

"When I attack, you'll find out about the defenses," Catriona replied without looking back.

The others sat there for a moment, unsure of what to do.

Then Erikoff hopped off his horse as well. "Hang on," the young mage said. "I'm going with you!" He ran after Catriona and soon caught up to her.

She gave him a brief, acknowledging glance.

He smiled at her and said, "After all, when walking into the dragon's lair, it's best to go with friends." He held out his hand to her. "Here, take this," he said.

"What is it?" she asked, looking down her nose at the small, golden trinket in his hand. It appeared to be a tiny heart surrounded by flames.

"It's the heart of the phoenix—a good-luck charm," Erik said. "One of the traditions of my order. It will also keep you warm on cold nights."

Catriona nodded. "The gods know I've had enough of those lately," she said. "Are you sure you want to do this with me?"

"No," he replied. "Are you sure you want to do it?"

For a moment, her good sense fought against her anger. "We need to surmount the defenses and find Viktor and Thane," she insisted.

"Yes, we do," he agreed.

"We need to do it now."

"That's certainly one option," he said. "It's just a matter of how recklessly we do it."

"You think I'm being reckless?"

"A bit," Erikoff said. "What would Rohawn think?"

The question stung Catriona, and some of the fire in her breast died away. Would he have wanted her to go rushing in to get killed in glorious battle? No. She owed it to Rohawn not to get killed—not before she killed Viktor and Thane.

"I'm still going," she said stubbornly.

Erikoff glanced back at the others, who were still waiting nearby, and said, "Then let's do it." He took a charm from his pocket—a charm that looked the same as the one that he'd just given her— kissed it, and put it back.

She followed his lead, kissing the charm before tucking the

blazing golden heart into her belt. Then together the mage and the warrior knight hiked through the towering petrified monuments and the craggy ravines toward the fallen sky castle.

Dragonlord Viktor adjusted his purple cloak so that he wouldn't sit on it, and then plopped down on his gilded throne. The throne rested atop a sturdy wooden platform because the floor slanted at a steep angle—as did the entire castle, a result of the fortress's sudden precipitation from the sky at the end of the War of the Lance.

Viktor had long since grown accustomed to the castle's odd angles. He hardly noticed them any more, and his kobold minions didn't seem to mind either. They were glad for the protection that he and Thane brought them—and the wealth, of course. The dragonlord had done well by the kobolds, and they treated him with due respect.

The warlord had also done well by himself and his dragon. Their pillaging and extortion of the surrounding lands allowed them to live in the lavish style to which they had become accustomed. They never seemed to have enough coin to fix the castle's crooked flooring, walls, battlements, and so on. But fine food, strong drink, and obedient slaves, those they had in plentitude. Indeed, Viktor was quite pleased with his life, skewed castle and all.

He removed his horned helmet and gazed admiringly at the purple-draped throne room around him. He lingered lovingly over the looted silver serving ware that decorated his table. He admired the delicate tapestry carpets covering the room's slanted floor.

The place was truly worthy of a king, which was what he hoped someday to be: the king of Ansalon—or maybe all of Krynn. No sense in setting his ambitions too low. He wished only that his citadel were still able to fly. Viktor smiled thinking about it—floating over the countryside, raining terror on his subjects below. Those must have been glorious days for the castle's original owners, whoever they might have been.

They were long gone by the time Viktor and Thane arrived, of course. The original owners probably abandoned the castle when it fell. That seemed a waste to Viktor. Aside from the floors, the place was perfectly serviceable—and nearly impregnable.

The clearing of a froggy throat interrupted his happy reverie. "Excuse me, my lord," the croaking voice said.

Viktor turned and found Chortog, the chief of the castle's kobolds, standing near his elbow. Chortog was a fat, lazy creature with piglike eyes and wet, drooping whiskers. His pointed ears twitched this way and that as he spoke. The horns on his head were little more than nubs, not the proud, curving horns usual with kobold chieftains. He wore purple and red, in homage to—or perhaps imitation of—the fallen castle's lord.

Chortog usually liked to be carried around the citadel on a litter by four of his servants. At the moment, though, he was standing on his own flabby feet.

"What is it, Chortog?" Viktor asked, his high, thin voice echoing through the chamber. Viktor found the kobold chief useful, but he didn't much like him and didn't want to spend any more time talking to him than necessary.

Bowing obsequiously, Chortog said, "I was wondering, my lord, how soon you intended to send another shipment to our allies in the undermountain."

"More slaves, you mean?" Viktor asked. He wished the kobold would speak more plainly. Obtuse references, such as calling slaves a "shipment," annoyed him.

"Yes," Chortog said. "The new slaves."

Viktor held out his right hand, and a house slave—a young boy—scurried forward and put a ripe peach in his hand. Viktor bit the peach in half and spat the pit on the floor.

Chortog watched the pit fall near his bloated feet. He then fastened his beady eyes on a skinny girl with short, dirty hair scrubbing one corner of the room. "Cinder!" he croaked.

The girl, who was crawling on her hands and knees as she scrubbed hard with a bristle brush, looked up. Her eyes met the kobold's, but she didn't blink.

Chortog scowled. "What are we paying you for?" he asked, pointing to the peach pit. "Pick that up!"

The girl scrambled across the floor and picked the pit up. "You're not paying me at all," she grumbled.

Chortog kicked her and she slid, sprawling, across the slanted floor. "And well I know it, slave," he said. "Remember your place here, Cinder, or I'll have your tongue on toast for my breakfast."

The girl didn't say anything, but her gray-green eyes burned with hatred.

"No need to spoil the merchandise," Viktor said, finishing his peach with a second bite. "Much easier to sell the surly wench if she acts up. Much more profitable too."

The girl bowed her head to the flagstones. "Beggin' your pardon, my lord," she said. "I didn't mean no insolence . . . to you."

Chortog snarled angrily, but Viktor just laughed. "Keep her around, Chortog," he said. "She amuses me."

Chortog bowed deferentially. "As you wish, my lord," he said. "Though, are you sure you don't want to sell her to the durogar? It would help our . . . balance of accounts."

Viktor glowered at Chortog. Again, he wished the kobold would speak more plainly.

"What do you mean?" he asked.

"I mean that your outflow of income is nearly equal to your intake," Chortog explained. He smiled, showing rows of sharp but rotting teeth.

A rumbling from nearby shook the throne room, and a deep

voice said, "I don't understand that."

Viktor turned to the left as Thane's huge blue head poked in through a big window near the throne. The warlord hadn't noticed Thane's approach, but the dragon came and went as he pleased. "Ask the imp what the kobold means," Thane said.

Viktor smiled. He and the dragon were often of a single mind. He clapped his hands three times and a small, blood red imp flew out of a shadowed corner near the top of the vaulted ceiling. His tiny ally was always lurking close at hand.

The imp fluttered down on her batlike wings and perched on the high back of Viktor's throne. She crept forward and spoke in the warlord's ear. "The fat one is implying that you are low on steel," she said. "He's suggesting that you need to sell more slaves to make ends meet."

Viktor scowled and nodded his understanding. "How is it that we always seem to be low on steel?" he asked Chortog.

The kobold shrugged, rippling his flabby flesh. "You and Thane live well, my lord," he replied. "You want for nothing."

"We *take* what we want," the dragon said. His deep voice shook the whole room.

"But one cannot loot *everything*," the kobold pointed out. "Some things must be purchased, or they will not be available at all. The amount of fine goods that can be won by combat is finite." He bowed obsequiously.

Viktor glanced up at the imp. "He is right, Lord Viktor," the small red humanoid said. "Burn the wheat fields and soon there is no bread."

"We've burned no wheat fields," Thane grumbled. The dragon's hearing was exceptionally keen. "I don't even like bread."

"She doesn't really mean bread," Viktor said, catching on at last. "She means things like bread, but better—vineyards for wine, herds of fine cattle."

"Exactly, my lord," Chortog said. "Resources can run thin."

"You're a fine one to talk, fat toad," Thane said.

The kobold chief bowed to the dragon.

"Enough," Viktor said, rising from his gilded seat. "We may sell the girl, but not today. Meanwhile, I will break some new prisoners so that they will make better slaves," he said. "There's one in particular that I'm looking forward to."

Catriona and Erikoff edged closer to the broken battlements of Viktor's fortress. The mage moved warily, keeping to the shadows between the towering standing stones and the hidden recesses of the craggy ravines around the fallen castle.

Catriona strode quickly and boldly, her eyes focused on their objective.

"Please, Catriona," Erikoff pleaded. "Keep out of sight as much as you can. There's no sense in alerting them to our presence if we can avoid it."

"How are we supposed to get to the fortress if we're always hiding?" she asked.

"Do you want to get to the fortress, or do you want to die trying?" Erikoff asked.

She stopped a moment and the fire burning inside her breast died just a bit. "I want to get there," she said.

"Then slow down," Erikoff suggested. "Maybe let me take the lead for a bit. I think I saw a good course to take."

"Better than the one I've chosen?" she asked.

"Maybe," he said. "Follow along a few minutes and see."

So she turned to Erikoff and nodded. "All right," she said. "You take the lead for a while."

Erikoff's face remained hidden behind his golden mask, but he seemed relieved. "Good," he said. "Just keep low and try to stay in the defiles as long as possible. We'll make for that breach in the hill there." He pointed to an area of broken wall quite a ways up on the fallen rock.

"We can reach those two breaches more quickly," she said, pointing at a different section of the wall. "They're closer."

"And more likely to be guarded because of that," he replied. "If you *really* want to get killed, we could try the road to the main gate as well. Reaching the upper break will be more difficult and take longer, but it'll be safer once we get there."

Catriona nodded, knowing he was right. She chided herself for letting her emotions get the better of her. It was that kind of thinking that had made her leave Rohawn behind, rather than taking him with her to Purespring.

"I know how you feel," Erikoff said.

"Pardon?" Catriona said. She wasn't even sure she knew how she felt herself.

"We've all lost people we loved, especially during the war."

They kept moving, more cautiously than before, picking their way through the defiles and between the rocks. "Who did you lose?" she asked.

He paused a moment and took a breath. "A girl I knew."

"Who was she?"

"Her name was Aliza," he replied. They'd made their way to the base of the fallen mountain. He found a handhold and pulled himself up the rocky slope.

Catriona followed right behind. "Did a dragon kill her?"

"No," he said. "Spells killed her, during the war."

"Evil wizards, then," she said.

Fire lit Erikoff's eyes. "Yes," he said. "Wizards. I vowed to pay them back. Every single one of them."

"Then why are you here?"

Erikoff pulled himself up over a small shelf of rock. He stopped a moment and caught his breath. She scrambled up after him. "The paths of our lives do not always run in straight lines," he said.

"So this is one of the crooked points."

Erikoff nodded. "For both of us, it seems."

"Yes," Catriona replied. The broken sword strapped to her backpack felt very heavy at that moment.

He started to get up to resume their climb, but she put a hand out and stopped him.

"Shh!" she hissed, and pointed to the sky above and to their left. As the two of them watched, a blood red gargoyle flew out of the west and landed on one of the castle's upper battlements.

"So, this is where the gargoyles came from too," she whispered.

"Rohawn said gargoyles attacked your caravan," Erik said.

"Yes."

The mage nodded. "Viktor has a lot of evil to answer for."

"Then let's make our questions to him as painful as possible," she suggested. A hard smile tugged at the corners of her mouth.

The last hundred yards was more of a steep walk than a climb. They dodged between boulders to stay out of sight as they went. When they reached the break in the wall, they paused. Inside, two kobold guards walked patrol. The small humanoids with rusty orange skin wore leather armor and carried short swords. They chattered to each other as they went, speaking in a language that Catriona didn't understand.

"What now?" Erikoff whispered to her.

"Now we start," she said, drawing her dragon claws.

When the kobolds passed again, she leaped through the breach and knocked them out before either knew what was happening. Erik followed her in. They bound and gagged the kobolds and dragged the bodies behind a broken portion of the wall.

Looking around, they found themselves in a courtyard. The fractured mountainside lay to their left. Ahead of them, another wall just as steep circled the buildings of the main citadel. Catriona gazed at the length of the inner wall. It ran from the original mountain to a squarish tower, and then farther on to the fortress's main gate house. Beyond the wall nearest to them lay part of the inner keep, crushed against the mountain face.

A waterfall tumbled down the mountain and into what Catriona assumed must be a courtyard next to the squarish building. The water exited the hidden courtyard through a small, stoutly barred culvert. From there, the stream ran into a deep crevasse between the mountain face and the inner gatehouse.

"There must be a courtyard at the bottom of those falls," Catriona said, pointing. "If we can get there, we should find access into the inner parts of the castle."

"How long do you think we have before they discover the guards?" Erik asked.

She shrugged. "Long enough, I hope."

"Long enough for what?"

"Revenge."

He took a deep breath. "I don't suppose you've given any thought as to how we're going to get out of here."

"If we kill the dragon and the warlord, I don't think getting out will be much trouble," she said. "And if we don't kill them . . ." She shrugged again.

"But if we can't win, I mean, if it's obvious we're *doomed*, we'll turn back, right?" he said. "This is just scouting."

She didn't reply.

He put his hand on her upper arm, and she looked at it as though it were a snake. "Just scouting," he reiterated.

"We'll see," she said.

They dashed across the open space between the walls. Many tall piles of rock littered the ground, and they found cover behind a heap leaning against the inner wall.

Erikoff looked from the stones to the mountain above. "These must have crumbled when the citadel crashed into the side of the peak," he mused softly.

"Who cares," Catriona whispered back. "They're providing cover and a way to climb this inner wall. That's all that matters."

Erik nodded, but his eyes narrowed behind his golden mask. "You first," he said.

Catriona nodded back. They climbed quickly but cautiously, trying not to make any sound as they went. She reached the apex of the pile first and leaped up to grab the top of the wall. Her fingers gripped the low spot between two crenellations and she pulled herself over. She glanced right and left down the battlement, but saw no sign of any guards patrolling the top of the wall.

Erikoff had jumped, but didn't catch hold. He clattered back to the rocks below and looked around, afraid that someone might have heard him.

"Hsst!" Catriona called, sticking her hand down.

He jumped again and she caught him. She pulled while he climbed, and a few moments later, he stood beside her.

"Where to now?" he asked.

A rectangular inner courtyard stretched out below them. The mountain formed the left-hand wall and the back wall of the courtyard. One portion of the tall, square keep formed the third side, on the right. The fourth was the parapet wall they'd just climbed. That wall dead-ended in the tower wall on one side and the mountain on the other. There was a door in the keep wall at the courtyard level below them. The only way down from the rampart was a rickety wooden staircase leading into the yard.

Catriona pointed at the door and nodded. Erik nodded back. The two of them moved cautiously down the stairs.

Soft white sand covered the courtyard. The sand seemed to have been raked into some kind of swirling pattern, but Catriona couldn't make out the design. The waterfall they'd seen from outside cascaded down the mountain face on the far side of the courtyard. The downpour ended in a rock-lined stream that exited through the barred culvert in the parapet wall.

The bottom of the stairway creaked as Erik stepped off. Both Catriona and the mage froze. When nothing happened, they hopped across the stream and walked to the door.

Catriona laid her hands on the door handle. Before she could open it, though, a deep voice behind her said, "What are you doing?"

Catriona and Erikoff turned and found themselves face-to-face with the dragon.

CHAPTER

17 THANE

Catriona froze, whether from surprise or dragonfear, she couldn't tell. She noticed that Erik wasn't moving either.

The immense, blue head of the dragon protruded from the waterfall at the back end of the courtyard. Clearly the falls hid some kind of cavern where the beast lived. Catriona cursed herself for not assessing their surroundings better.

The dragon stared at the two of them with bright yellow eyes. Thane's fangs were each as long as Catriona's hands, and his jaws were large enough to swallow her in two or three bites. The beast's armored head surmounted a wide serpentine neck covered with thick scales, blue on top and a pale cream color underneath. A large central horn surrounded by many smaller hornlets decorated the dragon's head, and spines ran down his long neck. How big the dragon was remained difficult to determine, as most of Thane's body remained hidden behind the waterfall.

"Did you bring my dinner?" the dragon asked imperiously.

Catriona tried to say something, but no words came out. Somehow, Erikoff found his voice.

136   "Um, no," the mage replied, bowing. "We thought you might be

sleeping, and we didn't want to disturb you. So we came to find out first. We're terribly sorry if we woke you. What will you be having for dinner, Lord Thane? Your usual?"

The dragon's eyes narrowed. " 'Usual' . . ." he said, as if mulling the word over. "You're not my *usual* servers. In fact, you don't look like slaves at all. Why are you wearing a mask?"

"I'm being punished," Erikoff said. "The inside of this mask is rough with thorns. I can hardly stand the pain."

The thought of that appeared to please the dragon, but then his baleful gaze settled on the dragon claw blades strapped to Catriona's hips. "Those aren't slave tools," he said. "They look like something that would belong to a warrior."

"She's my guard," Erikoff said quickly. "We slaves aren't trusted, you know. Not that any of us would be so *foolish* as to attack you or otherwise cross you, great and mighty Thane."

He shot Catriona a wary look that she interpreted as, "This is too much for us. Let's get out of here!"

Thane continued to study Catriona with suspicion. Despite increasingly desperate looks from Erik, Catriona remained frozen, caught between her own contradictory impulses.

She knew the sensible thing to do was play along with Erikoff. That was the best way to get out of the courtyard alive. Despite her training and her combat experience, another part of her just wanted to turn and run—a move that would surely get both of them killed. And a third part, so powerful as to nearly overshadow the first two, wanted to launch herself at the dragon and kill him—or die in the attempt—for all the terrible things he'd done, to do it for Rohawn, for Purespring, and the gods only knew how many others the dragon had destroyed.

Her hands crept toward the handles of her dragon claws.

Erikoff must have guessed her intention, though, for he suddenly threw himself at her feet. "No, no, mistress!" he cried. "I'm sorry!

I didn't mean to disturb the great Thane! Please don't kill me!"

The sight of the mage's pathetic, pleading form forestalled Catriona's death wish. Who would it help if they were to die? Certainly not Erikoff.

She scowled at the mage and kicked him away. "Fool!" she barked. "Next time, you'll know to wait until Thane calls for his dinner!" She turned to the dragon and bowed. "A thousand pardons, great and noble Thane! Come, slave."

Catriona reached down, grabbed Erik by the collar, and hauled him to his feet. She pushed him toward the aged oak door in the stone wall.

Erikoff grasped the door latch and pulled, but the door didn't open. He pushed, but it didn't open that way either.

"If you came through the door to find me," the dragon rumbled, "why can't you get back through it?"

Thinking quickly, Catriona replied, "Because this fool of a slave has locked it behind us." She cuffed Erikoff on the ear and whispered to him, "If you have any magic for locks, now would be the time to use it."

Before Erik could reply, though, Thane said, "That door has a *bar*, not a lock. How can you bar a door after you've passed through it?" His voice sounded puzzled but on the verge of anger. "I think I was right in the first place—you're not my servants at all."

"Any thoughts?" Catriona asked urgently.

"How about this?" Erikoff whispered. He turned suddenly, fire brimming from his hands. "Aaa! Aaa!" he screamed. "She set me on fire!"

Thane, who had been looming closer to the pair, stopped, puzzled as the mage ran away from Catriona. When Erikoff got close to the dragon, though, he suddenly stopped and blew on his flaming hands.

As he did, a huge billow of black smoke erupted from the flames.

The smoke sparked and sizzled, and completely surrounded the startled dragon's head.

"Run!" Erikoff cried to Catriona. He dashed for the stairs. She was closer and beat him there.

The dragon roared as the two of them raced up the rickety flight toward the parapet.

Suddenly, a sound like thunder split the air, and the wooden stairway shattered beneath them. Catriona grabbed the top of the wall with her left hand and seized Erikoff's robe with her right. His sudden weight almost wrenched her arms out of their sockets, but she held on.

"Scramble up!" she said to Erik through gritted teeth.

The mage quickly climbed to the parapet and then helped her up as well. Thane's head was still encased in the choking, sparking smoke, but the rest of his huge, reptilian body had begun to emerge from the cave behind the waterfall.

"He can't use his breath again for a bit . . . I hope!" Erikoff said as they ran. "That should give us some time to get away."

Catriona hissed at him. "Keep quiet! He can still hear, even if he can't see."

But her warning came too late. Thane splashed through the stream and lumbered in their direction.

"Jump!" Catriona cried as the dragon charged toward the wall.

Catriona and Erikoff leaped between the merlons atop the parapet and onto the rock pile below. Thane hit the wall, his immense bulk shaking the whole castle. Catriona landed solidly, but Erikoff slipped on the crumbling stone and fell.

"My ankle!" he cried.

She grabbed him around the shoulders, lifted him to his feet, and hauled him down the pile as the wall behind them quaked with Thane's fury.

"How long will that smoke last?" she asked as they ran.

"Not long enough," Erikoff replied. He was limping, and she kept supporting him so that he wouldn't fall behind. "Enemies to your left," he noted.

Catriona turned as a half dozen kobolds hurried around the corner of the main keep. "Spells or weapons?" she asked.

He winced. "It'd be nice if you could buy me a bit of time," he replied. "It's hard to concentrate on casting with my ankle throbbing."

Catriona nodded and hustled him to her right side so she stood between him and the enemy. The kobolds and the dragon were making a lot of noise, but Cat thought she could hear even more clamor from within the castle. Behind the wall of the courtyard, Thane roared again and the whole mountain shook with thunder as his lightning breath seared through the air. He was aiming blind, though, and only succeeded in blasting off a section of one of the fortress's topmost towers.

"I think we made him angry," Erikoff puffed as they ran. Catriona couldn't see his face behind the golden mask, but it sounded like the mage was smiling.

As they reached the breach in the outer wall, the kobolds finally caught up to them. Erik stumbled ahead while Catriona turned and faced the enemy. There were six of them—three with swords, three with spears. The spears were about six feet long, though the kobolds were barely half that size.

They shouted with glee as they attacked, thinking Catriona and Erikoff easy prey. Catriona smiled grimly. In an instant, the curved dragon claw blades were in her hands. The left blade flashed backward along her arm, acting like a shield. With it, she beat back two sword attacks and slashed through the haft of a spear. Her right blade feinted a thrust, and then turned into a savage cut on the backswing.

The remaining two spears fell, sliced in half. The third kobold on

Catriona's right barely parried a deadly slash as her weapon angled toward his neck. His sword stopped the blade, but shattered in the process. He dropped the broken weapon and fled.

Catriona turned both dragon claws to the offensive. The kobolds were so startled by their initial failure that the sudden switch in tactics caught them completely by surprise.

All three spearmen died, bleeding from neck wounds before they could even raise the broken shafts of their weapons. Two of the remaining swordsmen actually parried Catriona's thrust. But one kobold's parry came a moment too late, and he lost his sword hand.

That kobold fled, screaming and holding the stump of his arm. Finding himself suddenly alone, the last swordsman beat a hasty retreat.

Catriona stepped over the bodies of her enemies and climbed through the gap in the outer wall. A quick glance back told her that kobold reinforcements were coming quickly.

"Remind me . . . never to make you . . . angry," Erikoff puffed as she caught up to him.

"Consider yourself reminded," Catriona replied. "There are more kobolds on the way, and I can't get them all. Move faster."

Erikoff stumbled down the slope toward the ravine-scarred landscape. "I would if I could," he said. "If you want to carry me, I'd be fine with that."

"I'm hoping it won't be necessary," she replied.

"Me too. Look out!"

Catriona spun as a blood red gargoyle dropped out of the sky in front of them.

"Terrific," she said, meaning just the opposite.

"*Api belit!*" cried Erikoff. A bright flame shot out of his hands and struck the gargoyle in the face. It didn't harm the beast much, but it did startle it.

That gave Catriona the chance to close in. She ducked under the gargoyle's guard before it had a chance to clear its eyes.

The monster swung wildly with both claws. She deflected the blows with her left dragon claw and swung for its neck with the right. But the gargoyle brought its left hand around, blocking the cut. It lost two fingers, but didn't seem to mind.

Before Catriona could attack it again, the gargoyle took to the air and darted out of her reach. It swung around them, trying to dive on Erikoff.

Catriona pulled the mage out of the way and thrust him into the ravine closest to them. Erik barely managed to catch hold of the ledge and avoid falling. He landed clumsily, but without further damaging his twisted ankle. "Catriona, come on!" he called.

"Busy fighting a retreat here," she replied.

The gargoyle swooped down at her. She ducked out of the way of its rear talons and cut back at its legs with both dragon claws. Neither blow connected.

"Fight faster, or we'll be up to our eyeballs in kobolds," Erikoff said. He pointed back the way they'd come.

Catriona looked where he indicated. Sure enough, a huge swarm of the goblinlike creatures was pouring through the breach in the wall.

She ducked as the gargoyle tried to take her head off. The monster's claws missed her face by less than an inch and sliced off a lock of her red hair.

"We don't have time for this!" she said, making it sound like a curse.

"Get down in the ravine," Erik suggested. "The gargoyle will have less room to maneuver.

Catriona fended off one more attack and then leaped down into the ravine after the mage.

"We'd better hope that the kobolds don't bring bows," she said, "or we'll be skewered like pickles in a barrel."

"Maybe I can help in that regard," Erik said. He concentrated a moment, whispered a few words of magic, and gestured toward the lip of the defile. As he did, a line of fire sprang up at the ravine's entrance, cutting the kobolds off from the beleaguered pair.

Catriona didn't have time to admire Erikoff's handiwork. The gargoyle swooped in, all four of its claws extended. Catriona batted the left talons aside and lunged straight for the creature's chest.

She flipped her left dragon claw backward and stabbed the gargoyle through the heart. As before, the creature didn't die—but she hadn't intended it to. The blow pinned Catriona to the gargoyle, and her extra weight made it unable to lift off immediately. The monster clawed at her. She ducked her head to one side, but its nails still traced two long scratches down her cheek.

She ignored the pain and slashed with her right dragon claw, severing the gargoyle's head. It toppled into the ravine and turned into reddish dust.

"Well done!" Erikoff said. Then he froze and his eyes went wide with fear.

Catriona turned just as Thane, with Viktor on his back, soared over the ravine.

CHAPTER

18 BADLANDS

"G et down!" Catriona cried. She threw herself against Erikoff and carried them both to the side of the ravine. As she did, a thunderclap shook the air and bright white light flashed across the badlands. Thane's lightning coursed over the defile and smashed into the huge rock at the base of the fallen sky fortress. Clouds of dirt, dust, and stone pelted Cat and Erikoff.

Catriona, lying flat on her stomach in the bottom of the ravine, craned her neck, but couldn't see anything through the dust. Erikoff, lying on his back beside her, said, "That was close. Thanks."

"We can't stay here," Catriona whispered. She got up, pulled him to his feet, and thrust him down the ravine ahead of her. The two of them stumbled through the dust, away from the castle. "If we can make it to the rock pillars, we might stand a chance," she said.

He winced but nodded his head.

"Do you have any spell that might bring down a dragon?" she asked.

"A dragon *kite*, maybe," he said. "I'm barely more than a novice. I can handle some kobolds, goblins, and maybe a few gargoyles, but dragons? I might as well try to stop the moons from circling the sky."

Catriona cursed. She'd killed a dragon once, but those circumstances had been very different. Catriona doubted that Viktor and Thane would let her get close enough to even attack them.

She heard a *whoosh* overhead, but still couldn't see through the dust cloud. The dragon and warlord were looking for them. Catriona didn't say anything for fear of giving their position away. She hoped that Erikoff would be wise enough to remain silent as well.

At the same time, a series of whizzing noises cut through the dusty air around them.

Catriona gasped as something struck her hard in the back. An arrow, she realized. The kobolds. But they were shooting blind. She felt where she'd been hit, but didn't find any blood. Her chain mail had protected her. Erikoff didn't have any armor, though. If one of those arrows hit him, he could be killed. Or, just as bad, he might cry out, revealing their location to the dragon.

As much as she hated to do it, she had to chance speaking. "Keep low!" she whispered. "The kobolds are shooting at us."

He nodded his understanding and moved closer to the left-hand wall of the defile, hugging the rock as he loped along. She did the same, hoping the ravine ledge might intercept arrows coming from near the fortress.

The dust was clearing before them, revealing several large stands of boulders in the badlands ahead. Between the cover of the rocks and the shelter of the ravines, perhaps they'd be able to give their pursuers the slip.

"Get back! Get back!" Erik whispered, stopping so quickly that Catriona almost crashed into him.

The two of them pressed up against the wall just as a pair of gargoyles darted past the opening at the ravine's far end. The blood red creatures were searching for them, but Catriona didn't think that she and Erik had been seen.

"Do you think we can make it between those big rocks?" Erikoff asked, pointing.

About twenty yards from the end of the ravine, two tall rock formations stood like pillars at the entrance of a temple. Beyond the pillars lay a winding maze of similar rock formations. If they could make it that far, they might be able to conceal themselves.

But the terrain between the end of the defile and the huge natural pillars was open and ran uphill. Anyone from the castle looking in their direction would certainly spot the pair.

Catriona looked at the rapidly clearing dust around them. Even if they stayed put, the ravine wouldn't cover their escape much longer.

"We'll have to chance it," she whispered. Both she and Erik made one final, cautious scan for enemies. Seeing none, Catriona said, "Let's go!"

They dashed the few yards to the end of the ravine and then up the smooth, rocky slope toward the towering rock formations. Erikoff was still limping slightly, but not enough that Catriona needed to help him.

As they neared the two great natural pillars, a cry arose from the pursuing kobolds.

Erik cursed. "We've been spotted," he said.

"Keep going," Catriona urged. "The rock maze is still our best chance, whether we're facing an army of kobolds and gargoyles or a dragon."

They passed between the pillars and into the rolling, rock-strewn highland beyond. Catriona wondered if Gillean and the others were still waiting for them, but she saw no sign of their friends. She wished that Rohawn were with her—she knew she could count on her squire in this kind of situation. Her heart ached, and the desire for revenge sparked up within her again.

Erikoff cried out as a kobold arrow grazed his shoulder. A dark stain of blood spread on the sleeve of his orange robes. He staggered and Catriona stopped to help him.

"I'm all right," he said. "I'm all right. Keep going."

He didn't look all right. His skin was pale and sweaty. He wasn't giving up, though. Behind his golden mask, his deep brown eyes remained fierce and defiant.

More arrows rained down around them. They were at the edge of the kobolds' range, and the shot that hit Erik had been more luck than skill.

With a squawking cry, two gargoyles swooped down on them from behind. Catriona turned, parried with one dragon claw, and slashed with the other. She caught the gargoyle's attack with one weapon and cut off its head with the other. The body fell to the ground and crumbled into red dust.

Erikoff spun at the same time. He summoned a fire to his hand and blew it into the gargoyle's face. The flame sparked and smoked, blinding the monster. Erik and Cat kept running.

"Know any other tricks?" Catriona asked as they crested the hill and turned down slope.

"Sometimes the old, reliable ones are the best," he replied.

Suddenly, in front of them at the bottom of the stony rise, barely thirty yards away, Viktor and Thane dropped down out of the sky. "No tricks will save you now!" Thane's deep, inhuman voice boomed.

The dragon crashed into a slender stone pillar, smashing it. Thane spread his wings, blocking all forward avenues of escape.

Viktor reared up and threw a spear at Catriona. Her dragon claws flashed, knocking the spear out of the air before it could strike. Viktor's weapon clattered to the stone beside Catriona and rolled downhill, landing a dozen yards from the dragon's feet.

Viktor's high, reedy voice cut through the dusty air. "Impressive," he said. "Who are you? Why have you intruded here?"

"Curious travelers," Erikoff said quickly. "We'd heard of your prowess and wanted to see the mighty Viktor and Thane."

"Careful of that one," Thane rumbled. "He has the tongue of a snake."

"And that's why you knocked out our guards and tied them up, I suppose, to visit our magnificent palace," Viktor said. He laughed sarcastically.

Catriona wanted to kill him more than ever, but perched atop his fancy saddle on Thane's back, he remained too far out of reach. Then a new strategy occurred to her.

"I'm a traveling warrior," she said. "I heard you were the best fighter in this part of Krynn. I wanted to test myself against the best, so I hired this trickster"— she indicated Erik—"to help me get into your fortress."

"So, you came to slay me!" Viktor's voice crackled with anger.

"No!" she replied. "I came to challenge you to single combat, to see which one of us would prove superior."

Viktor's bearded face smiled as he said, "A truly superior warrior does not fight unnecessary battles. Kill them, Thane."

The dragon craned his long neck upward as he inhaled. White light seeped around the corners of his daggerlike teeth.

Catriona and Erik looked for cover, but the nearest rocks were too far away.

"When he breathes, dive to opposite sides," Erikoff whispered. "Maybe the lightning won't get us both."

His suggestion made sense, but Catriona decided to ignore it. If she charged the dragon, rather than diving aside, perhaps she could draw its fire and save Erikoff's life. And perhaps the move would surprise the warlord and his mount. Perhaps she'd even get a chance to strike at them. She tensed, waiting for the instant just before the blast.

Thane reared back, his head rising equal to the tops of the towering stone pillars on either side of him. His yellow eyes blazed with hatred, and his mouth brimmed with deadly electricity.

Just then, a small figure appeared atop one of the pillars near the dragon's head. The figure planted a long pole at the edge of the rock and vaulted into the air.

Catriona recognized the figure and gasped. "Shara!"

The pole retracted into the half-elf's hands as she sailed toward the dragon's head. As she soared past, Shara threw a yellowish powder into the monstrous reptile's eyes.

Thane howled with pain. Lightning blasted uncontrollably from his mouth, scorching the afternoon sky. Viktor grabbed the dragon's reins and held on for dear life. Thane bucked wildly and nearly toppled over backward.

Shara landed lightly atop the pillar on the dragon's far side and disappeared behind a rim of the rock.

Catriona raced forward. She sheathed her dragon claws and scooped up Viktor's fallen spear, hefting the captured weapon as she ran. She kept her eyes focused on the flailing monster and his master, waiting for her opportunity.

The rocky ground quaked as Thane crashed back to earth. He shook his head wildly, trying to clear Shara's powder from his eyes. Catriona took careful aim and threw.

Her spear sailed through the air, heading straight for Viktor's unprotected throat.

At the last moment, the warlord spotted the weapon and turned. The spear struck his left shoulder, sinking deep into the muscle. Viktor screamed.

Catriona drew her dragon claws and kept going.

"Up!" the warlord cried to Thane. "Up into the sky!"

The blinded dragon didn't need any more urging. He sprang into the air, beating his mighty wings and soaring high out of Cat's reach. Catriona cursed, wishing she had a bow.

She looked up and saw Shara standing atop the rocky pillar once more. Somehow, improbably, the half-elf had a bow in her hand.

Shara nocked a long, smooth arrow, took aim, and loosed.

The shaft struck Thane in the left wing, tearing through the leathery membrane just below the shoulder.

The dragon shrieked and lurched in the sky. For a moment, it looked as though he might topple to the ground or, at the least, that Viktor might fall from his back.

But Viktor gripped the saddle tightly with his one good arm and, a moment later, Thane righted himself. Dazed, the two of them flitted back toward the safety of their fortress.

Catriona wheeled, thinking she might follow the fleeing dragon and rider. As she turned, though, a hoard of kobolds appeared between the stone pillars at the top of the rise. The kobolds spotted her and drew their bows.

"Come on, Erik!" she called. She and the mage darted behind a huge boulder as the kobolds fired. Arrows rained like hail around the fugitives.

"What now?" Erikoff asked.

"Keep running," Catriona replied. They picked another stand of rocks for cover and dashed across the open distance between. One arrow grazed Catriona's calf, but the scratch didn't slow her.

"Was that Shara I saw?" Erik asked as they ran.

"I think so," Catriona replied.

"Should we go back for her?"

Catriona glanced back, but saw no sign of their friend atop the pillar. "I think Shara can take care of herself," she said.

The rock formations grew thicker and closer together as they ran, becoming a veritable maze within the badlands. Catriona and Erik dashed through them pell-mell. The sounds of the enraged kobolds echoed around the stone pillars, making it nearly impossible to determine how close their pursuers might be.

STEPHEN D. SULLIVAN

The fugitives moved right and then left, always away from the castle, hoping to lose the angry mob. With each passing moment, the pillars of the maze drew closer and closer together.

Erikoff abruptly skidded to a stop. "Wrong way!" he said.

Before them, the stones had closed together completely, forming a box canyon with no way out. The warrior and the mage turned and saw a huge contingent of kobolds right on their heels. Seeing the two humans were trapped, the kobolds stopped and drew their bows once more.

Catriona charged. She thundered into the front rank, killing three kobolds before any of them even knew what was happening. Her dragon claws whirled around her, parrying, striking, stabbing, cutting.

The kobolds in the front tried to fall back, but there were more behind them, so they had nowhere to retreat. Those in the rear of the group began calling to their comrades searching elsewhere in the maze of stone. "We've got them! Over here!"

Catriona killed four more before a kobold spear got through her guard and traced a long scratch up her right thigh. Her blades filled the narrow space between the rocks, and the kobolds didn't dare try to outflank her. Every kobold that tried to pass fell dead.

Catriona smiled, knowing that she could keep them off Erikoff, at least for a while. If she held out long enough, maybe she or Erik would come up with some clever plan to get them out of this mess. Of course, if she'd listened to Gillean and Karise, they wouldn't have been in this fix to begin with.

As Catriona killed the kobolds in front of the group, the kobolds in the rear started arching arrows over the front of the kobold line. With arrows raining around him, Erik drew a thin, curved dagger and limped up to stand beside Catriona.

"Keep out of my way!" Catriona cautioned. She cut down two more of the enemy with a whirlwind series of strikes.

"No problem," Erik replied. "I just figured standing near you was safer than hanging back and getting feathered with arrows. Here, at least, they risk shooting their own to hit us."

"And what makes you think they won't shoot their own?"

"Oh, I *know* they will," Erikoff said. "But at least it buys us more time."

"Time for what?"

"I wish I knew."

Catriona swore. "I was hoping you had a plan," she said.

Erik shook his head. "I was hoping the same about you."

Though the kobolds were taking terrible losses from Catriona's flashing blades—and now from their own arrow shots as well—they kept the two humans pinned inside the narrow box canyon. Catriona knew that if she and Erik didn't find a way past the kobolds soon, they'd be overwhelmed by the sheer force of numbers.

Erikoff stepped back, thrust his hands out, and said, *"Apibatuk!"* A shower of hot coals suddenly rained down on a rank of kobolds fifteen feet away. The creatures screamed as their clothes and whiskers caught fire.

Erik started to smile, but then an arrow slammed into his right thigh. He gasped, staggered back, and fell to the ground. More arrows rained around him. Catriona backed toward the mage, bringing the attacking mob with her, hoping that might foil the archers' aim.

Her ploy worked for a moment. Two arrows meant for Erik hit kobolds instead. The creatures fell dead at Catriona's feet and Erikoff crawled forward, trying to use their bodies as cover.

"Sorry I'm not more . . . help!" he gasped.

She didn't have time to reply. Sweat streamed from every pore of her body and her muscles ached. Erikoff's magical flames, still spreading among the enemy, had bought them a few more moments of life, but a few moments only.

Catriona stepped sideways to intercept a kobold trying to cut around her to attack Erikoff. She killed the creature with a stab of a dragon claw but as she did, her foot slipped in the blood of the many dead kobolds piled around her feet.

She staggered and fell to one knee, barely remaining upright. The kobolds howled with delight and pressed forward, slashing and stabbing, trying to get through Catriona's frantic defense. A spear traced a long cut across her left cheek. Another spear lanced into her left thigh before she could bat the weapon aside. Catriona groaned with pain and weariness.

Fatalistically, Catriona said a final prayer to the gods as her blades flashed around her. Three more kobolds died, but the rest pressed forward, filling the small canyon.

Then, just as they seemed about to overwhelm Catriona and Erik, the kobolds suddenly fell back. Screaming and wailing sprang up in the rear of the enemy ranks. Those in the front turned and backed up, trying to figure out what was going on. The rain of arrows stopped abruptly as the panicking mob pushed the archers out of formation.

Catriona surged to her feet once more, killing the rank in front of her. She looked for the cause of the disruption, hoping to capitalize on it.

In the rear, a few kobolds still burned with Erikoff's fire, but that wasn't the source of the commotion. Three warriors stood attacking the kobold archers, dealing death to the formation from the side.

"Gillean! Karise! Shara!" Catriona cried.

Gillean's long sword cut a kobold in two. He caught Catriona's eye and smiled. "Try to work your way to us!" he called.

Catriona nodded, her heart soaring with new hope. "Come on, Erik!" she said. She killed the kobold nearest to her and then pulled the young mage to his feet.

"Th-thanks," he said as Catriona helped him walk.

Even with one arm supporting Erikoff, Catriona was more than a match for the startled kobolds. Her lone dragon claw cut and stabbed and sliced as effectively as any sword. The kobolds fell back before her fury.

Karise cleared a path through the creatures with her mace while Gillean and Shara held the greater mass of the kobolds at bay.

"This way!" Karise said, indicating a path through the rocks.

Catriona nodded. She and Erikoff stepped between the stone pillars while Karise covered their retreat. As they went, Erik lifted his head and pointed one trembling hand toward a dead kobold still burning nearby. *"Asapi sihir!"* he said.

The fire immediately sprang up into a cloud of black smoke.

Seeing it, Gillean turned to Shara and said, "Come on!"

He and the half-elf dodged back around the bodies and between the pillars, following Catriona and the others.

Karise took Erikoff's other arm, and she and Catriona kept him moving at a good clip. Catriona's many wounds screamed with pain, but she knew there was no time to tend them. Now was their chance for escape, and if they didn't take it, they might not get another.

They darted through the rock formations with Karise leading the way. Gillean and Shara guarded the rear, though Erikoff's smoke cloud seemed to have bought them time.

"Why didn't you bring the horses?" Catriona gasped. She glanced behind, fearing she would see the dragon at any moment.

"The rocks were too treacherous," Karise told her. "The horses kept slipping when we tried. We were afraid they'd break their legs."

Catriona nodded, unable to find the breath to reply.

They ran for long moments, until Catriona's every muscle ached and her lungs burned even more than they already did. Sweat poured from her body, mingling with the blood flowing from numerous cuts. The towering rocks around them thinned as they moved away from the fallen castle.

"The dragon," Catriona gasped. "Keep watch for the dragon!"

"We're on it," Gillean replied. "But I don't think he'll be back after the wound Shara gave him."

"Unless he has a good healer at his disposal," Karise noted. "Keep going until we're sure it's safe."

She and Catriona were practically dragging Erikoff. The mage was slipping in and out of consciousness, his feet moving clumsily.

"H-how far to the . . . horses?" he asked.

"Not far," Karise assured him. "We tied them up safely while we rescued you."

"Th-thanks," he replied.

"Yes, thanks," Catriona said. "Thanks for coming after us. You didn't have to."

"So you were expecting us to just run away and leave you to get killed?" Gillean asked rhetorically.

The remark stung Catriona more than he could have guessed, but she said nothing in reply.

They hurried around a pair of tall boulders and into a U-shaped shelter of rock. There they found the horses carefully tethered, waiting for them.

"Thank the gods," Erikoff gasped. "I couldn't have walked another . . . step." With that, his knees gave way. He would have fallen except that Karise and Catriona caught him.

"He can ride with me," Karise said. "The three of you take the other horses."

Catriona and Gillean nodded, but Shara was standing at the corner of the rock, peering back the way they'd come.

"What is it?" Catriona asked. "What do you see?"

"We're being followed," Shara said.

CHAPTER

19   DEFEAT

atriona looked, but she didn't see anything. The rock they were hiding behind obscured much of her view.

Her gut clenched involuntarily at the idea that the dragon might be coming. Perhaps Karise had been right, and the dragonlord had access to a skilled healer.

"Is it the dragon?" Gillean asked, mirroring Catriona's thought.

The half-elf shook her head. With a few deft pulls and twists, she transformed her walking staff into something resembling a longbow. Amazed, Catriona looked on as Shara drew a long, straight arrow from within the bow staff's casing.

Noticing Catriona's astonishment, Shara said, "The staff is a gift of my people." That didn't explain it much more as far as Catriona was concerned, but the half-elf didn't seem inclined to offer further details.

Shara removed two feathers from her earrings and fitted them to the arrow shaft. "None of you move until I've loosed the shot," she said. "My staff holds only two arrows, and this is the last. I need to make this shot count."

She took a deep breath to steady herself, then stepped around the corner of the rock and loosed.

Catriona and Gillean stepped out next to her and watched the arrow's course. As they did, they saw what had been following them—a blood red gargoyle. Catriona noticed burns around its head and shoulders and deduced that it must have been the one Erikoff used his magical fire on earlier.

Shara's shot took the gargoyle completely by surprise. The monster hung in the air, apparently searching for the group, as the arrow sped toward it.

Catriona wondered why Shara had bothered to shoot it. She knew as well as Cat did that the gargoyles could be killed only by decapitation. The next instant, though, she realized cleverness of the half-elf's attack.

The arrow struck the gargoyle in the wing, right where the wing joint met the shoulder. The shot pierced between the bones, cutting the ligaments that held the wing to the monster's back.

The gargoyle gasped as the wing went limp. It tried to stay aloft but, with only one wing, it fell from the sky in an awkward spiral and crashed to the ground amid the field of towering stone pillars.

"That won't have killed it, you know," Gillean said.

"I know," Shara replied. "But by the time it walks back to its masters, we'll be long gone."

"Only if the rest of you mount up," Karise said. She had gotten Erik onto her horse and was sitting in the saddle behind him. The half conscious mage slumped over the horse's neck.

Catriona and the others mounted and all five of them galloped off.

"We need to find good shelter before Viktor and Thane come looking for us," Catriona said.

The others agreed, and they rode through the rocky hills until Erik began to slip from the saddle. Then they found an overhanging rock for shelter and dismounted. Shara left to scout for enemies as the rest of the group tended to Erik.

Catriona and Karise laid the unconscious mage down and removed his golden mask, revealing his sickly pale face. His robes were soaked with sweat, and his skin felt clammy.

"That's a pretty bad wound in his leg," Catriona said. "Can you heal it, Karise?"

"Sirrion willing," Karise replied. She began chanting in a low voice.

"You look pretty beat up yourself, Catriona," Gillean noted.

"I've had worse," she replied. Every muscle ached, but her soul hurt worse than her body. She'd had the murderers of Rohawn and her family within her grasp, but they'd slipped away. If only she'd gone alone, if only Erikoff hadn't been there for her to worry about, perhaps she could have avenged her loved ones.

She limped to a low boulder and sat down. Gillean sat down beside her, poured some water onto a clean cloth, and dabbed at some of the cuts on her arms. His gentle demeanor reminded Catriona very much of the Alric Arngrim she had loved.

She put up her hand to stop him. "You don't have to," she said.

"I want to," he replied, and kept working. "What you did was very brave. Foolish, but very brave."

"I guess I wouldn't make a very good mercenary," she said.

He paused a moment, as though stung, then continued cleaning her wounds. "I don't make such a good mercenary either," he admitted. "Mercenaries are supposed to be paid—or so I'm told. I, on the other hand, have an unfortunate tendency to work for very little . . . sometimes for free." He finished with her arms and began gently washing the wounds on her legs.

"Like now?" she asked. "You and the others didn't have to come back for me and Erik, but you did. Thank you."

Gillean smiled at Catriona, and her battle-hardened heart melted just a little.

"You're welcome," he said. "I'll say one thing, though. We may not be great mercenaries, but at least we're alive. And we seem to have escaped."

Catriona, unable to find her voice, nodded and smiled.

Shara returned, having walked all around their rocky shelter, looking for signs of pursuit. "Gillean appears to be correct," she said.

"We've lost them?" Gillean asked. "We've escaped."

Shara nodded. "Yes."

"You're both wrong," Catriona said. "We didn't escape. We *lost*."

For a moment, the only sound was the distant whisper of the wind.

"Well, pardon me if I don't see it that way," Karise said, joining the trio. "Could I have some of that water, Gil?" She held out her bloodstained hands.

"Sure," Gillean replied. He poured some water from his water skin, and Karise scrubbed the blood off her fingers.

"How's the patient?" he asked.

"He'll live," Karise replied. She dried her hands, built a small fire, and muttered a quick prayer. Then she continued, "With a little rest, he should be as good as new."

Catriona let out a long sigh. "Well, that's a relief," she said. Knowing Erikoff would recover seemed to drain the tension out of her. She suddenly felt very, very tired. She leaned back against the rock and closed her eyes.

"Now let's take a look at you," Karise said to her.

"I'm all right," Catriona replied.

"She says that, Kari, but the wound in her thigh looks pretty bad to me," Gillean countered. "I tried to clean it, but it won't stop bleeding."

"Let me see," Karise said, taking Catriona's leg in her hands. "Gil's right. This is serious. We're lucky you didn't open it up while you were riding."

"So, can you fix it?" Catriona muttered. She felt warm and sleepy.

"Catriona, stay with me," Karise said. "Cat?" She shook the warrior slightly.

Catriona forced her eyes back open. Karise looked blurry and her voice seemed to be coming from very far away.

"I need you to stay awake while I work," Karise said. "If you pass out, you may slip away. Can you stay with me?"

Catriona nodded. "I think so."

"Good. Now concentrate on staying awake." Sirrion's cleric laid her hands on either side of the wound.

Catriona felt the supernatural fire of Kari's healing coursing into the wound. It was like tiny, hot fingers reaching into her leg. Catriona looked up at Gillean, trying to stay awake as Karise had ordered. Gillean looked so concerned.

Gradually, the fiery sensation changed, and it felt as though the tiny fingers were pulling on her flesh, pinching the sides of the wound together. The fire of the healing lanced deep within her leg, then subsided, leaving only a warm tingling behind.

Gillean smiled at her.

Catriona looked down. The wound was gone. Karise slumped to the ground, exhausted. Gillean patted the cleric on the shoulder and helped her wash her hands again. "Good work," he said.

"Thanks," she replied.

Another smiling face appeared above Catriona. It was Erikoff, without his mask.

"I must say, Catriona," he said. "You're made of pretty stern stuff. I'm impressed." The mage looked pale and weak, but otherwise well.

"You're pretty tough yourself," she replied, sitting up once more.

"Oh yes," he said. "I was thoroughly impressive while losing consciousness and having other people carry me to safety. I don't think even Sturm Brightblade himself could have done better."

Everyone but Shara laughed.

"Who is Sturm Brightblade?" she asked.

"He was a hero in the War of the Lance," Gillean explained. "He died bravely."

Shara nodded. "We should travel farther from the fortress if we can," she said.

"I agree," Gillean said. He stood. "The horses have had enough time to rest. We should put as much distance between us and that dragon as we can—assuming your patients are up to it, Kari."

"I can ride," Catriona interjected.

"Me too," Erik put in.

"If they think they can do it, I won't object," Karise said. "That dragon moves a lot faster than our horses. The more distance we put between us and the fallen fortress, the more area he has to search to find us."

They mounted up again and rode well into the evening, angling roughly to the south but varying their path in hopes of throwing off pursuit.

As night deepened, they found a small copse of scraggly juniper pines to take shelter in. Karise fetched wood and built a small fire, and they all ate. A tiny, muddy watering hole amid the trees replenished their water skins. Karise chanted a prayer over the water to purify it.

As the silver moon, Solinari, climbed high in the night sky, they all gathered around the fire. Shara folded her legs under her and sat down in a rough circle with the rest.

"So now what do we do?" Gillean asked.

"We cut our losses and head for home," Karise replied. "We were fortunate to get out of this alive. No sense pressing our luck any further."

Catriona nodded. Their defeat had quenched the fires of vengeance inside her, at least for the moment. "We could go back to Silverpurse, help with the rebuilding," she said. "Or I could return to Cairngorn Keep and try to help my other friends."

"But there's no guarantee that Silverpurse won't be attacked again," Karise said. "In fact, given what the innkeeper said, it's a virtual certainty."

Erikoff pushed his mask onto the top of his head and scowled at the rest. "I can't believe what I'm hearing," he said. "We've seen Viktor's fortress and we've seen his army. The castle is impressive, yes, but it's not impregnable, and his troops are little more than rabble. As to the man himself, Catriona gave him a wound I'm betting he won't soon forget."

"You did?" Gillean asked. "That must have been before Karise and I arrived."

"I stuck one of his own spears into his shoulder," Catriona said.

"It was a good throw," Shara noted.

"And a good shot you put through the dragon's wing," Catriona said. "What is that weapon of yours, anyway—a staff or a bow?"

"Both," the half-elf replied.

"People, people," Karise said, breaking in. "You're all missing the obvious here. The point is that we're not just fighting Viktor, we're also fighting his dragon."

"But the dragon's not much more impressive than the man is," Erikoff said. "Sure, he's big, but he panicked when I blew a cloud of smoke in his face."

"A clinging, burning cloud," Catriona pointed out.

"Yes," Erik admitted. "But it was still just a minor bit of magic, and he couldn't handle it. He had the same reaction to whatever Shara threw into his eyes."

"Whitherstem powder," Shara said. "It's an astringent. It burns the eyes."

"And the two of them couldn't get out of there fast enough once they'd been hurt," Erikoff continued.

"So what are you saying, Erik?" Karise asked. "That we should go back there and assault the place again?"

"Yes!"

"Why?"

"Because we almost won!"

As the mage spoke, Catriona realized he was right. They *had* almost won. Despite charging in like amateurs and facing overwhelming odds, they'd almost defeated the masters of the fallen castle. The fire began to burn inside her once more.

"But we almost got killed too," Gillean noted.

"So did *they*," Erik said stubbornly.

"Even if we do go back, even if we *do* defeat them, why should we?" Karise asked. "What's the point?"

"Well, you said yourself that the two of them must have built up a considerable fortune," Erikoff said. "They've been looting the surrounding countryside for months now. That kind of steel could do a person—or a religious order—a lot of good."

"*Or* a budding magical order," Gillean pointed out.

"So is that why you want to fight them, Erik?" Catriona asked. "To line the coffers of the Fellowship of the Phoenix?"

"No," Erik said. "I want to kill them because they terrorize and destroy everything they come in contact with. Because their kind is a dying breed on Krynn and deservedly so. Only when the old is swept away can revolutionary ideas truly take hold."

"So you're a revolutionary now, Erik?" Karise said. "A revolution of what?"

"Of freedom!" Erik cried. "Personal freedom without ancient traditions telling you how things should be, or what you should do or think."

"That's a funny philosophy for a mage," Gillean said. "The orders of magic are among the most controlled organizations on Krynn."

Erik turned slightly red. "Well, yes," he said. "I suppose. But that's not what I mean. I mean, the war is over, but it isn't really—and it won't be so long as there are villains like Viktor and Thane still roaming the land, doing what they please."

"I agree with Erik," Catriona said. "But we got lucky this time. If we go back, they'll be ready for us."

"But we'll be ready too!" Erik said.

Gillean shook his head. "Catriona's right," he said. "Even though Viktor and Thane are vulnerable, trying to attack the fortress now would be like putting our heads on the chopping block."

"But—" Erikoff protested.

"I'm with Gil and Cat," Karise said. "It's too dangerous. If we attack the fortress now, we'll just get ourselves killed."

Erikoff looked around the circle, hoping to find some support. His deep brown eyes settled on Shara, who had remained silent.

"Shara," he said. "What do you think?"

The half-elf stared thoughtfully at the fire. "Sometimes, the best way to defeat your enemy is *not* to attack him," she said.

"What do you mean?" Catriona asked.

Shara looked at her and smiled ever so slightly. "Sometimes, the best way to defeat your enemy is to get him to attack *you*."

CHAPTER

20   The Dungeon Cell

The slave girl called Cinder crouched in a corridor outside the dungeon cells of Viktor's fortress. She was ostensibly scrubbing the floors. Viktor liked everywhere that he might visit in the castle to be clean. Even his torture chambers were scrubbed after each "session."

Usually that odious duty didn't fall to Cinder, but to some other unfortunate member of Viktor's "staff." Cinder knew that the warlord didn't trust her, and with good reason. She'd have killed him in an instant if she thought she could have managed it without getting killed.

Since that seemed beyond her means at the moment, the girl settled for spying on the master, trying to ferret out his secrets. That way, if a slave revolt ever came, she'd be ready.

So while Cinder was supposed to be scrubbing the floors of the dungeon corridor, what she was actually doing was spying. Currently, she'd stationed herself near the cell of Viktor's favorite captive, a youth the dragonlord had captured during one of his many raids. Cinder herself had been taken during one such raid.

She was young and small, though, and could do little to fight the powerful dragon rider. Little, except to watch and listen and bide 165 her time, and hope for the chance to strike back at her captors.

Viktor liked to "soften up" his captives before turning them over to the slavers. The young man in that particular cell had proven more difficult to tenderize than most. Viktor had been working on him for a long time, a very long time, which was why Cinder thought of the youth as the warlord's "favorite." Whenever Viktor had a bad day, he'd come down and beat his favorite prisoner. The dragonlord often had bad days, and today was another of them.

Cinder crept forward and peered through the feeding slit cut into the bottom of the cell's oak door. She saw Viktor's maroon suede boots pacing the floor. Beyond that, she glimpsed the bare feet of the prisoner. His ankles were shackled to the wall, and Cinder knew his hands were shackled as well. Viktor didn't like to beat prisoners who might have a chance of beating him back.

We'll see who gets beaten soon! Cinder thought.

Viktor's reedy voice echoed from inside the cell. "How a group like that could elude my forces for so long is beyond me!" the warlord raved. "How they got into the castle in the first place remains a mystery. Thane thinks they used some kind of magic, but I don't know."

"There's a lot you don't know," the shackled youth said. "Whole buckets you don't"— he coughed—"know."

The sound of a fist hitting flesh echoed in Cinder's ears. She winced. The ugly thuds kept up for a few minutes before stopping.

"You think you're so smart!" Viktor taunted the prisoner. "But you'll feel differently when I turn you over to the durogar. Their slave pits will make your stay in my dungeon seem like a picnic in the park."

"M-must be why I'm e-enjoying this place so much," the prisoner replied. "How's your sh-shoulder, by the way? Looks to be healing nicely. Your dragon stopped w-wailing about his scratches yet? *Oof!*"

Cinder backed away from the door as the beating began again. Even though she couldn't see through the crack under the door

STEPHEN D. SULLIVAN

that Viktor was hitting the boy, she couldn't bear to be so close to the horrible sounds. How could one human being treat another that way?

And why didn't the prisoner have the good sense to just shut up? Didn't he know he was only making things worse for himself?

After a while, Viktor tired of hitting the young man and began pacing again. "Why I don't just kill you or turn you over to the slavers, I don't know."

The prisoner didn't reply. Viktor had probably beaten him senseless again.

Cinder knew why the warlord didn't just sell the boy and be done with it—because he liked beating this prisoner. Viktor liked beating this particular young man more than he liked abusing any of his other many victims. Cinder couldn't guess why this prisoner was the warlord's favorite. Perhaps he'd been particularly defiant before Viktor and Thane captured him.

Yes, that was probably it. The only way to know for sure would be to ask the warlord, and that was something she'd never do.

The door to the cell suddenly flew open and Viktor stalked out. He slammed the door shut and locked it. Cinder crept into the shadows of the corridor, trying not to be seen.

She noted the blood on the warlord's knuckles as he passed. She couldn't be sure whether the blood belonged to the master or his victim. Though Viktor was fastidious in most ways, he seemed to enjoy beating his prisoners up close. The dragon rider rubbed his bloody knuckles and smiled. He laughed softly as he walked away from the cell and toward the stairs leading out of the dungeons.

In that moment, Cinder hated Viktor more than she'd ever hated anyone in her life. It was all she could do to resist throwing herself at him and biting his leg.

But no. That wouldn't do anyone any good, her least of all. What *else* could she do?

She could help the prisoner. There must be a reason Viktor hated him so much. Maybe he was a powerful knight or lord. Maybe he knew some secret of Viktor's—a secret that might doom the warlord and his dragon.

With that thought in mind, Cinder crept out of the shadows and toward the big oak door. She had a key—hidden within her rags—that she'd stolen from one of Viktor's other servants, a key that opened most of the doors in the castle. Usually, she used it to filch a few extra scraps for herself from the larder. Now, though, she tried it on the door to the young man's dungeon cell.

She turned the key slowly, keeping her senses alert in case a guard should happen to come down the corridor. Getting caught would be very bad indeed.

Her whole body thrilled as the lock clicked open. She pulled on the door, which was very heavy. But she'd worked hard in Viktor's service, and her muscles were strong. The door creaked open. Cinder slipped inside and pulled it closed behind her—not shut all the way, but enough that it might not be seen as open from the outside.

The prisoner groaned faintly as she entered. The room was dark except for a brazier of glowing coals set next to a small table. A pair of maroon gloves and several irons, obviously to be heated in the coals, rested on the tabletop.

The prisoner hung on the wall opposite, his wrists and ankles clapped in irons. The girl's heart ached to see him. He would probably have been good looking, save for the many bruises covering his body. A dark tangle of hair obscured his face, and Cinder couldn't tell whether he was awake or not.

"I've come to help you," she whispered. She crept over to the boy and began undoing the bolt that held his right ankle cuff together.

"N-no . . ." he mumbled. "Wrists first."

She looked up at him, not understanding.

STEPHEN D. SULLIVAN

168

"F-free my . . . wrists first," he said.

Cinder nodded and stood, twisting at the bolt holding the cuff on his right wrist. It was rusted and squeaked loudly as she worked it.

"Yes, by all means," boomed a reedy voice behind her. "Free his wrists first . . . *if* you can."

Cinder wheeled around to find Viktor blocking the doorway to the room. Behind him stood two of his kobold guards looking on with glee.

The warlord crossed the chamber in two quick strides and cuffed Cinder on the side of the head. She fell hard to the straw-covered floor. The world spun around her.

"It's a good thing I forgot my gloves," Viktor said. "If I hadn't, I might not have discovered your treachery until it was too late."

He picked Cinder up and hit her again. The kobolds laughed with delight.

"L-leave her alone!" the prisoner gasped.

Viktor nodded at the young man and the two kobolds rushed forward, slamming their scaly fists into the prisoner's stomach until he gasped for breath.

Cinder's senses reeled. Bright flashes of light danced before her eyes. She felt herself being roughly dragged out of the room and down the dungeon corridor.

"Little troublemaker!" Viktor growled. "I should have sold you a long time ago!"

Cinder tried to claw at his hands, but it was no use. He was much stronger than she, and her head was still swimming.

He dragged her down a set of stairs, heading even deeper into the tunnels beneath the castle.

Cinder realized with horror where he was taking her. She cried out and tried to kick, but he bashed her head against the corridor wall. She felt sick, but fear knotted her stomach and she couldn't even throw up.

The corridor opened out into a wide walkway across one side of a torch-lit cavern. The walkway ended in a set of stairs leading to the cavern floor, but Viktor stopped before he reached the steps.

Cinder blinked the spots from her eyes. The floor of the cavern teemed with slaves and Viktor's monstrous allies. All the human beings in the cave were shackled together in a long line. Their captors were smaller, with knotted faces and shifty eyes. Cinder knew these creatures—she'd seen one or two of them occasionally in the upper corridors of the castle. They were Viktor's dark dwarf allies, the slavers of the underworld. The durogar.

Before she could even cry out, Viktor threw Cinder off the walkway and into the sea of writhing bodies below. The other slaves didn't so much catch her as break her fall.

"Another one for your pits," Viktor said. "A young, strong one. Should fetch a good price."

One of the durogar, the eldest and most vile looking, glanced up at the warlord. The evil dwarf smiled, showing his rotten, pointed teeth. "Price is ours to determine, dragonlord," he said.

Viktor frowned. "Very well," he said. As he spoke, a blood red imp fluttered out of the darkness and settled onto his shoulder. The tiny creature spoke to the warlord, and he turned to go.

As he walked away, he called back, "Just so long as I'm rid of her."

"Don't worry, Lord Viktor," the durogar chief said. "We'll make sure you *never* see this one again."

Finally, Cinder found the voice to scream.

CHAPTER

21   SANDUSK

The village of Sandusk sat on the western edge of the dusty plains of northern Solamnia, in the shadow of the Vingaard Mountains. It was a small, bucolic village populated by several dozen dirt farmers and their families, all trying to scrape a living from the parched earth.

The town consisted of twenty or so mud-brick houses, a small temple, and an even smaller trading office. The temple was little used—the town didn't have a proper cleric—and the trading company had closed down completely in recent months, for the townsfolk had nothing to trade. Times were often hard in Sandusk, and lately they'd become even harder, which was why the village interested Catriona and her friends.

Sandusk wasn't the first village the companions found after fleeing the fallen fortress. They'd seen plenty of villages, all impoverished by Viktor and Thane—towns stripped of resources, towns with half their populations taken for Viktor's slave pens, towns filled with despair.

Of all the towns they visited, Sandusk was the only one suited to their plans—the only town in which some hope survived.

The buildings of Sandusk stood clustered around a square plaza in the center of the village. The townsfolk called the tiny, close-cropped rectangle of yellow grass "the green," but that was an optimistic name given to the square in better times.

The only actual green grass in the green stood nearest the big stone well in the square's center. Those few tiny, tangled blades benefited from the water spilled from the well.

Karise Tarn sweated as she pulled the long rope attached to the well's bucket. She emptied the water into a large earthen jug in Gillean Rickard's arms. Then she dropped the bucket back down into the well and mopped her brow.

"By Sirrion's fiery eyes, I don't know why I ever agreed to this plan," she said. "I mean, look at us, Gil, will you? Drawing water for a bunch of dirt-poor dirt farmers on the edge of nowhere! How can I—how can *we*—have sunk so low?"

Gillean shrugged as best he could while holding the big container. "Water needs to be drawn," he said.

"Well, then why can't the villagers draw their own water?" she complained.

"You know why they can't," he replied. "They're busy. Do you think they have the tarps and nets and the other things we need just lying around? Now, if you could draw the next bucket up quickly? This jug is getting heavy." He looked from the well to the cart nearby, where a half dozen jugs, already full, waited.

"Yeah, sorry," she said, drawing up the water again.

"If you like, we can switch places after this jug," Gillean said.

Karise sighed. "Anything to break the monotony." She sloshed the water into the jug, filling it nearly to the top. Gillean carried it the half dozen steps to the wagon, set it down, and picked up an empty jug to fill. He handed it to Karise and began to draw the water bucket up himself.

"Why can't the mage or the elf draw water?" she asked.

"They did it yesterday," he said. "Today it's our turn."

Karise rolled her blue eyes. "And it'll be their turn tomorrow, and our turn the day after that, and so on until . . . well, until when, exactly?"

He shrugged and poured water into the jug. "Until we're ready to put our plan into action."

"This godsforsaken plan may not even work!"

"And if it doesn't," said a pleasant voice from nearby, "then we still have the knowledge that we have done good for these people."

Karise and Gillean looked up and saw Shara walking toward them. She looked serene, as always, striding across the green with her carved walking stick in hand. "If not to do good, why do we venture forth into the world?" she concluded.

Karise and Gillean looked wearily at each other.

"I didn't become a mercenary to do good," Karise said. Then she backpedaled and said, "I mean, of course, I *intend* to do good, but that's not the *only* reason I became a mercenary. I also wanted to make some *steel*."

"And clearly that part of the plan isn't working out so well," Gillean added. "For either of us."

"What good is money without happiness?" Shara asked. "What use is money without goodness?"

Karise set the newly filled jug down on the cart and fetched another empty one. "Maybe I'd like to find out for once," she said.

Shara frowned at her.

"So, Shara," Gillean said. "Have you come to relieve us?" His blue-gray eyes sparkled with hope.

The half-elf shook her head. "No," she replied. "I just came to see how you were doing and to tell you that Catriona says the training is going well."

"*Well* . . . ha!" Karise said. "As if the people of this village will ever be anything but farmers—and not very good ones at that."

"You're wrong, Karise," Shara said. "The crops are doing better since our arrival."

"Will the villagers be able to feed themselves after the harvest, do you think?" Gillean asked.

"Perhaps," Shara said. "If the rest of our plans bear fruit."

"And what's your opinion on that?" Gillean said.

"I think that all is proceeding as planned," Shara replied. "The village elders—Kuro and Sawa—think so too."

Karise plopped down on the side of the well and put down her half full jug of water. "So, now we're trusting the opinions of that batty old bunch, are we?" she said.

"Kari, what's wrong with you?" Gillean asked. "We've thrown our lot in with this village. We all agreed to it. You're not thinking of backing out, are you?"

Karise shook her head and ran her fingers through her short brown hair. "Sorry, Gil," she said. "I'm just tired of all this waiting. I want something—anything—to happen."

Just then, the alarm bell atop the temple rang out.

"It seems you may get your wish," Shara said.

"And sooner than you'd hoped," Gillean added.

Gillean, Karise, and Shara raced across the green to the front steps of the temple. It was a small building, only a bit more than three stories tall, counting the fifteen-foot-tall bell tower.

Karise and Gillean drew their weapons and scanned the skies from the mountains on the west to the arid plains on the east.

"Anything?" she asked.

He shook his head. "You?"

She shook her head in reply.

As they stood looking, every person in Sandusk arrived in the square. Some shambled in from the nearby buildings, others ran in from the fields. The last to arrive were Catriona and Erikoff.

With them came several dozen farmers armed with pitchforks and makeshift spears.

The doors to the small temple opened, and an old woman dressed in the dust-colored robes of a village elder appeared. She walked down the temple's brief flight of steps and bobbed her head.

"Sawa," Karise said, "where's the threat?" She continued to scan the horizon for enemies.

"No threat, Karise Tarn," the old woman replied. "It's what you call a . . ." She screwed up her wizened face, unable to remember the word.

"A *drill*," said the old man who came out of the temple behind her. His name was Kuro, and he, too, wore the robes of an elder. "Is that not right, Catriona?" he asked.

Catriona nodded. "Yes, Kuro," she said. "A drill."

"How'd we do?" Sawa asked.

Erikoff, standing beside Cat, consulted a piece of parchment and made check marks. "Passing well, I think," the masked mage said. "Though I don't see Jimal in the crowd. Where is he?"

"Here I am!" cried a young man dashing toward the square. He was pulling on bits of armor as he ran—a badly dented helmet, a shoulder guard, a shin protector.

Catriona frowned at him. "Jimal," she said. "I've told you before—arm yourself, then arrive. You'll be cut down in an instant if you show up for battle dressed like that."

"But this isn't a battle," Jimal said. "It's only a drill."

"He's right," Karise agreed. "Though it would have been nice for you to let us know, Catriona." She glared at the warrior.

"Announced drills are over," Catriona said. "Everyone needs to be on their toes all the time now. We're getting close to the day we've waited for."

A murmur of mixed agreement and dissent rumbled through

the crowd. "What about our harvest?" one woman asked. "The time is near for that as well."

"What good does the harvest do if someone steals it from you?" Kuro asked.

"As they've stolen from us before," Sawa pointed out.

"We'll help you with the harvest, as we've helped with your other chores," Catriona said. "But if we're going to accomplish our goal, we need to stick to the plan. We need to keep preparing, keep practicing."

"The flame-haired warrior is right," Sawa said. "We've all agreed to the plan, and we need to stick to it. If we don't, we'll never be any better off than we are now."

"Well, if this drill is over," Karise said, "I have water that needs hauling." She looked at Catriona as though for permission.

Catriona nodded. "All right, everyone," she said. "Good job. You can go back to work."

"But remember, next time the bell rings it may not be a drill. Next time, it may be for real," Erik said.

Catriona sat with her back against an adobe wall, looking out of the small doorway of the room she shared with Karise and Shara. She'd pulled back the ragged curtain so that she could have a clear view of the stars.

Karise snored softly on a cot in one corner of the room. A few embers smoldered in a tiny brazier nearby, remnants of the cleric's evening devotions. Sweet smoke from the incense wafted up into the still night air. On another cot nearby, Shara sat up.

"You can't sleep?" the half-elf whispered.

Catriona shook her head.

"Are you worried that the plan might fail?" Shara asked.

"No," Catriona replied. "It's a good plan—as good as we can make it."

"You're worried about the villagers, then."

Catriona shook her head again and said, "Not so much. Our preparations are almost done. We've had to scrounge and scrape for every last thing we needed—especially the wood and ropes—but these people are nearly ready. They'll never be a real army, of course, but at least this time, they'll be able to defend themselves."

"Then, what?" Shara asked, puzzled. As she spoke, Karise groaned and tossed uncomfortably.

"Let's talk outside," Catriona said. "Karise deserves her sleep. She's worked hard."

Shara nodded. "As have we all."

She and Catriona stepped outside and closed the ragged curtain behind them.

They walked a short distance from the small room they shared behind the trading post. The night was clear and cool, and the stars shone brilliantly overhead. The red moon, Lunitari, was sinking low, while Solinari, cautiously poked its silver head up above the horizon. The two found a quiet place near the stables.

"If not the plan or the villagers, are you worried about our companions—Karise and the rest?" Shara asked.

"No," Catriona replied. "That's not it either." She took a deep breath of the cool night air. "It's myself I'm worried about—*me*."

"You're worried that you might die?" Shara asked, again puzzled.

Catriona shook her head. "No, not *my* dying. I've faced death many times. It's *other people* dying I'm worried about—the villagers, Erik, Kari, you, Gil."

"None of us can choose our fate, Catriona," Shara said.

"That's true," Catriona replied.

Shara tilted her head and looked compassionately at her friend.

"Then why do you think *you* can choose other people's fates?"

"I . . ." Catriona began. Then she hung her head. "A lot of people I cared about have died because of me," she said.

"But you did not kill them," Shara said. "You did not choose their fate."

"No," she said. "But I didn't save them either."

"You cannot save everyone, Catriona," Shara replied quietly. "Do not waste life mourning what you cannot change."

Catriona couldn't decide whether to thank Shara for her gentle wisdom or curse her for being so calm in the face of danger and death. She remembered what Shara had told her in Purespring about losing her own mother in the war. Clearly, the half-elf had taken her own advice—she had moved beyond guilt and loss to build a new life for herself. But what kind of life?

The mystery of the half-elf's movements and motivations remained. Catriona trusted her yet couldn't quite say why.

She turned to find Shara staring at her, as though the half-elf might be reading her mind. The thought disturbed Catriona, and she went back to looking at the stars.

The two of them sat alone in the quiet evening for some time, until movement from beyond the stables caught Catriona's attention. She peered into the starlit night, trying to make out the person moving through the darkness.

"Is that Erik?" she whispered to Shara.

The half-elf nodded.

"What's he doing?"

Shara shrugged. The mage had left the small room that he and Gillean shared and was creeping deliberately to the north. Cat wondered what lay in that direction. Only one thing sprang to mind—the fortress of their enemy. She stood. "I'm going to find out what he's up to," she said. She turned to find Shara already standing beside her.

STEPHEN D. SULLIVAN

The two of them moved cautiously through the back alley of Sandusk, following the furtive mage. Erikoff paused at an adobe house near the temple. He whispered something to the back window, then waited. A few minutes later, a girl about the mage's age came out the back door. Catriona recognized her as one of the daughters of Anaska, the woman who tended the temple.

Erik held out his hand and gave the girl something small that glinted in the light of the rising moon.

It was a charm, the kind the mage had given Cat and her friends.

The girl took the token and smiled at Erikoff. She gave him something—another charm?—in return. Then she took his hand and led him out into the darkness beyond the houses.

Catriona sighed and shook her head, silently cursing herself for being paranoid. "Even mages have feelings, I guess." She turned and walked back toward her room. The half-elf followed.

"I suppose it's good that Erikoff's found someone," Cat said.

"We all need . . . friends during stressful times," Shara said.

A feeling of overwhelming sadness welled up within Catriona's breast. "I . . . I wish I had someone like that," she said. "I don't, though. I have friends scattered here and there, but it's not the same thing. I have no one . . . no one like that."

The half-elf arched her eyebrows. "No one?" she asked. She glanced from Catriona toward the building where Gillean and Erik were staying.

Catriona blushed. "No," she said. "No . . . I . . ." But she couldn't finish. She didn't know what she meant to say.

How could she even think of having a relationship with Gillean when any of them—all of them—could die at any moment?

Catriona watched Gillean shovel dirt from the trench at the edge of town. Sweat poured from the mercenary's brow, and his dark hair fell in rivulets over his blue-gray eyes. How like Alric Arngrim he looked. Yet at the same time, how unlike.

No matter how difficult things became, how hard he worked, Gillean always had an air of optimism about him. He was brave and strong and plainspoken. The only strike against him was his mercenary nature—and even that wasn't so bad. If steel was all he loved, why would he be digging ditches, camouflaging tarps, building weapons, and training farmers for a few meager meals a day?

Catriona clipped her dragon claws to her belt, picked up a shovel, and went to join him. He glanced up and smiled as she arrived. "Weren't you training the crossbow recruits?" he asked. "I thought you were done working for the day."

"I was," she said. "But this still needs doing." She shrugged.

"I can't say I'm sorry for the help," he replied. He grabbed his water skin from atop the trench and offered it to her. She took it and drank, washing a bit of the dust from her mouth.

"Thanks," she said and began digging.

They worked side by side for half an hour without talking. Finally, Catriona turned and said, "Gillean, I know why I'm here, and I know why Erik is here, and I kind of understand why Karise and Shara are here. But why are *you* here?"

"In the ditch?" he replied, smiling. "Because digging ditches is my job today." He threw another shovel of dirt on top of the nearby pile.

She frowned. "No, that's not what I meant. I mean, why did you come to this town with us?"

He thought for a moment and seemed about to answer when someone said, "Find any gold down there yet?"

Gillean and Catriona looked up. Karise stood at the top of the pit, carrying an armful of wooden spikes.

Gillean smiled at her. "No," he said. "No gold yet. Why don't you come down and dig with us? Maybe together we can turn some up."

Karise laughed. "I might just do that—if I thought it'd do any good. Here. You'll need these when you get done." She tossed the spikes down into the hole next to where the two were digging.

"Thanks," Catriona said, though she barely meant it.

Karise nodded and left to finish her assignment. When Catriona turned back, Gillean was working again, her question forgotten.

Gillean set his plate down on the table between Karise and Catriona and smiled, but said nothing. All of them had worked hard for weeks, and they were all very tired. Dust and sweat covered all three warriors.

Shara sat across the table from them, barely dirty, not sweating, staring serenely off into some uncertain distance. Gillean didn't know how she managed it. Perhaps it had something to do with the elf half of her heritage. He'd met only a few elves in his life and had never spent much time with one before.

Erikoff sat next to her, his golden mask gleaming in the evening candlelight. Whether the mage was sweating remained difficult to determine, though his orange robes certainly looked grubby enough. He and Shara ate and drank very little, which was good, as there was little food or drink in the village of Sandusk.

Gillean poked at the maize and the tiny bit of meat on his plate. What was he doing here? Catriona had asked him that the other day. He didn't have a good answer then, and he didn't have one now.

Sure, there weren't many jobs to be had in this area, and those that he'd taken had turned out badly. But working for a bunch of poor farmers, trying to form them into a militia? It seemed completely mad.

He glanced to his right at Catriona. Her red hair fell over her smooth shoulders like a cascade of fire. She caught his eye and flashed a brief smile. Even covered with dirt from the fields, she

181

was still one of the most compelling girls he'd ever met.

She was the source of the madness. This was *her* obsession, not his. How was doing this going to help his family get out of debt? Sure, his prospects of a big payday had seemed larger with her at first, but this? This was all nobility and duty with a payoff only if they won the day—and then only if they were lucky. Did sticking with Catriona make any sense?

He glanced toward Karise on his left. She caught the look and smiled back as well, her blue eyes flashing. Clearly Kari thought there was some coin in this venture. She wouldn't be there if she didn't think so. She did have some measure of a cleric's altruism, but not enough to overrule her good sense—not enough to make her abandon hope of becoming a full-fledged priestess of Shinare.

What has happened to *my* good sense? Gillean wondered silently.

The sensible thing to do would be for him to leave right then. He could make his way south, go home and try to start over, loot or no loot. Yet here he sat between two girls he liked very much, two girls who seemed to represent the dual sides of his nature.

How could he choose between them? How could he do what was right? And what, indeed, was the right thing for him to do?

Gillean shook his head and ate his maize.

Catriona stood beside Gillean, Karise, Shara, and Erikoff at the edge of town.

She surveyed Sandusk, admiring the results of their preparation. The village militia ran through their drills in the green, looking almost as though they knew what they were doing. Beyond them, a smaller group worked a half dozen makeshift presses, turning harvested maize into volatile oil.

Aside from those two things, everything seemed normal in the village. Catriona's plan of camouflage and concealment had worked. To all appearances, Sandusk was just another poor farming town on the edge of the mountains—a farming town that happened to lie within the territory of Viktor and Thane.

The dragonlord would be coming soon. Catriona felt it. She thought the others could feel it as well.

She stooped down, picked up a handful of dust, and spread it across the top of a straw mat that concealed a spike-filled pit.

"Well?" Gillean asked. "What do you think? Are we ready?"

Catriona stood and brushed the dust from her hands. "As ready as we'll ever be," she said.

"So . . ." Erikoff said. "What do we do now?"

"Now we wait," Shara said.

Catriona nodded. Waiting would be the hardest part of all.

CHAPTER

22   WAITING'S END

Viktor and Thane circled in the sky above their fallen citadel. The dragon's wing had healed nicely, as had the warlord's shoulder. In the courtyard below, their force of kobolds, servitor gargoyles, and human commanders massed, waiting for the order to march forth and work the warlord's will upon the land.

Behind his horned mask, Viktor smiled. This was going to be a good venture—a profitable campaign indeed.

"Things have been quiet around the castle since you sold that brat to the durogar," Thane rumbled.

Viktor nodded. "I should have gotten rid of her ages ago," he said. "If I had any idea of the trouble she'd been causing behind the scenes, I would have. Misplacing things, stealing food, leaving doors unlocked, whispering rumors, and encouraging discontent among the other servants . . . that little ratbag kept busy, I'll say that for her. But she's gone now, and we're richer for it."

"And that's even better than if I'd eaten her," Thane added. He laughed a wicked, hissing laugh.

As they circled in the air, a small red shape fluttered up toward them. Viktor recognized it as the imp, a messenger from his far-off allies, the ones who had sent the gargoyles for his army. The imp hovered before him and bowed politely in the air.

Viktor nodded to her and she settled onto the front of the saddle, folding her batlike wings along her back. "Greetings from my masters, Lord Viktor and Lord Thane," she said.

"Return our greetings to them as well," Viktor replied disinterestedly.

"We perceive that you are making ready to leave the fortress," the imp said.

"We have tribute to collect," Thane rumbled. "It's expensive being a lord, like Chortog said."

"Indeed, my lords, indeed," the imp replied, her high voice squeaking above the wind. "That is why my masters were hoping you would accept our offer for the piece from your trophy collection that we discussed earlier. You need coin and we can supply it. No need to risk yourselves campaigning."

"Risk?" Thane boomed. "There is no risk. Our kingdom is pacified. We take what we want."

"Just so," the imp said. "But still, more steel in your coffers could not be a bad thing. Surely you can part with so insignificant a trinket."

"That big jeweled jar?" Viktor said. "I don't understand why your masters would want it."

"It has some sentimental value to them, as I explained before," the imp said.

"And we didn't believe you then either," the dragon boomed. "If your masters want the thing, there must be some magic about it—some important magic."

"Indeed, we have never denied it," the imp said. "But the magic it contains is useless to you. You cannot wield it."

"Useless," Viktor noted, "except that it keeps us allies."

"We are allies regardless," the imp replied.

"And how long would that last if we gave you the jar?" Thane said. "Not long, I'd venture."

"That's why we'll keep it," Viktor said. "That way, we and your masters can use it together, when the time is right."

"If that is what you wish, we are at your service," the imp said. She bowed. "When the time is right." She lifted off from the saddle and fluttered down toward the castle once more.

"I don't trust that thing," Thane said when she'd gone. "She's too clever—never quite means what she says. She annoys me."

Viktor nodded. "She makes me tense as well. I think I'll go punish my prisoner, loosen up a bit before we leave."

"Aren't you done with that human yet?" Thane asked. "If you don't finish soon, there won't be enough of him left to sell."

"Ah," Viktor replied. "But think of how much more we'll receive in payment, once I've broken him."

"I could break him with one pinch of my claws," Thane said.

Viktor smiled. "But where's the fun in that?"

He tugged on the dragon's reins and angled down toward the castle courtyard below.

"This stinks," Karise said. "This stinks both figuratively and literally." She shot a disdainful look at the many peasants working in the fields nearby and sniffed the air. Then she reached down and scythed off another stalk of maize and threw it into the cart behind her. "Picking ears was bad enough, but this silage cutting . . . ! If there wasn't a whole castle full of treasure at the other end of this, I wouldn't put up with it."

"Catriona said waiting would be the hardest part," Gillean replied. He sliced a stalk of maize and threw it into the cart as well. Another cart rumbled across the fields, returning from its trip to the silo where the stalks would be chopped up and fermented into cattle feed.

"Yes, but I thought she meant hardest on my nerves, not hardest on my *back*," Karise said. She straightened up for a moment and rubbed her hands at the base of her spine.

"Here, let me do that," Gillean offered.

"Cut my maize?"

"No, rub your back."

She smiled at him. "I'll rub your back if you rub mine."

"It's a deal." He lay down his scythe and put his hands on her shoulders, gradually working down to the small of her back.

"Mmm," she said. "You missed your calling."

"Does being a masseur pay better than being a mercenary?"

"It would almost have to, wouldn't it?" she replied. "At least the way we've been going." She wiped the sweat from her brow with one sleeve of her tunic. "Sorry," she said. "I'm as ripe as those villagers."

"No worse than I, I'll venture," Gillean said.

She shrugged. "It's manly to smell a bit, especially while working on a hot day."

"Speaking of which, we should get back to cutting," he said.

"Why?" she replied. "They're not paying us."

"We have been housed and fed," said Shara from two rows over. "What more could we ask?"

"A pocket full of steel and a banquet of something other than maize?" Karise suggested. "I mean, if our plan succeeds, this village will benefit far more than we will. They'll have their freedom, while we—"

"Yes, Karise, what *will* we have?" Catriona asked, stepping between the rows.

"Come to bend your back with the rest of us?" Karise asked.

"Yes," Cat replied. "But go on, Karise. What will we have if we win?"

"A chance to fight and risk our lives again, most likely," the warrior-cleric replied.

"In a good cause," Catriona reminded her.

"All causes look good to someone," Karise shot back.

"Don't mind her," Gillean said. "She's been out in the sun too long."

"All of us have," Karise said. "Except maybe the mage."

"Erik's done his share," Catriona said.

"It's just that his share doesn't include the backbreaking work," Karise concluded.

"Most mages are ill suited to physical labor," Shara said. "Their strength is of the mind."

"Well, I wouldn't *mind* if Erik would lend some of his *strength* to these fields," Karise said.

Gillean smiled at her. "Because what we really need is another sweaty man stinking up the place."

Karise rolled her eyes, "You know what I mean."

"Erik is *watching*," Catriona said. "That's his job. You should get back to yours."

Karise frowned at her. "Just as soon as you do."

Catriona cut the maize as quickly and efficiently as she could. The coarse stalks grated against her hands, quickly rubbing them raw. The dust from the field and the brightness of the afternoon sun stung her eyes. Still, she wasn't about to complain or give up—not until Karise did, anyway.

The cleric had remained silent since her earlier outburst. Perhaps she was just blowing off steam. Everyone needed to do that from time to time. Catriona wished that she could afford to do the same. As the presumed leader of the project, she could be seen to neither bend nor break. The villagers needed to be confident in her leadership, and so did her friends.

Yes, Shara and Gillean might understand if she broke down and let her feelings show—they might even respect her afterward. But would Erik? Would Karise? Catriona thought that she'd pushed everyone involved just about as far as they would go. Two questions still nagged at her, though: Had she pushed the villagers and her friends far enough to see their plan through to completion? Or was she leading them all to their deaths? Catriona wished she knew.

She'd done everything she could think of. Yet she still had the nagging suspicion that it was not enough—that it could never be enough. Even the best commander could not consider all the possibilities.

What had she missed? What fatal flaw in her plan might spell doom for all of them? And was the whole venture mad to begin with?

Was she really helping the villagers of Sandusk, or was she merely dragging everyone down her own private road to the Abyss?

As the thoughts and worries spun thorough her head, a sound broke her concentration—a repeating, tolling sound.

The alarm bell!

They had abandoned practice drills days ago, after finishing the fortifications at the town's perimeter. This was the real thing. This was the time they'd prepared for.

Catriona, Karise, Gillean, Shara, and everyone else working in the fields dropped their farm implements and ran to the village square.

Erikoff dashed out of the temple to meet them.

"There's a dust cloud moving on the northern horizon and something large flying above," he said. "The enemy is coming!"

CHAPTER

23   The Battle of Sandusk

A wave of fear washed through the assembled villagers. Most whispered anxiously, while some actually ran from the crowd into their mud-brick houses.

Catriona held up her hands and called, "There's no need to panic!" But no one was listening. The crowd grew more restless and confused with each passing moment. Cat feared that the whole village might run, even after all their careful planning.

"Stop!" Catriona cried. "Listen to me!"

But the din of the mob drowned out her voice.

Gillean climbed to the top of the well wall, stuck his fingers in his mouth, and whistled loudly. The piercing sound cut through the air and, for a moment, everyone stopped and listened.

"Everybody, stay calm," Gillean said. "We knew this would happen someday. This is what we've planned for."

"The mercenary is right," said Sawa. The ancient, robed woman stepped to the center of the crowd and held up her gnarled walking stick. All eyes in the village turned to her. Kuro pushed through the throng and took his place beside the other village elder.

"Are you all rabbits?" Sawa asked. "Will you run and hide at the

first sign of trouble?"

"It is as Gillean said," Kuro concurred. "We knew this day would come. Months ago, when the troops of Viktor and Thane first came to our village, we knew they would return for tribute."

"They've returned twice, and each time taken almost more than we could bear," Sawa reminded her people. She turned and pointed at one man in the crowd. "Vedec," she said, "is your farm thriving on what they've left you?"

The man lowered his eyes and shook his head. "No, Sawa," he said. "Viktor's tributes leave me barely enough to carry on."

"Anaska," Kuro said, turning to a woman in white robes. "Did the dragon's troops not threaten to destroy our temple if we could not pay them what they demanded?"

Anaska, the temple's caretaker, bowed slightly. "They did," she replied. "And every time they return, their demands increase. If I had the power of the gods, I would smite them! But, alas, I am merely a caretaker."

"The warlord demands *everything!*" Jimal blurted from the back of the crowd. "Soon we will have nothing left! That is why we must fight! That is why we agreed to the plan that Catriona and the rest brought to us!"

Catriona stepped up onto the well wall alongside Gillean. "And now is the time to put all our plans and preparations into action," she said. "We can defeat these villains if we stick together."

"But what about the dragon and his rider?" someone called from the crowd. "They can destroy our town in an instant!"

"Viktor won't come himself," Karise said. "Not at first. He'll let his henchmen do his dirty work for him. He'll send underlings to collect his tribute."

Kuro nodded. "Is that not the way it's been before?"

"The last two times, yes," said someone else in the crowd. "But the first time, the dragon came!"

"That was just to scare you," Catriona said.

"And it seems to have worked," Erikoff said in a sly whisper.

"Think about it," Gillean said. "Remember what we told you when we first came to your town: Viktor and Thane don't want to destroy your village—destroyed villages don't pay."

"He's destroyed villages before," said the first speaker, a weathered, one-eyed man named Elops.

"But only to make an example of them," Karise said. "Once a village is pacified, he just wants tribute, which only makes sense. Perhaps a dragon can live on carnage forever, but humans need food and steel. And Viktor is only human."

"But now we're fighting him," said a woman named Sheli. "Now he'll fight back and maybe destroy us! What will happen to our children?" She clutched a small child clad in dirty rags to her breast.

"What will happen to your children if you *don't* fight him?" Catriona asked. "Will you have them live as slaves to this dragonlord for the rest of their lives?"

"And Viktor *does* take slaves," Erikoff added. "He took them from every town between here and Silverpurse. In every town we stopped at before we came here, people told us of mothers, fathers, *children* . . . all lost. Those towns are too weak to fight back now. Will you wait until Viktor and Thane decide you're worth more as slaves than you are as farmers?"

"They took some of us when they first came here!" Vedec said. "They took my brother and my niece."

"And my sister too, and others as well," added a young woman. "They said our people were hostages against our good behavior. You mean to tell us they are slaves?"

Erikoff nodded. "More than likely."

The crowd seemed less frightened now. An angry murmur built up among them. The thought of being enslaved was worse to the villagers than the thought of being killed outright.

Kuro held up his staff. "We have discussed this before," he said.

"We made our decision when these five warriors came to town. We will *not* be slaves to this dragon and his warlord!"

"We won't let them drain the lifeblood from our town any longer!" Sawa added. "We've trained to fight, and now we will fight! We'll fight and kill the dragonlord and his army!"

A great cheer went up from the assembled crowd.

Catriona smiled. Now, they were ready. "Fetch your weapons and go to your stations," she called. "Gillean, Shara, and I will ride out and deal with their advance scouts. The rest of you, make ready!"

The crowd cheered again and hurried to fetch their weapons.

The stable master brought three horses for Catriona, Gillean, and Shara. After the three mounted up, Catriona looked down at Karise and Erikoff. "Can you handle the villagers until we return?" she asked.

Karise nodded. "No problem," she said.

"We'll keep their morale up while you're gone," Erik added.

Gillean smiled at the two of them. "We'll try not to be long."

"Just be sure to come back in one piece," Karise told him.

"If I don't," he replied, "you'll just have to patch me up."

Catriona shook her horse's reins. "Let's go."

The three of them galloped out into the arid foothills surrounding the small village. They rode to a spot they'd chosen previously, where a stand of large rocks overlooked the northern trail into the village. The rocks were big enough to conceal both horses and riders, while still giving a good view of the incoming path.

They stationed themselves so they could see the trail below and intercept the warlord's scouts. Then they waited.

"How many do you think there'll be?" Gillean asked after they'd been sitting about an hour.

"Probably just two or three," Catriona replied. "Viktor will want to remind the village of his hold over them without slowing down his main force if he can help it."

Gillean nodded. "And that main force will be pacifying new villages in the area," he said.

"Or taking slaves," Shara added.

"Or both," Catriona concluded. "As Viktor drains the coffers of villages he's already conquered, he'll need new villages to take their place."

"So he steals their goods and, when a village has nothing left, sells their people into slavery," Gillean said. "Quite a racket."

"One worth stopping, even if there's no profit in it," Catriona said as she turned away from the road and gazed at him.

"Yeah," he agreed, his face somber and determined. "But if some loot falls my way out of this, I hope you won't mind if I take it."

"Just so long as it doesn't jeopardize our goal," she said.

"They're close," Shara announced, cocking her head to the north. The hot breeze tugged the half-elf's wavy hair away from her pointed ears. She took her staff and, with a few deft twists, transformed it into its bow form. She'd carved new arrows to replace the twin shafts inside the staff, but she wouldn't be using those now. Instead, she'd strapped a normal quiver, with a dozen ready-made arrows, to her back.

Gillean had brought his bow too, and Catriona carried one as well. Catriona hefted the weapon confidently. Gillean and Shara had tutored her during their spare time over the past weeks, and now she was quite a good shot, though not as good as either the half-elf or the young nobleman.

She peered around the rocks and saw a dust cloud coming toward them over the rolling foothills.

"Four, I think," Gillean said.

"Five," Shara corrected.

"Let them ride past," Catriona said. "Make sure we know how many we're facing. Then take them."

"Shooting bandits in the back isn't very sporting," Gillean noted.

"Believe me, they wouldn't have the same compunction about where they shoot you," Catriona said. Besides, protecting the town is the important thing, not chivalry."

Gillean nodded. "Point taken."

Viktor's outriders appeared atop the next hill. There were five—as Shara had said—and they were humans, not kobolds. Each rode a lean, muscular horse. The men wore chain mail and were armed with swords and shortbows, though their weapons were sheathed. None of them seemed concerned about meeting any resistance. Their harsh voices echoed over the hills as they joked about the gruesome details of Viktor's conquests.

As the bandits passed beyond their hiding place, Catriona, Gillean, and Shara each took aim.

"Now!" Catriona whispered.

As one, the three of them loosed their arrows.

Viktor and Thane circled high above their army, looking down on the forces massed below. The army looked impressive, but nevertheless, Viktor frowned.

Even though the force was composed mostly of kobolds, it still cost quite a lot of steel to maintain. Kobolds would fight for love of war, but they still had to be fed, armed, and sheltered. The castle served for the last, but the first two required resources—ever more resources, it seemed.

The few humans who worked for him required all that and more. They were more powerful and more reliable than the kobolds, though. Without humans to lead it, Viktor's army might fall into disarray.

The only troops that weren't in some way costly to Viktor were the gargoyles. They went where he told them to and carried out his orders without question. Of course, the gargoyles weren't, strictly speaking, *his* troops. They belonged to his allies, the ones who wanted that certain trinket from him.

If he gave them the trinket, if he *sold* it to them, would the allies remain true? Would the gargoyles desert him?

Thinking about questions like that made Viktor's head ache. He much preferred fighting, and so did Thane. Fighting was simple, direct. No deals, no bargains, no politics, just force against force. That was why he and the dragon got along so well—they were both of the same mind.

At that moment, their minds were troubled, not only with the state of their ongoing finances, but also with the progress of the campaign. "I don't see them," the dragon rumbled for the fourth time. "I think something has happened. Maybe they got lost."

"They didn't get lost," Viktor scoffed. "That's why we sent the humans, so they wouldn't get lost." He gazed to the south toward the small village of Sandusk. Why hadn't his scouts returned yet?

"Maybe they've stolen the tribute and run off," the dragon suggested.

Viktor shook his head. "Kobolds might do that, but not humans. Humans are smart enough to know that we'd hunt them down and kill them if they ran off with our loot. Besides, that's one of our farming villages—they usually pay us in grain, not steel."

The dragon nodded, which made Viktor bounce up and down in his saddle. "You'd have to be an idiot to run off with a bunch of grain," Thane said. "And what good is grain anyway? We should make the villagers sell it and give us the steel."

"Our army needs to eat, doesn't it?" Viktor asked, feeling a bit peeved. "If they don't eat, they don't march, and if they don't march, then we can't collect our tribute."

"We could collect it ourselves," Thane suggested, "*if* it wasn't being paid to us in grain. What do we need a whole army for, anyway? We could do this job ourselves."

"But if we collected all the tribute ourselves, when would we have time to enjoy our riches?" Viktor asked.

The dragon frowned as he considered that question. Finally, he said, "So where are they? They're late."

"Yes," Viktor said. "They are."

He and Thane gazed across the distance to Sandusk. The village appeared the same as it always had. So why had his tribute collectors failed to return?

"We should find out why," the dragon suggested.

"Yes," Viktor said. "Swoop low and I'll tell the troops to follow after us."

"You think there's been an uprising?" Thane asked.

Viktor gazed at the town, which was so close that it was almost within sight of the top parapets of his castle. All looked quiet. "I don't know," he said. "But it doesn't pay to take chances."

"Why not send that red imp to find out?" the dragon suggested.

"Because the imp is never around when I need her, of course," Viktor replied.

"Off doing her masters' bidding, I suppose," the dragon said.

Viktor thought of the imp and her fascination with the artifact in his treasury. "I suppose," he replied. "That is why I left Chortog at the fortress to look after things."

"You think we can trust that fat kobold?"

"I think we can trust his fear of death," Viktor replied. "Come on. I'm starting to get hungry. Let's get this done so we can fly back to the castle and have a proper, relaxing dinner."

They dipped low over their army and relayed marching orders to the human subcommanders. The commanders turned the mass of kobolds, humans, and gargoyles toward the town. Then Viktor and Thane set course for Sandusk.

It didn't take them long to reach the sleepy village in the foothills.

They circled the town twice but saw no one—no one walking the streets, no one working in the fields. As they completed the second pass, though, a robed figure came out of the town's shabby temple.

Thane laughed. "They're afraid of us," the dragon said. "They're hiding. None of them want to show their faces."

"Yes," Viktor agreed. "They've sent out one lone elder to speak with us." He smiled and pulled back on the reins.

Thane arced around the village once more and then landed at the edge of the green. His enormous wings beat up huge clouds of dust as he touched down. His long talons cut into the parched grass and dry earth. The robed figure sank to one knee in supplication as they landed.

Viktor stood in his saddle. "We are Viktor and Thane," he said. "The time for tribute has come, and we demand our due."

The figure rose and, as she did, the hood slipped back from her head. Her hair shone flaming red in the afternoon sunshine. Catriona looked the dragonlord in the eye and smiled. "You'll get your due, all right."

"Now!" Catriona cried.

She dived to the ground as two dozen villagers popped out of concealment and threw their spears at the dragon. Simultaneously, four other groups threw the tarps off the huge crossbows they'd constructed and hidden near the square. The bows all fired.

The air above the green filled with deadly missiles aimed at the dragon and his rider. Thane roared as spears and crossbow bolts as thick as a man's arm pelted his armored body. The dragon's scales turned many of them aside, but some got through. One crossbow bolt pierced his right shoulder, and another sank into his hip near the base of his tail. A spear lodged in the middle of his throat, while another stuck in the scales of his belly. A third spear pierced his right wing, and a fourth scraped across the ridge above his left eye. Blood dripped down the dragon's face.

Viktor brought his sword up as quickly as he could, but it still wasn't quick enough. He batted two spears from the air and barely dodged a huge crossbow bolt aiming to take his head off. Several spears glanced off his armor, while several others traced long cuts down his arms and legs. One got through his defenses and found the seam in his armor's left side. The spear pierced his flesh, but stopped at his ribs. The dragonlord screamed in pain.

"Lift off!" he cried. "Lift off!"

"Keep firing! Keep firing!" Catriona called from where she lay. She drew her dragon claws and prepared to rush in the moment the missile fire let up.

Thane, maddened with pain and half blinded, tried to comply with his rider's order. He stumbled back and opened his wings, but they smashed into the buildings on either side of the street.

Jimal appeared on the rooftop next to the dragon and threw a spear at Viktor's back. The warlord saw it coming out of the corner of his eye and ducked. The spear missed him but struck the back of Thane's head, between the spiny ridges behind the dragon's eyes.

Thane bellowed with anger, stepped forward, and stretched his wings again. Spears and crossbow bolts battered and pierced the scaly membranes between the veins. The dragon flapped wildly.

Catriona saw Jimal rise with another spear in his hand. "Get back!" she cried. But the youth didn't hear her. The dragon's wing struck Jimal, knocking him off the roof. He toppled to the street below, hit the ground, and lay unmoving.

Viktor and Thane lifted into the air despite the numerous holes in the dragon's wings. As they did, Gillean's piercing whistle echoed through the square.

A swarm of villagers rose from their hiding places on the rooftops.

As one, they threw their weighted nets. The nets sailed over the dragon, ensnaring his wings and entangling Viktor.

The dragonlord screamed with fury as the dragon crashed to the ground. They landed hard, shaking the whole village with the impact. A huge cloud of dust rose into the air. As it did, a cheer burst from the villagers.

A dozen or more rushed from their concealment, spears in their hands, looking to pin Viktor and Thane to the ground and finish them off. As the jubilant villagers ran forward, the rest stopped throwing their spears and firing their crossbows, for fear of hitting their friends.

Karise stepped from between two buildings, a frantic look on her face. "No! Idiots!" she cried. "Stick with the plan! Don't forget about the dragon's—"

The village quaked with the sound of thunder. Catriona and the other combatants closed their eyes as Thane's lightning scorched through the air. The building nearest the dragon's head exploded in a shower of clay and splinters. The three people stationed atop the building screamed as it collapsed under them. The lighting hit two villagers directly. They died before they could even cry out.

All the peasants near Thane fell back in shock and surprise.

"Fire, curse you! Fire!" Gillean called at the top of his lungs.

But the Sandusk villagers seemed to have forgotten the plan. As the dragon reared up, they scattered like scared rabbits.

Catriona cursed as she rose to her feet, dragon claws in hand. "Fight!" she cried. "Fight or we're all doomed!"

Two villagers stayed their ground, stabbing at the dragon with their spears. Thane swatted them aside. One villager crumpled where she stood, while the other sailed through the air and crashed into the front of the temple. Neither villager rose again.

The respite gave Viktor time to cut himself free from the entangling net. He spotted Catriona running toward them and pointed at her. "There!" he said. "She's the ringleader! Kill her, Thane!"

The dragon lumbered toward Catriona, but he was still tangled in the nets. Cat smiled.

Thane swiped at her clumsily with his left claw. She dodged aside and slashed twice across his elbow. The first blade slid off his armor, but the second bit into the joint. Before she could cut further, though, the dragon reared up and threw his arm wide. Catriona sailed through the air and landed hard near the well.

Viktor grabbed a spear from the rack in front of his saddle, hefted it, and aimed for the downed warrior. Gillean rushed forward and stabbed his long sword into the dragon's side. Thane roared and spun toward the young nobleman. Viktor's throw went wide, thudding into the ground a yard from the stunned Catriona's head.

Gillean barely avoided having the weapon ripped from his hands as the dragon lurched toward him. He pulled his sword out and ducked as the dragon's claw sailed past his head. Thane's tail flashed toward him, which he spotted and tried to jump over.

The tip of his boot got caught on one of the spikes along the tail's ridge. Gillean toppled through the air and landed between two buildings, sprawling face-first into the dusty street. As he shook his head to clear it, the town's alarm bell rang out.

From the bell tower, Sawa cried, "Man the perimeter! Viktor's army is coming! The army is coming from the north! They're coming!"

Gillean looked up. Thane towered over the mercenary. The dragon flexed his huge muscles, shredding the remainder of the nets holding him. Seated atop the dragon's back, Viktor hefted his spear and aimed for Gillean's heart.

CHAPTER

24 Desperate Measures

Erikoff cast a worried glance toward the center of town. Things had gone brilliantly at first, but all their plans seemed on the verge of falling apart.

When the alarm bell rang out, the mage took a deep breath. "All right," he said. "This is what we've been waiting for. Man your stations!"

"B-but the dragon!" the conscript said.

"The kobolds will kill us just as dead if they get through the lines!" Erik snapped. "Man your stations!"

He looked to the southwest. Already Shara's ragtag archers were moving in their direction to help reinforce Erik's nervous foot soldiers. The mage nodded and started to prepare his first spell.

"Bring me that torch," he said to the young woman standing next to him.

She fetched one from a nearby brazier and handed it to him.

"Good," he said. "Now draw your weapon and prepare to fight."

The girl swallowed hard and pulled a rusty sword from its sheath.

Viktor's army thundered downhill to the flat plain surrounding the town. They came a hundred wide, intending to sweep past the ragged band of warriors standing in a line at the town's edge.

"Hold the line," Erik commanded. "Be ready."

He held out the torch before him. When Viktor's troops were two dozen yards away, he said, *"Asapi sihir!"* and blew into the torch.

Instantly, a huge cloud of smoke billowed from the flames. It fanned out across the line and blew toward their enemies, completely engulfing the kobolds and their human allies. Viktor's army kept coming. The brutal war cry of the enemy split the late afternoon air.

"Pull the bridge!" Erik shouted.

The two recruits nearest him chopped downward with their axes, cutting the ropes hidden just below the top layer of dirt. The secret bridge the ropes had been supporting, the one on the road leading into town, collapsed just as Viktor's army reached the camouflaged pit ringing the perimeter of Sandusk.

The first wave of kobolds burst through Erik's smoke, howling lusty war cries and brandishing their weapons. The camouflaged tarps covering the pit gave way under the weight of the kobolds, dropping them onto the sharpened wooden spikes below. They died before they even realized what was happening.

The second wave saw the pit, but their momentum was too great to stop. They plunged in screaming and died atop their comrades.

Those behind the first two waves heard the screaming and slowed down. When they emerged from the bank of smoke, they saw the pit filled with the bodies of their fellows. Some managed to stop, others toppled into the pit anyway.

Several human commanders who were riding horses had fallen into the trap on the first push. Those who survived reined in their troops. The kobold line fell back as they searched for a way through the perimeter. They found none—the camouflaged pit ringed the entire village.

Erikoff smiled. All their planning and preparation had paid off.

Shara's archers raced forward and fired into the disorganized ranks of kobolds. Many more kobolds died until Viktor's human commanders ordered their troops to fall back out of range.

Erik smiled behind his mask and gave Shara the high sign. She shook her head, though, and pointed to the sky. Erikoff looked up just as the gargoyles dived on them.

Catriona clipped her dragon claws to her belt and scooped a fallen spear from the ground. She aimed at Viktor's head and threw.

The warlord reeled back his spear to pierce Gillean's heart. But Thane spotted Cat's spear aimed at his rider. The dragon moved slightly at the last moment.

Catriona's spear crashed into Viktor's helmet as the warlord let loose his throw. The impact of the blow tore the helmet from Viktor's head, and his throw went awry. Viktor's spear crashed into a building's wall, inches from Gillean's head.

Viktor swore, looking around for his new enemy. Thane reared up, intent on squashing Gillean, who still lay stunned below them.

As the dragon rose, though, Karise darted from the shadows and yanked Gillean to his feet.

"Run!" she shouted to him. She turned back to face Thane, summoned a small ball of fire into her hand, and threw it at a wooden spear imbedded under the scales of the dragon's chest.

The spear caught fire instantly. Thane howled and leaped into the air. He slashed out with his tail, smashing two buildings at the edge of the green.

Karise saw the buildings falling and pushed Gillean forward, but the cascading rubble buried them both.

The tide of battle swirled all around Erikoff. The gargoyles swooped down on the village militia and attacked mercilessly. There were only a handful of the blood red beasts, but neither Erik's fire spells nor Shara's bowmen could stop them.

"Cut off their heads!" Erik cried. "They'll die if you cut off their heads!" But he couldn't tell if anyone was listening to him.

The gargoyle attack bought Viktor's troops the time they needed. Concentrating on one point in the defensive trench, the kobolds cleared the spikes from the pit and swarmed across a makeshift bridge built from the bodies of their fallen comrades.

The wind shifted and Erik couldn't maintain the concentration needed to keep his smoke at bay. The billowing cloud blew back across the trench, mingling with smoke from fires caused by the dragon's lightning.

A kobold appeared out of the smoke, swinging an axe at Erik's head. The mage side-stepped and drew the curved dagger from his sleeve. He plunged it into the kobold's belly, only to yank it out again as the creature fell at his feet, dead.

Erik backed away from the body, heading for what he hoped was the center of town. He couldn't be sure because of the smoke swirling all around him, but the noise of the fighting seemed louder in that direction and he thought he heard the bellow of the dragon above the din.

He cursed himself for not having done a better job holding the perimeter. True, they'd inflicted heavy casualties on the enemy, but it was anyone's guess whether the villagers would win out over what remained of the warlord's army.

He wished he knew where Shara was. The last he'd seen, she was fighting a gargoyle. The half-elf had been holding her own, but it was difficult to decapitate an enemy using a wooden staff. Smoke and the swirl of battle had separated Erik from her before he could try to help.

The mage kept running forward through the smoke and fire, toward the sound of the fighting in the square. His feet stumbled across chunks of rubble in the gloom, and he wondered how many buildings had been destroyed.

Then the smoke parted and he saw the dragon's tail flashing toward him. He barely registered the shapes of Karise and Gillean diving for cover nearby before the tip of the tail caught him full in the chest.

Erikoff flew through the air and landed hard as the building beside him toppled onto his friends. For Erik, the whole world went dark.

As the dragon rose skyward once more, Catriona picked up another spear. The spears they'd made for the villagers were clumsy and ill balanced, but she couldn't use her dragon claws to fight at a distance.

Viktor already had another spear in his hand. He threw before she could, aiming for Catriona's chest. Catriona turned sideways and batted the spear out of the air. She spun and hurled her weapon straight for the open mouth of the startled dragon.

Thane breathed. Lightning seared the air, turning Catriona's spear into ash.

But Catriona had already moved. The lightning bolt shattered the ground where she had stood moments before.

She ran for the small alleyway between the temple and the building next to it. The alley was small, too small for the dragon to enter. Catriona knew Thane wouldn't be able to breathe lightning again—not for a while, anyway. He'd need to catch his breath first.

Thane circled awkwardly in the air. The battering his wings had taken in the initial barrage had hindered his maneuverability.

Catriona smiled. Then she wondered whether her friends were all right. She had seen Karise and Gillean go down under a rain of rubble, but she hadn't seen Shara and Erik. Had she led even more of her friends to their deaths?

She pushed the grim thoughts aside as she ran down the alley, glancing back over her shoulder. "Come on!" she muttered. "Come on!" But she didn't see the dragon behind her. Where was he?

A tingling on the back of her neck made her throw herself flat on the ground.

Thane's jaws passed over her, snapping shut where she'd stood just a breath before. The dragon swooped over the alley, his neck stretched down, like an immense bird bobbing for fish.

Catriona rolled to the side, pressing herself against the wall. As she'd anticipated, one of Viktor's spears clattered to the stones beside her.

She grabbed the weapon and rolled to her feet again, but she didn't throw. The dragon and Viktor arced away over the rooftops to circle back again.

Catriona dashed to the far end of the alley and waited, letting Viktor and Thane see her clearly.

The time for running was almost over. She only hoped that she would live long enough to see her plan through to the end.

CHAPTER

25 A Blaze of Glory

Shara struggled to kick free from the dead kobolds clinging to her legs. Bodies lay all around—some were of her village militia, but mostly the corpses of her enemies.

The leaders of the enemy—the handful of humans on horseback—she'd slain with her bow during the opening minutes of the attack. The village militia fought magnificently, pitting their homemade spears against the rusty swords and axes of the kobold invaders.

Her archers and Erik's troops held the line for many long moments, fighting bravely. But soon the number of kobolds became overwhelming. The enemy pushed through the guard like a sea of angry ants, sweeping the militia apart. In the confusion, Shara became separated from the rest.

At close range, her bow proved useless, so she transformed it back into a staff and wielded it with all the skill she possessed.

Many kobolds fell before her, their bones broken and their skulls crushed. But they kept coming. They kept clawing and grabbing, even after she'd bashed their heads in.

She looked up and saw a gargoyle diving toward her. It was the

last one remaining in Viktor's army, but that would matter little if it killed her. She kicked again, trying to free herself from the pile of dead kobolds.

The blood red beast swooped low, clawing at Shara with its rear talons. Shara swung her staff hard, breaking its shins as it came. The gargoyle's feet pawed at her, trying to pick her up, but the creature couldn't maintain its grip. Its clawed toes flopped wildly at the ends of its broken legs.

The gargoyle squawked and flapped a short distance away, trying to gain speed and altitude. Shara reached into the pile of bodies entangling her, searching with her long, slender fingers.

The gargoyle turned and swooped in headfirst, foretalons extended for the kill. Shara held her staff in her left hand, prepared to defend herself. With her right hand, she continued to fish among the corpses.

The gargoyle swiped for her head, and Shara parried with one end of the staff. The monster raked for her gut with the other hand. She parried with the staff's other end. The gargoyle grabbed both ends of the staff and pulled, yanking Shara from the pile of dead kobolds and lifting her into the air.

"Thank you," the half-elf said.

She brought her right hand around. In it, she held a kobold short sword—just what she'd been looking for. The sword bit cleanly through the gargoyle's neck. A startled look washed over the monster's face as it crumbled into dust. Shara dropped from twenty-five feet up.

She twisted in the air, trying to absorb the impact and break the fall instead of having the fall break her. She hit hard. All the air rushed out of her lungs and bright spots of light flashed before her eyes.

Shara blinked, trying to clear her head as the world spun around her. A breeze wafted past and the smoke around her parted.

In the distance, near the temple, she saw Thane diving toward

Catriona. The flame-haired warrior stood valiantly, waiting in an alley.

The half-elf wanted to help, but the dragon was too far away for a good bow shot. Instead of changing her staff into a bow again, Shara decided to pass out.

Catriona had stood and waited long enough. She turned and ran back toward the green. Viktor and Thane swooped in behind her, the man hefting a spear, the dragon craning down his long neck to snap her out of the alley.

The flame-tressed warrior didn't dare look back. She knew death was hot on her heels. She heard the dragon's tattered wings beating the air, smelled the monster's rotten breath, could almost feel his yellow eyes boring into her back.

As she neared the temple, she shouted, "Now, Kuro! Now!"

Viktor threw his spear at Catriona, but it missed, the weapon passing harmlessly over her right shoulder as she ran.

The dragon opened his mouth wide, and Cat felt Thane's hot breath on her back. She looked up just as Kuro launched the village's final trap.

With an earth-shaking groan and a crumble of aged mortar, the temple tower gave way, falling forward onto the green. The dragon's maw reached for Catriona, but she sprinted clear as the edifice smashed down on Thane's neck and shoulders.

The dragon squawked with surprise and crashed awkwardly to the ground. As he did, the tower walls and the barrels stored within them fell on top of him. The barrels were heavy, secured with strong netting and filled almost to overflowing with liquid. The nets entangled Thane, and the barrels' weight kept him pinned for several moments.

Catriona turned and ran straight for the netted, floundering dragon. She threw her recovered spear at his bleeding eye, which had been wounded in the first barrage.

Thane turned and caught the spear in his jaws, snapping it in half. But she'd never actually meant to hit him. In an instant, Catriona was past the dragon's deadly jaws. She used Thane's foreleg like a ramp, ran up his rubble-strewn back, and tackled Viktor before the warlord could regain his bearings and grab another spear. The two warriors tumbled down Thane's back and crashed to the ground. Catriona landed on top.

Thane thrashed to free himself, shattering the wooden barrels and spilling their oily contents all over his scaly hide. His careening tail struck Catriona and Viktor and sent them tumbling into a wall. The impact knocked the warrior and the warlord apart. Viktor recovered first and rose to his feet, drawing his sword as he charged. Catriona rolled into a crouch, dragon claws leaping into her hands.

Viktor brought his sword down hard, intending to cut Catriona in two. She twisted her left dragon claw so the blade protected her forearm. Viktor's sword smashed down and skidded off the steel.

Before he could recover, she slashed across his belly with the other blade. The dragon claw bit through the warlord's crimson armor and into the soft flesh beneath.

Viktor staggered backward. His fingers twitched open, and he dropped his sword. "Don't . . . !" he gasped.

Catriona whirled the dragon claw and buried it deep in his chest. Viktor's eyes went wide and he fell backward, dead. Catriona stood and stared down at the warlord's body. "That was for Rohawn and everyone else you've ever killed."

She turned to face the dragon.

As she did, the ground under her feet shook with a deafening thunderclap and the whole village filled with bright, yellow light.

Erikoff had opened his eyes in time to see the tower crash down around Thane's neck and shoulders, further pinning the dragon to the ground.

The mage struggled to his feet, pushing away bits of rubble that had fallen on top of him. He brushed himself off. Everything still seemed to be working. If only his head would stop pounding. Vaguely, he saw a red-headed shape that looked like Catriona run over a high mound, tackling something and tumbling out of sight. Once he regained his senses, Erik saw that the mound was Thane, who was covered in the slick oil that had spilled over him earlier. The dragon had turned toward a group of villagers as bright white light leaked around the corners of his mouth. Led by Kuro, the townsfolk were running forward with spears and pitchforks.

Erik knew he couldn't save them, but he had to try. If only he could remember the words! "A . . . ab . . ."

Thane's jaws opened wide.

Erik concentrated, trying to form the necessary phrases and images in his head. "Ap . . . api . . . api belit!"

Flames leaped from his hand just as the dragon breathed.

Lightning spewed from Thane's mouth, scattering the villagers as if they were tenpins and smashing a house on the far side of the square.

Erik's fire shot straight to the flammable maize oil, setting the dragon ablaze. Thane shrieked in agony, the scream cutting short his lightning blast. The dragon sprang into the air, bright yellow flames covering him from his head to the middle of his back. He flapped awkwardly once, twice, and nearly fell back onto the green. Then he straightened out and gained altitude, turning to the north.

Catriona emerged from the alleyway beside the fallen temple, bloody dragon claws clenched in her hands. Her eyes scanned the green, as if looking for something.

"Cat!" Erik shouted to her. He waved, but his legs wobbled when he tried to move, so he decided to stay put.

She spotted him and called, "A bow! Have you got a bow?" Her eyes darted from the mage to the rapidly retreating dragon.

Erikoff shook his head and nearly fell over in the effort. Catriona ran to him and put her arm under his shoulders to keep him from falling. She watched the blazing dragon recede into the twilight.

"We almost had him!" she said. "If only I could have gotten off a final shot!"

"Just be glad . . . that *he* didn't," Erik said. She followed his gaze to where a half dozen brave villagers lay dead or dying, their bodies scorched by the dragon's lightning.

A deep, trembling breath filled Catriona's lungs. "Are you all right?" she asked.

He nodded and said, "I will be if I can just sit down." She walked him to the well and sat him down against the stone wall surrounding it.

Erik nodded his thanks. As he did, a cry went up from the outskirts of town.

"They're retreating!" a villager called. "We've won!" cried another. "We've won!" A hearty cheer drifted over the square.

Catriona and Erikoff looked at each other. The battle for Sandusk was over, but at that moment, neither one of them felt very victorious.

"We haven't won yet," Catriona said.

CHAPTER

26 THE PRICE OF VICTORY

"O ver here," Catriona said. "I think I've found them!" She planted her torch in the ground and began digging in the rubble near the village green.

Shara and a handful of villagers ran through the darkness to help her.

After the retreat of Viktor's kobolds, Catriona had quickly organized the villagers into caregiving, fire control, and rescue teams. The groups combed through the wreckage of Sandusk, helping the injured, comforting the bereaved, and looking for people trapped under the ruins of the town. Nightfall soon made their tasks more difficult, but everyone worked as quickly and efficiently as they could.

Sawa took charge of her people as Catriona and Shara concentrated on finding their missing friends. Kuro had been killed in the final assault against the dragon. His body lay in a place of honor within the village square. Fortunately, Sawa remained uninjured.

Catriona dug through the rubble with scraped and bloodied hands. Sweat dripped from her dust-covered brow. She dug in the last place she'd seen Karise and Gillean, before the dragon smashed the building down on top of them. That was before sunset, though, and seemed ages ago.

She pulled a bit of roof matting up and saw Gillean's battered face. His eyes were open, and he smiled at her, though the smile seemed full of pain.

"So . . . we're not dead, then?" he gasped.

Catriona shook her head. Tears sprang to the corners of her eyes as she dug frantically to free him. "No," she said. "We're not dead."

"Did we win?"

"Yes," she said. "We won."

He groaned. "If this is winning, I'd hate to see what losing feels like!"

Catriona quickly cleared the rubble away from his head and face. He seemed to be breathing regularly. "When did you last see Karise?" she asked. "Do you know where she is?"

"I think," Gillean said through gritted teeth, "that she's lying on top of my legs." He took a deep breath. "She tried to push me out of the way as the wall fell."

Catriona nodded, and Shara and several villagers began digging where they guessed Gillean's legs might be.

"Good thing she gave you that shove," Catriona observed.

"Good for me?" Gillean asked. "Or good for her?" He glanced down to the rubble where the others were digging.

"Good for both, I hope," Catriona replied. She smeared more tears from the corners of her eyes with the dusty sleeve of her tunic and kept digging to free his chest and shoulders.

"We'll know soon enough," Shara said. She heaved a large section of plaster and wattle off the pile, revealing the still form of Karise Tarn.

"Is she—" Catriona started.

"She's breathing," Shara announced. "Come. Help me dig her out."

"Yes, by all means," Gillean said. His tone was lighthearted, but he gasped for breath as he spoke. "I can wait."

Catriona nodded and went to assist the half-elf and the villagers.

Working together, they quickly uncovered Karise. "She's pretty bruised, but I don't see anything broken," Catriona announced.

"Nor do I," Shara agreed. "Let's move her over by the well."

"Yes, please," Gillean gasped. "My legs are beginning to fall asleep. When she wakes up, we should ask her to lose weight before she falls on me again."

"I'll be sure to mention that to her the next time she's saving your life," Catriona said.

Gillean laughed, though the laugh quickly degenerated into a coughing fit.

Catriona and Shara gently lifted Karise out of the wreckage and laid her down on the green nearby. Sawa, standing near the temple and directing the village's efforts, sent one of Sandusk's healers to look Karise over. Catriona and Shara went back to digging out their other friend.

"How is she?" Gillean asked. He seemed more awake and alert with every passing moment.

"Her armor and helmet probably saved her life," Catriona replied.

"That's what they're for," Gillean said, smiling slightly.

"Though whether she will recover . . ." Shara continued.

"If she doesn't have any internal injuries, she should be all right," Catriona said. "Unfortunately, she's the only one who could determine that, and she's still unconscious."

"Where's Erik?" Gillean asked.

"Helping to put out fires," Catriona replied.

A few more minutes of hard digging freed Gillean from the rubble. He sat up, smiled, and winced as he gazed down at his right arm. It was twisted and clearly broken below the elbow.

"Funny," he said, looking a little queasy. "It didn't feel bad when I was buried under the rubble."

They gently carried him to the green and set him down next to Karise. A circle of torches ringed the square, giving light to those tending the injured and mourning the dead.

A village healer—one of the handful Karise had trained for their strategy—sat swabbing Karise's head with a damp cloth. Catriona mopped Gillean's forehead as well. Shara went to fetch the young nobleman some water.

"Thanks," he said when the half-elf returned. Catriona helped him sit up, and he gratefully sipped the water from the dipper.

"W-what's a girl gotta do to get some of that service herself?" asked a quiet voice from nearby.

Everyone smiled as Karise's bright blue eyes flickered open. Karise tried to smile as well, but it ended up being more of a wince.

"Do you think you have anything broken?" Catriona asked.

Karise thought a moment. Her arms moved slightly, as though she might check herself, but she looked stiff and soon gave up the effort.

"I don't think so, but my stomach aches as though a dragon had stepped on it," she said.

"That would be where you were lying across my legs," Gillean retorted. He winced again.

A look of concern passed over Karise's weary face. "What's wrong with him?" she asked.

"A broken arm," Catriona replied.

Karise took a deep breath and said, "Give me a moment and I'll see what I can do."

She closed her eyes and chanted. Blue healing sparks danced across her body from the top of her head to the tip of her boots. Then the sparks died away and she sat up, looking considerably better than she had before.

She knelt beside Gillean and took his hand. "How do you feel?" she asked.

"About as good as I look," he replied.

"I think I can mend the arm," Karise said.

Catriona and Shara stood silently as Karise chanted. Gillean gritted his teeth and closed his eyes.

As the cleric's chant rose, a glow of blue light grew around Gillean's body. Soon, bright blue sparks began to dance on his right shoulder. They moved down his arm, like a tiny river of fire, until they reached his broken forearm. Then the fire leaped up, blazing two feet off the ground.

Catriona stepped back reflexively. Shara stood still, watching.

"Great Sirrion, help me!" Karise cried. She tossed her head back, her eyes rolled into her forehead, and sweat poured from her brow.

The blue flames grew higher, higher. Gillean's body began to shake. His eyes went wide. His mouth parted in a soundless scream.

Then, as if snuffed out by an invisible hand, the magical fires suddenly died away. Karise slumped forward, her head nearly touching her knees. Gillean's body relaxed and lay still. His arm lay straight and whole once more.

Karise took deep, gasping breaths. "There was more damage than I thought," she said. "I had to . . . fix a few things inside him too."

Gillean sat up and flexed his fingers. Despite being covered with dust, grime, and blood, he looked much better. He kissed Karise on the forehead and said, "Thank you."

Catriona knelt beside the two of them. "Well done," she said, patting Karise on the back.

Karise looked at her and nodded. "Thanks."

Sawa walked over to the group from the other side of the green. There, her people were carefully laying out the dead and injured. "If you've the strength for it, missy," the elder said to Karise, "there are others as need your help."

Karise nodded and Catriona helped her to stand. "I'll do what I can," the cleric said.

Gillean stood as well, surveying the damage to the town. Most of the buildings around the square, including the temple, lay in ruins. Small fires were still burning throughout the village, though Sawa's people were working hard to extinguish them. Close to twenty people lay injured in the square, and an equal number lay dead beside them. Catriona led Karise to the line of wounded.

"So, we won," Gillean said tentatively as Karise knelt and began her healing work on the most gravely wounded.

Sawa gazed at him, her ancient eyes alive in the firelight. "Yes," she said. "We won. The dragonlord is dead. Lady Catriona killed him."

"But the cost was terrible," Shara noted.

Karise finished chanting and took a deep breath. "Then it's over," she said. "It's done."

Catriona shook her head. "No," she said. "It's not finished yet." She gazed sternly at her three companions.

"We still have a dragon to kill."

CHAPTER

27   THE FALLEN FORTRESS

T hane escaped?" Gillean asked.

"Yes," said Erikoff, as he walked across the green toward them. He looked dirty and bruised but little the worse for wear. His golden mask glittered in the torchlight. "The dragon's badly injured, but he still got away."

"And where have you been, Erik?" Karise asked, moving on to the next wounded villager.

"Helping fight the fires," he explained. "I didn't get hurt as badly as some, so I thought I might be of use there. I see the two of you came through it all right."

"Thanks to a little healing from Karise," Gillean said. He flexed the fingers of his right hand, working out the remaining stiffness.

"How are we going to find an injured dragon?" Karise asked. "He could be anywhere."

"He could be," Catriona said. "But in his state, I think there's only one place he would go."

"The sky fortress," Erikoff said.

Catriona nodded. "We need to take an expedition there, clean up the rest of Viktor's troops, and kill the dragon before he can recover," she told them.

"That's a pretty tall order, given the state of things around here," Gillean said. Even in the torchlight, the extent of damage to Sandusk was brutally evident.

"Not to mention the fact that we're running low on volunteers," Karise said, scanning the dead and injured lying before her on the green. "Still, I'd hate to have someone else recover the dragon's loot."

Sawa's eyes lit up. "I hadn't thought of that," the old woman said. "Do you think there's much treasure to recover?" As she asked, a small group of villagers, lured by the prospect of a dragon's hoard, began to gather around the companions.

"There's only one way to find out," Gillean said. "It'd be a shame to come this far and not see it through."

"I don't think anyone should do this expecting a reward," Catriona said. "It will be difficult and dangerous. Chances are more people will be killed."

"We've suffered enough already!" one villager from the crowd put in. "We lost Kuro and Jimal and a score of others! Why should we leave here to die fighting a dragon holed up in a castle?"

More than a few villagers grumbled in agreement. Some of those who had gathered drifted away from the green and vanished into the night. Others stayed, though, still intrigued by the prospect of recovering the dragon's wealth.

"We have to do it because it *must* be done," Catriona insisted. "If we don't kill the dragon now, he'll come back later and wipe us out. Everything this village has fought and sacrificed for will come to nothing if we don't act now."

Sawa nodded. "I will find some brave enough to go with you," she said. "But do not expect many."

"We'll take all we can get," Gillean said. He put his hand on Catriona's shoulder.

She smiled back at him and said, "I'm glad you're with me."

Karise nodded at them. "I'm with you as well," the warrior-cleric said. "Though I should finish healing the gravely wounded before we go. It won't take much time."

"And I," added Erikoff. "I didn't come all this way just to miss the final act."

"I will finish this job before returning to my people," Shara concluded.

"Good," said Catriona. "Then let's gather our crew, saddle our horses, and get going. Karise, you stay here. We'll bring your things to you. We haven't a moment to lose."

Sawa turned up a dozen villagers brave enough to make the trip with them. Anaska, the steward of the village's ruined temple, came along. One-eyed Elops came too, wanting to see the dragon's final demise. The farmer named Vedec went also, as he hoped that his brother and niece might still be captive within the fortress. Others came to look for their missing relatives as well, and a handful of villagers tagged along in anticipation of recovering the dragon's treasure.

"It's no more than we're owed, after all we've been through," said a man called Bosc. His daughter, Lynd, nodded in agreement.

There were barely enough horses in the village to carry all of them. Still, under Catriona's command, they set out before Lunitari had risen.

They rode through the night and into the next day. The horses started well rested, as they hadn't been used in the battle, and the company made good time. They stopped only briefly to water the animals and eat. Catriona kept the group going as fast as she could, though some of the villagers grumbled about the pace.

In the afternoon of the second day, they entered the badlands at the base of Viktor's castle. Their previous journey through the badlands proved invaluable, and they made good time navigating the mazelike pillars of rock and winding ravines. Shortly before sunset, they came within sight of the sky fortress's main gate.

"We're in luck!" Gillean said.

The gates to the fallen fortress stood open to admit the returning army of Viktor's kobolds. The once proud force had been reduced to scruffy bands of stragglers, retreating to their former master's stronghold.

Fire flared within Catriona's heart. "If we ride fast, we can be inside before they know what's happening," she said. "Come on!"

She spurred her horse forward. Gillean, Karise, Shara, and Erik quickly followed. Seeing they were trailing, the Sandusk villagers hurried behind as well.

The hoofbeats of their horses echoed like thunder as they crested the rocky shelf below the fallen fortress. They had no need for stealth this time, and were able to use the same smooth, uphill path that Viktor's army had used when going on patrol.

The ragged bands of kobolds heading for the gates turned at the sound of the horses and shrieked with fear. They panicked, falling all over themselves as they ran for the door.

"Close the gates! Close the gates!" screamed a fat kobold supervising from the top of the wall. "Keep them out of the citadel!" He pointed a flabby finger at a group of kobolds in front of the charging enemy. "You!" he croaked. "Stop them!"

The four kobolds he indicated halted in their tracks. "Yes, Chortog!" said the tallest of them. They drew their rusty swords.

Catriona and Gillean hit them at full speed, parrying the kobolds' blows. Slowly, groaning from the strain, the giant gates of the fortress began to grind shut.

Catriona pointed toward the entrance. "Erik, Karise," she called. "Can you do something about that?"

Both the cleric and the mage nodded. Karise closed her eyes, folded her hands in prayer and began to chant. Erikoff pointed to the kobolds pushing the door on the left and said, *"Api sentak!"*

Instantly, clinging orange flames sprang up on the kobolds' arms. The creatures screamed and tried to pat the flames out. Their side of the huge double door screeched to a grinding halt.

As Karise's chant built, so did the wind around the galloping riders, as though they rode at the crest of an invisible storm. The winds buffeted the fortress gates and the kobolds trying to close them. The kobolds staggered and fell. Some were blown entirely off their feet.

By the time Chortog's servants rose again, the riders had surged through the gates and into the courtyard beyond.

"Let them close the gates now, if they want to!" Gillean said with a laugh.

But the kobolds seemed to have no intention of doing so. In fact, few of them had any intention of staying to fight the riders invading their castle. The kobolds near the gates quickly scurried out of the fortress and fled into the badlands beyond. Those atop the walls bolted toward the shelter of the inner keep.

Catriona led the riders toward the gatehouse of the inner wall. Chaos reigned within the fortress. Despite Chortog's frantic cries, none of the kobolds seemed capable of mounting a defense.

The riders galloped through the inner gate before the kobolds could drop the portcullis and seal them out. Catriona wheeled her horse and rode it up the steps to the top of the gatehouse. Kobolds dived off the stairs to get out of her way.

She leaped from the back of her horse and with two quick cuts of her blades, killed the guards trying to lower the portcullis. The kobolds in the inner courtyard nearly trampled their own, trying to escape the keep.

"Let them go," Gillean said. "I'd rather they run than we fight to keep them from escaping."

Karise and the others let the fleeing kobolds pass. Soon the inner courtyard stood empty of Chortog's forces.

"I need two guards to man the portcullis," Catriona said. "We'll drop it now to keep the kobolds from rallying and trying a counterattack."

"Do you think that's likely?" Vedec the farmer asked.

"No," Catriona replied. "But we may meet resistance yet."

Two villagers, both from Shara's corps of archers, stepped forward to man the gate.

"Anyone who wants to get out, let them out," Catriona told them. "But don't let anyone in." The archers nodded.

"What should the rest of us do?" Bosc called up to Catriona from the courtyard below.

"We're going into the keep," Catriona replied. "We'll free any slaves we discover, and find and kill the dragon."

"And if we can recover some of the stolen goods," Gillean put in, "so much the better."

"We'll form search groups," Catriona said. "No one is to tackle the dragon alone. Anyone finding Thane needs to get the rest of us. Together, we'll plan how to take him."

"He might be in that courtyard where we encountered him before," Erikoff suggested.

Standing atop the gatehouse, Catriona looked west to where the mountain met the fallen fortress. The rubble that she and Erik had used to scale the wall had been cleared away since their visit. The path to the courtyard along the top of the wall was blocked by an intervening building.

"He might be there," Catriona called down. "I can't tell. But we can't climb over the walls the way we did last time. We'll have to try and find our way there through the castle."

"What's your plan?" Anaska asked.

"Some of us will search the citadel. Gillean, Karise, Erik, Shara,

Lynd, Bosc, Vedec, and Anaska, you're with me."

"What about the rest of us?" asked Elops.

"The rest of you guard the main doors to the keep, watch the horses, and help with the portcullis. Remember, we don't want to fight anyone who's running away, only those who are trying to defend the castle."

"What if the dragon comes out?" Elops asked.

"Retreat inside and call for help," Catriona said. "We'll come as quickly as we can." She looked around the group as she rode her horse down from the gatehouse. They were as ready as they'd ever be. The whole group dismounted. "Does everyone know their jobs?" Catriona asked.

Everyone nodded.

"Good. Then let's go."

The doors of the great keep swung open easily—its guards had long ago abandoned their posts. They'd also abandoned their weapons, which lay scattered across the floor near the doorway.

A wide, empty hall lay beyond the door. Light streamed in through small windows set high into the upper story. Rows of stone columns supported the vaulted ceiling. The whole thing slanted at an awkward angle, the angle the fortress had settled into after falling from the sky. Three doorways exited the chamber at the far end.

"Nice place Viktor chose for himself," Gillean said sarcastically. He kicked a kobold sword with his toe, and it skidded across the tilted floor until it hit the wall. The noise of it echoed in the hall for nearly a minute.

"I suppose one could get used to it," Karise mused. "I'm sure there are advantages that offset the crooked floors. It's pretty well fortified, for instance."

"*If* the fortifications aren't manned by kobolds," Erikoff noted. He looked around. "This reminds me of a test I had to pass to join my order—a maze that was meant to disorient initiates."

"We need to keep our bearings," Catriona said. "If we don't, we're liable to stumble into a trap or wind up as dragon food. The kobolds may have given up the fight outside, but that doesn't mean there aren't some lurking around in here, waiting to jump us."

"Which door to you want to try first?" Gillean asked.

"We want to cover as much ground as we can, so we'll break into three teams," Catriona said. "Gillean, you take Shara and Lynd. Karise, you and Erik take Bosc with you. Anaska and Vedec are with me."

Everyone nodded soberly. They walked toward the doors in the back of the hall. "We'll take the one on the left," Catriona volunteered. "The courtyard where we saw the dragon lies that way."

"W-we will?" Vedec asked.

"Don't worry," Catriona told him. "We're not going to do any fighting. We'll send for help if we find the dragon."

"We'll take the middle branch," Erik offered. "Karise and I always seem to be in the thick of things." His eyes flashed behind his golden mask, and Karise smiled back at him.

"Yeah, that's all right with me," she said.

"That leaves the right-hand passage for my merry band," Gillean said. "Stay alert, everyone. Yell if you find anything. With the acoustics in here, someone's bound to hear you."

Catriona looked at Gillean and Karise. "On the count of three?"

The other two nodded.

"One . . . two . . . three!" Simultaneously, they all kicked their doors in. Three empty corridors lay beyond. No kobolds jumped out to ambush them.

Gillean smiled at the other two groups. "Good luck, everyone," he said. "See you at the dragon's lair." He and his group disappeared through the right-hand doorway while Karise and her group walked down the middle passage.

Catriona led Anaska and Vedec into the hallway on the left. The corridor ran uphill, in the general direction of the waterfall courtyard, though Catriona couldn't guess how far away that courtyard might be.

The hall was lit by only a few small, soot-blackened windows high above. Low pedestals, the kind used to display armor or stuffed trophies, rested in niches on either side of the hallway. The niches were empty, their pedestals unoccupied. Cobwebs hung across the high ceiling like draped fabric.

"Not much of a housekeeper, was he?" Vedec remarked.

"I don't think Viktor entertained many guests," Catriona replied.

The corridor turned parallel to the original entryway then twisted back downhill. Catriona frowned. They were heading away from the direction she wanted to go.

They opened a number of doors as they went, but all led to small, shabby rooms formerly used as barracks by the kobolds. They shut those doors before the stench overwhelmed them.

The hallway turned again and suddenly became wider and taller. Some of the filth vanished as well. Sunlight streamed in through high-set windows on either side. A wide, red carpet trimmed with gold lined the flagstone floor. A set of large, polished oak doors stood at the far end of the hallway.

Catriona walked to the doors and pushed them open. On the other side lay a large room draped in hideous purple velvet. A gilded throne rested in the middle of the room. It sat atop a wooden platform designed to keep the throne level. A wide, open window on the left was big enough to admit a dragon's head.

Catriona motioned for the villagers to keep back. She ventured inside, dragon claws in hand.

A kobold rushed at her from behind one of the curtains. It seemed more frightened than brave, but it had a sword in its hand. Catriona blocked its blow with her right dragon claw and stabbed it with her left. The kobold fell to the floor, dead.

She looked around, wary of any more ambushes.

After a few moments, she motioned to Vedec and Anaska to stay in the doorway. Then she crept to the window. She looked out, but didn't find the courtyard she'd hoped to see. It wasn't the place with the waterfall where she'd met the dragon previously, but a wider court covered with black rosebushes and tangled wildflowers.

The flowers showed signs of having been trampled by a large beast—the dragon probably—but not recently. Most of the stems had rebounded upright. Catriona silently cursed.

"Come in," she said to the others. "There's nothing here."

"O-other than the k-kobold," Vedec said.

"Yes," Catriona replied. "Other than the dead kobold."

The two villagers walked cautiously into the room, looking at everything in awe.

"The man lived like a king," Anaska said.

"A pretty shabby king," Catriona pointed out. "Most of the stuff here is in bad repair—those tapestries he's used as floor coverings, for instance."

"But the throne!" Vedec said, running his hands over the golden surfaces.

"Gilded wood, most likely," Catriona said. She mounted the platform, gripped the chair arm, and lifted. It came up easily. "Yep," she said. "Just gold leaf over soft wood."

"Still, it might fetch something to pay recompense," Vedec said.

Catriona nodded. "It might at that."

"Quiet!" Anaska said. "I hear something,"

"The dragon?" Vedec asked fearfully.

"No," the temple steward replied. "It sounds like groaning—human groaning—coming from behind that curtain." She pointed to one of the purple drapes hanging to the right of the throne. Catriona strode to it and threw it back, weapons at the ready. Behind it, a stairway led down into the fortress bowels.

Catriona could hear the groaning now too, faint and far away. "Slaves?" she asked.

"Maybe," Anaska replied.

"We should find them and free them," Vedec said.

Catriona couldn't tell if he made the suggestion because he actually wanted to find the missing villagers or because wanted to avoid meeting the dragon. However, if there were people trapped in Viktor's dungeons, they needed to be freed just as surely as the dragon needed to be slain.

"We'll take a look," Catriona said.

She took a torch from a sconce on the wall and lit it. Then she headed down the stairs into the darkness, with Vedec and Anaska following close behind.

The stairway wound down the wall of a wide room with a high ceiling cut out of the rock below the fortress. Clearly the chamber had been part of the sky castle because its floor slanted at the same angle as the corridors they'd traveled above.

There were no windows, but a brazier of hot coals—set on a platform to keep it level—still smoldered in the center of the chamber. Tongs, hammers, flails, chains, and other instruments of torture hung from hooks on the walls.

There was an arched opening in the room's far wall. Catriona walked straight to it and into the corridor beyond. Cells with wooden doors lined the corridor until it ended in a **T** intersection. Most of the doors stood open—as if they'd been recently vacated. Catriona looked inside each one she passed, but found no one.

She stopped at the intersection and listened. Sure enough, a low

230

STEPHEN D. SULLIVAN

groaning came from somewhere down the right-hand corridor. There was only one closed door on that side.

"See if you can find some keys," she called to the others, who were taking their time crossing the torture chamber.

"Have you found something?" Vedec called back.

"Maybe," Catriona said. "Bring me some keys and we'll find out." She peered into the room, but couldn't see anything beyond the glow of her torch. "Hang on," she said to whoever was inside. "We'll have you out in a moment."

Moments later, Anaska jangled up to her with a ring of keys. Catriona looked them over and selected the one that looked the most worn as a good place to start.

The key slipped into the lock and turned easily. Catriona pushed the door open. Holding her torch before her, she stepped inside. As she did, her jaw dropped open and she gasped, unable to speak.

CHAPTER

28   MATTERS OF THE HEART

Karise kicked the axe out of the hand of the dead kobold lying at her feet. Two more lay nearby, both sporting fatal wounds from Karise's mace, like their comrade.

Erikoff stood behind her, near the door to the room, wiping blood off his curved dagger. The body of the kobold that had attacked him lay slumped against the wall.

Bosc, the big villager, stood next to Erik. He was sweating profusely, and a long cut traced down the length of his left arm. A fifth kobold lay dead beside him, its neck twisted almost completely around.

"There better be something worth it down here after all this trouble," Bosc said. He looked at the wound, then at Karise. "Can you do something about this?" he asked.

"Not now," she said. "It's barely more than a scratch."

"She's right," Erik said. "We may need her power later on."

"Easy for you to say," Bosc grumbled.

"Let's get moving," Karise said. "Our fight may have alerted more of the castle's guardians."

"This bunch wasn't guarding," Erik observed. "They were just cornered."

"Pardon me if I don't see the distinction while someone is trying to kill me," Karise snapped. "Let's go."

She left the chamber and walked deeper into the castle. Erik and Bosc followed behind.

Karise silently cursed herself for not figuring out a better way to search this maze of corridors. If she'd been a full cleric of Shinare, perhaps she'd have had some prayer to guide her to the treasure. That would have been really useful right now.

Despite Catriona's high-minded talk of slaying the dragon and making people safe, Karise had another goal in mind—finding the dragon's hoard.

After all, unlike Catriona, she hadn't gotten involved for altruistic reasons. She wanted the steel, pure and simple. Yes, she was more than willing to do some good along the way—Shinare would, annoyingly, insist on that—but the loot remained her main objective.

And what did she get for her help? She was stuck in a dismal castle playing bodyguard to a wizard and a thick-headed peasant. The gods only knew what she had done to deserve that.

Karise marched forward briskly, alert for any threats. But the corridor was empty, like all the others. Just moldy flagstones and rock walls. Ahead, the passage turned to the left. A bright purple curtain hung draped against the wall at the bend.

That was strange.

Karise frowned and yanked the curtain aside. Then she smiled. Beyond lay a passageway carved into the natural rock.

"This must be part of the original sky fortress complex," Erik said.

"How can you tell?" Karise asked.

"Because it's tilted, just like everything else here," he replied. "If they were building a new corridor, don't you think they'd have made it level?"

Karise shrugged. "With this lot, who knows?" she said. "I have to say, I'm not very impressed with Viktor's reign as dragonlord. The whole place is a mess—just like his plan for attacking Sandusk. I know a lot of people who could have done better."

"So do I," the mage agreed.

"What do you think?" Bosc said, finally catching up to them. "Is this where the dragonlord kept his treasure?"

"It could be," Erik replied. "It's certainly deep enough in the castle."

"Let's find out," Karise said, and led the way into the newly discovered tunnel.

Gillean produced a long, thin piece of wire from the hem of his glove and worked it into the ornate lock on the heavy, iron-banded door.

"An interesting skill for a young nobleman," Shara noted.

"I've learned a lot of interesting things since I left home," he replied with a smile.

"What do you think is behind the door?" Lynd, Bosc's daughter, asked.

"I don't know," Gillean said, concentrating on the lock as he spoke to her. "But they wouldn't have put it behind a door this sturdy if it didn't have some value."

"You think the door might lead to where they keep the slaves?" Shara asked.

"Not exactly," Gillean replied. He smiled as the lock gave a resounding *click*.

"See?" he said. "It's amazing what you can learn in a traveling carnival." He pushed the door open with his foot, looked inside, smiled, then stepped through.

"What is it?" Lynd asked. "What have we found?" She followed Gillean into the room with the half-elf right behind.

"It appears," Shara said, "that we have discovered Viktor's treasury." She held her torch high to spread the light throughout the chamber.

The three of them looked around, awed by the piles of iron-bound chests and the glittering bits of polished steel. The room was about seven yards on a side, and all but a small path through the middle of it was filled with boxes, sacks, and artifacts of various kinds.

Many of the items were plain or uninteresting—a copper sword, a bard's lute—but a few glittered with platinum, crystal, and gems, promises of more treasure to come in the room's many chests and coffers.

As Gillean and Shara took it all in, Lynd threw open the lid of the chest nearest her. She peered inside and her face fell.

"It's empty!" she gasped.

"What?" Gillean said. He felt as though he'd just been awakened from a particularly lovely dream. He opened the chest nearest to him. A few copper coins rattled around in the bottom of it, but aside from that, it was empty too.

Gillean and Lynd dashed around the room, opening chest after chest, looking in coffer after coffer after coffer, with the same disappointing result.

"This is the most treasure-free treasury I've ever seen," he declared.

He threw open a small chest near the door, one of the few unsearched chests remaining. A small cache of coins, mostly gold and silver with just a smattering of valuable steel, rattled in the bottom of the box.

"Well, here's something, anyway," he said.

Lynd peered into the chest and frowned. "That's not much," she said.

"It's better than nothing," he said. "And I'm starting to get the feeling that there's not much more to be found, aside from the

WARRIOR'S HEART

trinkets and jewelry we spotted from the doorway."

"And what about those?" the girl said. "Surely they're worth something."

"Probably less than you think," he replied. "The only choice piece seems to be that one standing in the corner over there, and I'm not even sure what it is." He pointed toward a jarlike object about three feet tall. It was made of crystal and entwined with golden tubes, each as wide as a man's finger.

"Well, that didn't come from *our* village," Lynd said.

"Viktor and Thane pillaged many towns," Shara noted. "Far too many to adequately repay."

"So where's the rest of it?" Lynd asked. "Where's the dragon's treasure?"

Gillean shook his head. "It looks like Viktor and Thane didn't manage their finances any better than my parents managed our family fortune," he said glumly.

"Unfortunately for the victims, the army of a dragonlord is expensive to keep," Shara said. She walked around the room, taking inventory of the warlord's meager savings.

Gillean sat on one of the big, empty chests, resting his chin on his hands. He felt as though all the wind had been taken out of his sails.

Time and again he had risked his life for *this?* After all the perils they'd faced, all they'd done just to get here, it didn't seem possible.

Gillean bowed his head and sulked as his two companions examined the treasure. After a while, he looked up and asked. "How much is there?"

"Enough to cover the damages to Sandusk," Shara said. "With a little left over for Purespring and the rest maybe."

"Very little," Lynd added. "Not counting the worth of the thing in the corner."

Gillean got up and wrapped his arms around the gold and crystal artifact. "Then I guess this is our share for protecting the town," he said. "Mine, Catriona's, Erik's, Karise's, and yours, Shara."

Shara shook her head. "Not mine," she said. "I never wanted any coin." She picked up a very long sword in a plain leather sheath and inspected it closely.

Gillean huffed with exasperation. "All right," he said. "We'll figure out the split once we get out of here. Come on. We'll lock the door behind us when we go and come back for the rest later."

Erikoff walked behind Karise and Bosc, taking in the course of the tunnel, the angles, the curves, details about the rocks they were passing through. Something about it all seemed familiar to him, though he couldn't quite figure out why.

A faint, fluttering sound caught his ears and he turned, peering behind them into the darkness. Something moved just at the corner of his vision. A bat? He couldn't be sure. And he didn't see anything.

"What's that noise?" Karise asked.

"What noise?" Erik said, wondering if she'd seen the same furtive shape. The mage suddenly became aware of a loud, hissing sound filling the tunnel. The sound grew progressively louder as they walked forward.

"It sounds like running water," Bosc suggested.

"Yes," Erikoff said. "I suppose it could be." He was still wondering about the fleeting shadow and why the tunnel seemed familiar to him. He'd been in dark, underground places during his training with the Fellowship, but none had been quite like this. Something subtle was nagging at the back of his brain, but he couldn't figure out what.

"How soon do we get to the treasure?" Bosc asked.

"How would I know?" Karise replied. "It's not like I have a map of this place."

"So you have no idea what that light up ahead is?" Bosc asked.

"Of course not," Karise replied. "I've no more idea what it is than I know what that rushing sound is."

"But it sounds like water," Bosc said.

"Yes, it does," Karise agreed.

There was a corner ahead of them, and the light—yellow-orange in color—grew brighter the nearer they got to it. The noise became louder too.

And Erik noticed something else: The air around them had started to feel positively damp. And the stone floor was wet too, almost slick.

The mage stopped and examined his boots. It was water all right, water on the floor of the passage. It pooled in small puddles atop the rough stone.

It was *pooling*—not flowing to one side.

The floor was flat!

The corridor wasn't part of the flying castle's original construction. Somehow, he and the others had passed out of the fortress corridors and into a natural passageway in the mountainside.

With a sudden, sickening drop of his stomach, Erikoff realized exactly where they were.

He dashed toward Karise and the big villager as the two of them reached the corner.

"No, wait!" he called. "Don't go that way! The *waterfall* is that way!"

Karise turned and looked back at him, but kept walking. "What waterfall?" she asked.

Erikoff rounded the corner behind them and skidded to a stop. His voice dropped so low that it could barely be heard above the crashing water.

"The waterfall where we met the dragon."

He stood still, unable to muster the courage to move. Karise and Bosc had stopped as well. All three of them stood at the entrance to a large, natural cavern.

A curtain of falling water covered the left side of the cave. The first rays of sunset leaked in through the waterfall, painting the cavern in shades of gold and orange.

Beyond the waterfall, only ten yards away from the startled explorers, lay an enormous, reptilian form—the scarred and battered body of Viktor's mount, Thane.

As Erik and the others stood transfixed, the dragon's yellow eyes flickered open.

CHAPTER

29   A Glimmer of Hope

"Rohawn!" Catriona gasped.

At the far end the cell stood the battered and dirty form of Catriona's young squire. The teenager was chained to a wall, and bruises covered him almost from head to foot. Long, ugly cuts and burns traced across his muscular body.

Catriona dropped her torch and ran to him. "Rohawn, are you all right? Can you hear me?" she asked.

"Dreaming . . ." Rohawn muttered. "Dreaming."

"No, Rohawn, you're not dreaming. I'm here," Cat said as she bent down and fumbled frantically to untwist the bolts on the manacles holding his feet. To find Rohawn, alive! It was beyond anything she could have hoped.

With his feet freed, she moved up to his hands. She worked more deftly, calm and focused, with a surety of purpose. Within minutes she'd freed both of Rohawn's hands.

She caught him as he slumped onto her shoulder. "It's all right now," she said quietly. "I'm here. It's all right now.

"Let's get him out of here," she said to Anaska and Vedec. "He needs fresh air."

240   "But what about the other prisoners?" Vedec asked.

"I don't think there are any others," Catriona said. "You can look, but be quick about it. I'm heading for the main doors, and I'm not going to wait."

She hefted Rohawn on her shoulder—he was surprisingly light—and strode back down the corridor and up the dungeon stairs. Vedec and Anaska did a quick check of the rest of the cells before following.

The halls of Viktor's castle became a blur as Catriona carried Rohawn through them. A mixture of joy, relief, and puzzlement swirled through her mind. How had he survived the dragon's attack? How had he gotten into that cell? Was he ill? Would he recover? Clearly Viktor had treated him terribly.

She pushed the thoughts aside. None of that mattered now. All that mattered was getting Rohawn to safety and helping him to recover. "I need to find Karise," she said to herself. "Karise will be able to heal him."

Catriona burst into the entryway at the same moment that Gillean, Shara, and Lynd entered through the opposite passage.

All of them stopped, thunderstruck. Gillean stared at the young man draped over Catriona's shoulders. Catriona stared at the large golden artifact cradled in the arms of her mercenary friend.

"Is . . . is that . . . *Rohawn?*" Gillean asked, stunned.

Catriona nodded. "Gillean!" she blurted. "You've found the *Heart of Purespring!*"

Her outburst snapped the young nobleman out of his stupor. "I have?" he said. "Yes, of course I have. Doesn't that just figure."

He seemed sarcastic, but Catriona couldn't figure out why. At that moment, she felt happier than she'd ever felt in her life.

"How did Rohawn get here?" Gillean asked.

"We can find out later," she replied. "Right now, he needs some fresh air, some water, and maybe something to eat, if he can stomach it."

Gillean nodded and handed the Heart of Purespring to Shara.

"Let me give you a hand," he told Catriona. He took Rohawn's legs and helped Catriona carry the young squire through the main door and onto the castle steps outside.

As they came through the doorway, the villagers guarding the entrance gathered around them.

"I need some blankets, some bandages, and some water," Catriona said. The villagers immediately fetched those things from the horses, and the supplies appeared almost instantly. Anaska arranged one of the blankets on the ground in front of the steps, and Catriona and Gillean laid Rohawn down on it. The temple steward draped the other blanket over the injured boy.

Catriona cradled her squire's head on her lap and put a water skin to his lips.

Rohawn's eyes flickered open and he smiled weakly. "I knew you'd come," he said.

"You're going to be all right," Catriona assured him. "Everything is going to be all right."

"We are dead. We are all dead." Karise mouthed the words, though she knew her companions would never hear her.

The dragon lay before them, almost within reach. His face was scarred and burned. Spears jutted from his scaly hide. He was bleeding profusely, and his wings were pierced and torn. He looked as though he might die at any time, but his bloodstained eyes were still very much alive, alive and filled with hatred.

Those eyes bored into Karise like hot pokers. She couldn't move, could barely stand under Thane's baleful scrutiny. How Erikoff and Bosc could bear that terrible gaze, she didn't know.

She wanted to scream. She wanted to run for her life. Yet if she did that, the dragon would surely strike. Her only chance—the only chance any of them had—was to remain perfectly silent and perfectly still.

Bosc screamed. He screamed at the top of his lungs—his voice high and shrill—the scream of a terrified child, the scream of someone about to die.

The dragon lunged forward, snapped the villager into his huge maw, and swallowed Bosc with three flesh-rending gulps.

Instantly, Karise and Erikoff dived back the way they'd come. The dragon's body was too large to follow them into the tunnel. If they could only get out of range of his neck and head, they might stand a chance. She and Erik ran for their lives, ran as fast as they could across the slippery stone.

The dragon breathed. The whole side of the fortress shook with the thunderclap. White lightning blazed down the stone corridor, searing the walls and shattering them at the same time.

Karise and Erik threw themselves to the ground and covered their heads. Rocks—some as large as fists—rained down on top of them. Tingling electricity coursed through Karise's armor. She felt the metal heat up. She knew she was going to die.

Then it all stopped. The bright light faded, the thunder died away, the rocks stopped falling. She lay facedown on the corridor floor next to Erik.

The mage coughed, and dust drifted up from his body. "I can't believe we're alive," he said.

Karise got to her feet. "Alive, but trapped," she said. "Look."

The tunnel beyond them had collapsed, blocking the passage completely. With their best avenue of escape destroyed, only one way out remained—past the dragon.

Karise swore. "The gods curse us for fools!" she said. "Even a wounded dragon is deadly!"

"Come out," Thane croaked, his deep voice shaking dust from the tunnel ceiling. "Come out and I will kill you quickly—as I did your friend."

Karise gripped her mace so tightly that her hand tingled. Was this her fate, to die here, trapped like a scared rabbit in its hole?

"Erik!" she whispered. "Erik, we need to confront the dragon now, fight it before it recovers its breath. Maybe if we're lucky, it won't kill both of us. Maybe one of us can get out through the waterfall."

Erikoff didn't respond. She turned and looked at him.

The young mage stood in the shadows leaning against the shattered wall, panting, sweating, tense. Yet somehow, he also looked strangely detached, as if he were thinking deeply, or listening to a voice that only he could hear.

"Erik, we don't have much time," she said.

Still he didn't respond. She wanted to rip off his golden mask and read the expression on his face. Was he too frightened to fight? Had he run out of spells?

She quickly cataloged prayers she might use in the battle—wind might help, fire would be better though. If only Erik would add his fire powers too!

"Erik," she hissed. "We have to do something *now!* Curse you, mage! Wake up!"

But Erikoff remained silent and unmoving.

This was the end, and Karise knew it. She ran through the prayer for a fireball in her mind. She held tight to her mace, took a deep breath, and prepared to charge around the corner.

As she stepped forward, though, Erikoff laid a pale hand on her shoulder.

She turned and saw his eyes glittering behind his mask.

"Wait," he said. "I have an idea."

CHAPTER

30 THE FINAL BLOW

Rohawn smiled up at Catriona. Already he looked healthier, cleaned up a bit. Despite the cuts and bruises, his old spirit was starting to show through.

He sat up slowly, as if every muscle in his body ached. Shara handed him a piece of bread and cheese, and he ate it eagerly. He took a swig of water to wash the food down and said, "Thanks."

"We thought you were dead," Gillean told him.

"I thought so too," Rohawn said. "I was fighting near the mayor's house. The dragon breathed lightning, and it seemed like the whole world exploded. Everyone near me died or got buried. I guess I got lucky. The dragon plucked me from the wreckage and carried me away. His rider, Viktor, said he had something 'special' in store for me." He looked at the bruises and cuts covering his skin. "I guess Viktor didn't like the way I stood up to him."

"He's dead," Catriona said. "Viktor's dead. I killed him. I'd have killed him twice if I'd known what he was doing to you." She put her arms around the boy and hugged him.

"Hey, I'm all right," he said. "I'm alive at least, and free. What about the other prisoners, the other slaves? Did you free them?"

"We didn't find anybody else," Catriona said. "You were all alone in the dungeon. Even the kobolds were gone. They fled after we crushed Viktor's army.".

"You killed Viktor *and* wiped out his army?" Rohawn said, impressed. "Gosh, I wish I could have been there!" Then he grew serious once more. "But if there weren't any other prisoners, if there were no slaves in the dungeon, then that must mean that Viktor sold everyone else before you arrived."

Catriona nodded and said, "You can't save everyone, no matter how hard you try."

"But you don't understand," Rohawn said. "Some of those people, some of those slaves . . . You have to find them!" His voice failed and he took another swig of water. "I heard the slaves talking while I was chained to the wall. You have a lot of time to listen when you're chained to a wall."

A cold snake of apprehension curled around Catriona's heart. "What did you hear?" she asked. "What were the people saying?"

"Some of the slaves," Rohawn said, "they were from *Purespring.*"

"Purespring!" Catriona gasped. "They must have been taken prisoner when Viktor stole the Heart."

"Obviously," Gillean said.

"The question is, where have they been taken?" Catriona said. "Who did Viktor sell them to?"

She turned to the villagers. "We need to search the castle again," she said. "We'll stop any kobolds we find, but we *won't* kill them. Understand? We need to find out what happened to the slaves."

"It sounds like you've found a new quest," Gillean commented.

She nodded. "Are you with me?"

"I've come this far," he said.

"I'm with you too," Rohawn said, standing on shaky legs. "I'll help you free the slaves. I know what it's like to be held captive by Viktor and his kind."

"If you're going to fight again, Rohawn, you might need this," Shara said. She handed him a long, leather-sheathed weapon.

"My greatsword!" Rohawn said. He took the huge blade from her, slung it on his back, and smiled.

"I found it in Viktor's treasury," the half-elf explained.

"You found the treasury?" Elops said, his single eye gleaming.

"Don't get your hopes up," Gillean told him. "There's not much there."

"What about you, Shara?" Catriona asked. "Will you come with us to free the slaves?"

"I will help search the castle," the half-elf said. "After that, I must go my own way. I have been away from my people for a long time, and I have much to tell them."

"I understand," Catriona said. "I guess you should give me the Heart, then."

Shara nodded and handed the gold and crystal artifact to Catriona.

Rohawn gawked. "What is it?" he asked.

"It's the Heart of Purespring," answered a familiar voice from above. "And it's something we want very much."

All of them turned and looked up.

Karise hovered in the air above the roof of the castle's main hall. The light of the setting sun reflected off her armor and helmet, making them appear blood red. In one hand, she clutched her spiked mace, poised to strike. In the other hand she held the reins of her new mount—the blue dragon Thane.

"Give us the Heart," Karise said, "or we'll have to kill you."

The story continues in . . .

WARRIOR'S BLOOD

GOODLUND TRILOGY, VOLUME TWO
by Stephen D. Sullivan

In the deserts of northern Solamnia, many surprises await Catriona Goodlund.

The treachery of a friend. The humiliation of captivity. The joy of a long-sought reunion.

With one shock after another, Catriona learns at last whether the blood of a warrior flows within her.

Available May 2007

Find out how it all began in . . .

TEMPLE OF THE DRAGONSLAYER

by Tim Waggoner